Books by D.E. LADD

A Dreamer's Dance

Circle of When

Moonlight Roses

Without Wings

Please visit **www.deladd.com/mybooks** for more information.

Please visit **www.deladd.com/connect** to gain access to free eBooks and audiobooks, sneak peeks at project concept art, merchandise, and giveaways.

CIRCLE of WHEN

D.E. LADD

Circle of When

Copyright © 2019 by Derek E. Ladd

ISBN #978-0-9723275-3-4 (trade paperback)
ISBN #978-0-9723275-7-2 (eBook)
IS-123019

Intended audience: Adult

Genres(s): Drama, Romance

This book contains the following: profanity, adult content and sexual situations, depictions of drug or alcohol abuse, mild violence.

Summary: Laura Alman crosses paths with a man who dredges up painful memories, causing her to redefine happiness, reconnect with her estranged mother, and revisit a past she's spent most of her life trying to forget.

This book was printed in the United States of America.

Published by Avian Wing Media, in association with Avian Entertainment, LLC.

Avian Wing Media
834 SW 15th Avenue
Portland, OR 97205
www.avianwingmedia.com

This story is dedicated to anyone who has had to fight through a battlefield of the past to find peace in the present. It is also dedicated to anyone who has ever taken a leap of faith to embark on a journey of the heart.

Forever Joined

Outstretched arms or waving oceans—
Wide and always changing
Mountains vast, so straight and structured,
So tall they crowd all sight

Icy tongues of snowflake on skin,
The innocence of rain
And stubborn cold shall fade in light—
The warmth of dawn's embrace

Whispering joy of wind through leaves—
Nature's children laughing
A breath-like breeze, the scent of spring
A lover's distant sigh

A boundless sea so smooth and calm,
A place for life to bathe
Where two can soar, and touch, and love
With streams forever joined.

~D.E. Ladd '97-

CIRCLE of WHEN

Laura first saw him on a rainy Monday morning around seven thirty. She was stuck in traffic again—part of a long, wet train of vehicles. Heavy droplets of rain splashed the windshield of her Mercedes CLS550, shattering and running down the glass in lazy, wriggling streams. The wipers thumped intermittently, matching the rain almost perfectly while the engine idled.

Laura Alman was a lovely, successful woman dressed in a sharply tailored business suit comprised of a navy skirt and coat. As usual, her dirty-blond hair was twisted into a series of thick braids tied up into a hard little bun. Her selection of complementary jewelry was always subtle: a small silver watch and earrings, perhaps a playful pin on her lapel or a thin chain around her slender neck. The same held true for her makeup, which she applied sparingly to the edges of her small lips, her large blue eyes, and the skin covering her prominent cheekbones.

Within the quiet confines of her luxurious car, she could barely hear the drumming of the rain above her. Everything was filtered by a stale gray, as if heavy clouds had fallen to smother the world. The line of cars in which she found herself inched along ten or twenty feet every few minutes.

"C'mon, dammit." She drummed her slender fingers on the wheel, inspecting her polished red nails for flaws.

The radio hummed with a steady swelling rhythm created by strings that she knew immediately was Vivaldi. Laura also knew she would be late again, which concerned her, even though she answered to few people. She removed her phone from her briefcase and dialed her office. The phone made a little beep, indicating that the battery was low—*again*. She'd forgotten to recharge it the night before. The ringtone purred and clicked a few times.

"Rockwell and Associates. This is Kate." The older woman's sharp tone gleamed with an edge of authority and intimidation.

Laura cleared her throat and took in a quick breath. "Hey, Kate, it's Laura. I'm stuck on Wilson Road again."

"Ugh. I *hate* that road. Where are you now? How close to the beltline?"

"Just past Whistler's Restaurant. About a half mile from the loop." Laura leaned over to see ahead of her.

Kate made a whistling sigh. "Get here as soon as you can. We've got a meeting this morning with Harvey Kessel."

"I know. I should have left an hour earlier. I promise I'll be…" Laura stopped talking as she turned to her right.

Beside her was an old Jeep with no doors and nothing but a small strip of vinyl over the driver and passenger seats. The man behind the wheel looked to be around Laura's age—in his early to mid-forties. Rain pasted his light-brown hair to his forehead, and he wore a bright smile as if it were a beautiful day. Laura noticed his lips moving. When she cracked her window, she realized he was singing.

Laura stared at the spectacle beside her: a man dressed in a pair of worn-out shorts, a loose cotton shirt with rolled up sleeves, and hiking sandals. To her, he looked like a vision, something that warranted skepticism—like a rippling pond in the middle of the desert. When the wind attacked the flank of the man's Jeep, spraying him with rain, he paid no mind. He slicked back his wet hair with one hand and kept on singing. Laura was shocked when he turned to face her, but she couldn't look away. His eyes were like two bright emeralds set in pearl, and when he smiled, exposing his white teeth, his eyelids came together slightly, hiding those two magnificent gems.

He sang in her direction, something as slow and bluesy as the day itself. Then he waved at her, holding up his right hand as if he knew her. Normally, Laura would never have stared at someone for so long. But she watched the man as he sang in the rain, wiping the water from his hair and smiling. He glanced at Laura several times, seemingly amused that his unusual behavior and demeanor had captivated her. Finally, he faced front again, cut the wheel, and eased the Jeep onto the median to roll past a delivery truck blocking the left lane. Laura watched as he drove slowly along the grassy island before easing back onto the road and vanishing from sight.

"Laura? *Hello?*" Kate's sharp voice erupted over the phone.

"Oh. What? Yes. I'm…I'm here. What's the matter?" Laura's words spilled out as she struggled to blink away the mirage.

"I *said* hurry up and get here. Mr. Kessel just walked through the door." Kate hung up on her.

Twenty minutes later, Laura finally arrived at the parking garage. She zipped into her reserved space and hurried to the elevators. She did her best to maintain a professional appearance as she hurried down the corridor toward the west boardroom, her heels clicking on the off-white tile floor. She had to force herself to slow down, lest she step wrong and twist her ankle.

Rented pieces of high-end artwork added splashes of color and texture to the oak-paneled walls. A four-foot vase at the end of the corridor held a plant with several leafy stalks poking out. It had always reminded Laura of a deadly upside-down squid with its dark-green tentacles reaching for the ceiling.

As Laura approached the boardroom, she found Kate waiting by the door, looking prim and polished in a gunmetal-gray suit, burgundy polish on her nails, and her fire-kissed hair twisted into a braid. *If the Devil was a woman...*

"Well, *hello!*" She wrapped her left arm around Laura's shoulder and squeezed her close in a motherly way. "How're you feeling? Okay? Good. I have no doubt at all about you. Give it to 'em hard and fast, just like you did in front of Mason and the rest of us last week."

Kate slipped in behind Laura and began massaging her shoulders as if they were entering a boxing ring. "We both know what landing this account means for us. It's a big one. Right? That means you *have* to be at your best. You sleep enough last night? You look a little peaked."

"Actually, I was sort of *shaken* awake at three this morning—"

"You'll be all right. You hear me?" Kate spoke with a sense of impatient urgency, staring hard at Laura with her blue-flame eyes. She spun Laura around and kneaded her shoulders from the front. Laura almost dropped her briefcase in the spin but managed to recover.

"We're all counting on you, Laura. Okay? You land this account, there could be a promotion for you."

Laura nodded and forced a smile. "I'll get 'em."

Kate smiled with a touch of malevolence, a look that hinted of consequences if Laura should fail in some way. "I know you will. Know why? 'Cause people *like* you."

The words gave Laura pause, but her brief reflection was interrupted when Kate spun her around again and ushered her toward the doors. "This is it. Give 'em hell."

The double doors swung wide, and Kate shoved Laura inside the room like a lone gladiator. The company president himself, Mason Rockwell, was there to greet her personally. That alone was a firm testament to how big this particular account was. He stood up and mechanically buttoned his gray pinstriped jacket, grinning at the sight of her, his light-gray eyes kind and generous.

"Well, *there* she is. We almost sent out a search party." He laughed as if his comment were terrifically funny.

Some of Laura's coworkers were also in attendance, those who would assist with project development—assuming the deal went through without a hitch. Laura found herself uncharacteristically nervous in their presence. She'd landed more than a dozen large accounts before, and yet, she suddenly felt as if she'd never done such a thing before.

"Nice to see you, gentlemen, ladies. I apologize for my tardiness. *Traffic.*" Laura moaned with a demure smile, playing up to them.

She stood at one end of the expansive gothic boardroom. Coffee and water urns dotted a thirty-foot ebony-wood table. The eight men and three women who served in positions at or above Laura's sat in high-back leather chairs, all staring back at her with quiet anticipation, a few through wire-rimmed glasses. Everyone looked sharp in their navy, black, or gray suits. Pens clicked and paper crinkled as legal pads flipped open.

Harvey Kessel was a wealthy entrepreneur who stood six foot, six and weighed probably three hundred pounds. He had a kind face and soft brown eyes, and he was smiling, apparently not the least bit concerned or bothered by Laura's tardiness.

Laura launched into her proposal, employing the trademark blend of marketing strategies she understood and presented so well. She explained to Mr. Kessel that Rockwell and Associates could market and promote his product from beginning to end more aggressively and more efficiently than anyone else. She outlined campaign ideas and marketing strategies with half a dozen examples and presented a chart that displayed the best way to track their results and make adjustments along the way.

Mr. Kessel was impressed, but he started asking questions that rattled Laura's timing. And twice, while she was rearranging her slides, he was forced to repeat himself. Flustered, Laura explained that she hadn't slept well the night before, which wasn't necessarily a lie. But making excuses in front of such a high-caliber prospect was unprofessional, and she knew it. Her lack of sleep wasn't what was bothering her anyway. She was simply *off*—unable to find her usual groove. As the meeting dragged on, the sensation of being off the mark tormented her more and more. In the end, she barely managed to quell Mr. Kessel's more pressing concerns. He seemed relatively pleased with the overall package they were offering but insisted that he be given a week to make his final decision.

In the eyes of Laura's superiors land equals—especially Mason— that was not acceptable. They'd hoped for a decision that day and blamed Laura for Mr. Kessel's hesitation. After Mason and Mr. Kessel left together, a vice president named Hugh Parsons, a large man with bushy salt-and-pepper hair, leaned over and whispered something to Kate before leaving the room.

Kate approached Laura and smiled weakly. "He says it could have gone *much* better. He wasn't too happy. *Me?* I've had bad days too, but this isn't like you. You hardly ever miss. Something wrong?"

For the ten-plus years she'd worked for Kate, Laura had never completely trusted her. To anyone who *didn't* know her, Kate was an attractive woman of fifty-five, tall and fit, with thick, reddish hair and a kind smile. But Laura knew the woman that lurked beneath all that confident beauty and that sparkling smile. She'd seen Kate yell at underlings many times. One girl who'd sent Kate into a rage had pressed her hands over her face and burst into tears in front of everyone. Kate hadn't stopped yelling at her.

Now, as Kate studied her with what could easily pass for deep concern in her eyes, Laura suspected that Kate's empathy was less about Laura's health and more about the account. A kind of silent desperation radiated off Kate. Or perhaps it was anger threatening to explode to the surface. To Laura, it felt as if Kate were teetering on the edge of flying into a bloody rage, all while using a sterile brand of maternal consolation as cover.

Laura had come to expect deception from people like Kate; it was just the way things were. Kate was someone who infiltrated the social structure of those working beneath her. Part of her job was pretending to be on *their* side, that is, the lower echelon of management. Laura knew this because during the past six years, she'd developed an open lane of communication between herself and those directly beneath her.

"I'm fine," Laura assured her. "I just couldn't sleep last night. I was a little nervous about this morning."

"Don't worry. He won't make a decision without speaking with us again." Kate flashed a tight-lipped grin. "Just…brush up on your presentation. Okay? How's everything else? How's Don?"

"He's fine."

"Yeah? Good. I like him. Anyway, I gotta run. I'll see you later?"

Kate turned on her heels and was gone in a few quick strides.

Laura remained where she stood for a while. It was strange the way people avoided her, acting as if they couldn't see her…even though she was standing almost in the middle of the hallway.

Returning home that evening, Laura battled the same traffic she'd fought on the way in. After retrieving the mail, she opened the heavy front door and crossed the hardwood foyer, snapping on the light without looking around. The house was a beautiful two-and-a-half-story Cape nestled among many others like it along a well-lit street. It belonged to Don, but most of the furnishings were hers—including all the dishes and appliances. The majority of the gadgets—like the food processor she never had the time to use—were gifts she had thoughtlessly purchased for herself.

The kitchen floor was laid with Italian tile; jade-and-black granite countertops gleamed under recessed lights, and the cabinets were made from smoky maple the color of coffee with heavy cream. Elaborate Persian rugs sprawled on the hardwood floors, cathedral ceilings stretched twenty feet high, and a massive television she hardly ever watched hung on the wall. A state-of-the-art computer sat in the study just down the hall, which was lined with half a dozen tables adorned with expensive antiques and ornaments. Chandeliers with hundreds of diamonds tied together with invisible thread twinkled, while the huge windows never let in enough sunlight. It was a spectacular display of wealth and success—which oftentimes felt more like a museum than a home.

Still, Laura found a strange sense of comfort as she walked along the high-ceilinged hallways, stepping into any of the five bedrooms, or the den with its stuffed bookshelves. That familiar, reassuring sensation evaded her now, driven away by the pervasive sense of failure she'd suffered at work. It wasn't *really* a failure, but it wasn't "as good as it could have been." So she sank into the leather sofa, kicked off her shoes, and stared up at the twinkling sparks of light bouncing off the chandelier crystals.

She attempted some kind of inner reflection and wasn't successful at that, either. It felt strange: whenever she tried to seriously think about something, she hit a wall. She groaned and rolled into the puffy chair to one side. In this new position, she found herself staring out the French doors at the street. A car drifted by in the mellow shades of evening. The rain had stopped by afternoon, and the purple skies and crooked little shapes of tall buildings framing the horizon helped her to focus. What was it her shrink had told her? *"Sometimes, it's possible to think too much about something. You have a good life, you have much to be thankful for, and sometimes, people feel guilty when confronted with abundance."*

Laura had stopped seeing the shrink shortly after that. He had almost made sense with the whole guilt-abundance thing. Except that Laura was not born into money the way many of her associates had been. Laura had *earned* everything she had: the scholarships, the countless As, the high-paying jobs…

She'd earned *all* of it. So why did she feel that menacing presence of guilt all the time? She asked herself that at least a few times a week. No answer ever came.

And what was the true source of her anxiety? Her shrink had never been able to answer that one, either. Of course, she had withheld *some* things from him. Laura wasn't foolish enough to tell a stranger— even if he was her shrink—*everything*.

The door opened and closed, announcing Don's arrival. "Hello?" he called out.

Laura rolled back the other way as her fiancé, Don Woodruff, entered the great room. A boyish-looking man with sculpted brown hair and a Wall Street ensemble, he set his briefcase beside hers and approached her.

"Hey, babe. How's your day?" he asked.

She stood to embrace him, but it didn't bring the calmness she was longing for.

"Something wrong?" He flashed her his winning smile—the one that had closed a thousand deals.

Don was and always had been the picture of happiness. He was a salesman. People liked him. *She* liked him. Laura had met him three years ago at a staff party. He worked for a company whose marketing interests Laura had been assigned to handle. There was no resisting his charm and cheerfulness or his contagious smiles and laughter. Nor could she deny the fact that Don had seemingly found his place in the world—a place he would gladly occupy until he could no longer. He was the sort of man who had plans, had everything worked out, from their marriage date to their retirement date.

"Got my ass kicked today. Sort of." Laura felt the smooth fabric of his jacket.

Don stroked her hair and kissed her on the forehead. Laura waited patiently for an excuse to elaborate, a word or gesture that would prompt her to go on.

Oh? What happened?

Do you want to talk about it?

I'm sorry to hear that. Is there anything I can do?

Instead, Don kissed her quickly on the mouth and pulled away. "Tomorrow's another day. I'll make you dinner. That'll cheer you up."

Laura's arm fell away as he moved off toward the kitchen. She remained where she stood, her small feet planted on the thick carpet as Don went to work on dinner, whistling all the while.

He prepared breaded lemon chicken with sautéed mushrooms and carrots, served on rice pilaf, paired with a glass of white wine. During the meal, Laura listened semi-attentively as Don described how well things were going at work and the number of new contacts he'd made in a single day. Laura nodded while she chewed, offering little sounds of approval without really listening.

As Don continued, Laura thought about Kate. Several times, she'd either dreamed or imagined Kate hurling one of her subordinates out of a sixth-story window for losing a page of an important presentation. Such an incident suddenly seemed quite possible to Laura, which made her begin to seriously question her own sanity.

She wondered how—or why—she'd tripped up at work earlier that day. Retracing her steps, she recalled having seen something odd, but couldn't for the life of her remember what the hell it had been exactly.

"Honey?" Don said.

Laura looked up and raised her eyebrows at him. "Hmm?"

"I asked if you'd like some more wine."

Laura forked another bite of chicken into her mouth and nodded. "Mmm," she said with a forced smile.

After two days of feeling out of place for reasons she couldn't put her finger on, Laura reverted back to her usual routine. And three days after that, she was completely back to normal.

During the second meeting with Harvey Kessel, Laura informed him that she had adjusted her presentation to answer all of his questions and concerns. Employing a razor-sharp blend of candor and professional conviction, Laura not only recommended that Mr. Kessel hire their firm, but also made it clear that he would be foolish to hire anyone else.

In the end, Mr. Kessel and his team applauded Laura. Mr. Kessel then turned to Mason. "I think we're ready to discuss the terms."

That same day, Kate took Laura to lunch at Julian's—a four-star restaurant known for catering to celebrities in days past. It was a celebration of sorts, a way of patting Laura on the back for landing such a large account single-handedly.

"Actually, Ross Chaplin and his team did a lot of my research," Laura pointed out. "I'd like to see them recognized for this, as well."

"Of course, but that's their job. They already get paid for what they do." Kate sipped her red wine and winked.

Laura responded with a troubled smile. Nothing ever changed.

"By the way," Kate said, beaming at Laura as she eyed their surroundings, "did you hear about Walter?"

"Walter Preston? What about him?"

"The old codger used his corporate account to get a pedicure, of all things. Hugh is a little peeved about it. He may let him go."

"What? For *that*?"

"Sure. Problem is, you let someone like Walter get away with it, *every*one thinks they can."

"But, um, Walter's due to retire in two years, isn't he?"

"*Was* my dear…*was*." Kate sipped her wine. She looked over the glass at an attractive young man with a rich bronze complexion. She tapped her wedding ring against the wineglass and studied it pensively. "I do wish the damn thing would come off. It may be coming off soon anyway. For *good*."

Laura pretended not to hear, and Kate tactfully changed the subject.

"You'll be rolling in it soon, dear Laura. Two percent of first-year earnings—that'll be a good slice."

Laura's face wrinkled with confusion. "You mean…*four* percent. That was the deal, wasn't it?"

Kate turned to face her slowly, the way an animal on the hunt turns toward the sound of its prey. She smiled, exposing her perfect teeth. "Negotiations only allowed for two. But it's still a good bit. Cheer up! I'm sure the raise you get will be more than enough to offset whatever you lost in commissions."

Kate was obviously quite pleased with how things had turned out. Laura had an idea about where her other two percent had gone, but she didn't say anything.

Kate kept talking throughout the meal, and while Laura tried to enjoy her lunch, she couldn't help but consider that the meal had cost her two percent of her commissions.

After lunch, on the way toward the exit, Kate occupied herself with admiring the handsome busboys and waiters, smiling at them and winking at Laura. When she and Kate reached the parking lot, Laura stopped in place. Kate was busy fishing in her purse for her cigarettes…when *he* came into view.

As traffic zipped by, Laura stared at him on the other side of the street. The sun was shining, and the air was scented with the emerging perfume of spring. Upon seeing him, Laura was at last able to recall the strange thing she'd seen before—the same anomaly that had caused her such unrest.

He was standing beside his white Jeep, dressed in olive-green shorts and brown hiking shoes. His cream-colored shirt was unbuttoned halfway down. The sleeves were rolled to his elbows, and his skin was lightly tanned. He stood near a farmer's vegetable stand, holding a basket of assorted produce she couldn't make out. But it *was* the same guy who'd been singing the blues in the rain—the one who'd waved to her as if they knew each other. His hair had seemed darker then, perhaps from the rain, and it looked lighter now, with streaks of darker brown mixed through. Laura didn't understand what she found so captivating about him or why she found his presence so intriguing. She didn't know him, he was dressed cheaply, and he drove an old Jeep with scratched paint and no doors. She wondered about the strange attraction and suspected that it came from somewhere too deep within for her to reach without digging for it. And she had no interest in doing that.

"Laura? Hey? What's the matter?" Kate shook her by the shoulder.

"What? Oh, nothing, I was just…"

When she looked up, he was driving away. The engine hummed and paused while he shifted, then the Jeep carried him out of sight again.

"I thought I saw something."

Kate lit up a cigarette. "Well, we should be getting back to the office. There's all that research on Lefty Tool Company. Remember?"

Laura nodded as she walked to her car in a daze. She rose onto her tiptoes and searched far and wide for the man, but he was gone. Even worse than the idea of the stranger's sudden absence bothering her was the fact that she didn't want to go back to work.

That night, after Don had gone on and on about how wonderful business was for him, Laura sprang the good news about landing the Kessel account. It felt odd, delivering the marvelous news with detachment and rigidity, even though she smiled as she spoke. The way she stared absently through the bay window in the dining room didn't seem to bother Don, and that gave her the creeps. Frustration crept in and curled around her neck, making it hard to breathe.

Don was elated about her success. He hurried over to her end of the table and embraced her, planting a kiss on her lips before returning to his own seat. His affection made her breathe a little easier. He called no attention to how distant she was, how silent and pensive, and Laura wondered if she was simply thinking too much—like she always did. She explained to Don how good it felt to achieve the acceptance of her coworkers and supervisors, and what landing this account would mean for them. The more she spoke about it, the better she felt. Don listened attentively, smiled, and told her how proud he was. Frustration, or whatever it was, slinked away.

After dinner, the two of them watched a video. Something about a businessman who gets framed by the mob, the movie was almost three hours long, and Don fell asleep before it was over. As Laura helped him to bed, he mumbled something about playing golf with Ted and Victor in the morning.

Lying in bed, Laura remained on her back for hours, replaying the images of the strange man she'd seen—first getting soaked by the rain then being kissed by the wind and sun. He'd been smiling on both occasions—a subtle, warm smile that blossomed on his face slowly and naturally, the way a smile is supposed to. It wasn't forced or artificial. It wasn't an expression that surfaced from fear or implied obligation. It was just a smile. Simple.

Contemplating that one detail about the stranger, Laura suddenly felt far removed from simplicity. The image of a man smiling was nothing so uncommon—Don did it all the time. But the way the stranger smiled was different.

Laura worried that thinking too much about the stranger in the Jeep would throw her off her game again. She hadn't been worth a damn for the rest of the day after seeing him at the vegetable stand. Luckily, her full mental attendance hadn't been required that afternoon. Aside from the numerous pats on the back she'd been forced to acknowledge, the remains of the day had been insignificant. Even so, Laura wondered about what problems her daydreaming might lead to.

Whenever she closed her eyes, he was there, smiling, his hair sweeping at the bridge of his nose… And that more recent image of him led her back to the first, which lingered in her mind with equal parts menace and clarity.

Laura rolled over and groaned. Don had been asleep for almost two hours. Any help he might have been capable of administering was negated by the fact that her problem involved another man.

Hey, Don. Don, wake up! I can't get this guy out of my head. Any suggestions?

She laughed aloud at the thought, and little by little, the images of the stranger—placed delicately beside one another in some intangible scrapbook—faded. After another hour, Laura drifted off to sleep and was moderately disappointed that the man who drove the Jeep wasn't in her dreams.

Over the next week Laura got tripped up at least once a day by internal questions about the man in the Jeep. Sometimes, her search for answers ended almost as quickly as it began. Other times, Laura would barricade herself in her office, lean back in her leather chair, and mumble aloud one speculation after another.

"Maybe I met him somewhere." She would immediately shake her head and curse the improbability. "He's not *that* attractive…is he?" From there, she would swivel around in her chair and stare out the window. And she never came up with a decent answer. She could never decide whether it was something about *him* or something about *her* that kept tripping her up. It began with *him*, though. Before seeing him, she was simply—

"Miserable. I was miserable before… Now, I'm confused." Laura wondered where that word had come from. "*Am* I miserable?"

But who was she to complain when millions of people the world over had it so much worse? She had a damn good job, a decent fiancé, friends…not many of them, but Kate… *Well, maybe not* Kate, *but there are others…aren't there?*

That little nugget of introspection lodged itself in her brain, and she was embarrassed suddenly. Do *I have any friends? Besides the people I work with? Do those people even count?*

"I never should have given up therapy." She shook her head.

Laura attempted to get some work done and failed. Her

concentration was blown—it hadn't really been there all day. She wondered how long it would be before others started to notice.

"That's all I need—more anxiety in my life. Jesus, what the hell is wrong with me?"

Dead silence rang in response to her question—no help from within or above.

The following Wednesday, after battling the same barrage of pointless questioning and aimless thoughts, Laura left work for an appointment she didn't really have. When she announced her departure, she didn't even know why she was doing it. The day—a cool sixty-five degrees and sunny—was gorgeous, and she reasoned that her sole motivation was to treat herself to some fresh air and open space. Therapy without a therapist getting in the way.

It was ten in the morning, and she assured Kate and the others that she would return after lunch. She drove across town without any idea at all where she was headed. The usual sensation of accomplishment delivered by motion wasn't there, however, and she was frustrated by the absence. Then the questions started: *Is that sensation of accomplishment you enjoy really nothing more than a petty illusion? Maybe you're not going anywhere, Laura—did you ever consider that? How lost and empty does a woman have to be before she finds such pleasure in simple motion the way you do?*

Laura exhaled in frustration. She brushed a few strands of hair out of her eyes and cursed them when they fell back down again. The sun was beating in through the window, and she started to sweat. But putting down the window would surely result in messy, unruly hair. She tried the AC, which made her too cold. She shook her head, feeling as if she didn't know what she was doing.

At a stoplight, Laura noticed a young woman with long flowing chestnut hair with her arm hanging out the window. Laura studied the woman for a long time, blinking at her. The light changed, and they drove on, the young girl with her flowing hair, and Laura in her car with the windows up. Laura kept watching the girl until she glanced forward and had to slam on her brakes. Rubber shrieked against the pavement, leaving two long marks in the road. She'd come inches from rear-ending a truck waiting for the light to change.

Laura's cheeks instantly flushed with embarrassment. She felt a thousand eyes staring at her. People at a roadside café snickered and pointed. She stared straight ahead and gripped the wheel as if trying to strangle it. When the light changed, Laura made a right then another. In a state of frustration and anger, she retraced her short course back to work.

The next day was every bit as beautiful, and Laura bravely decided to make another attempt at sneaking out of the office to clear her head. She explained that her appointment wasn't for yesterday, but today, hence her early return the day before. The excuse was greeted with casual dismissal, and she ventured out again.

In the parking lot, she sat in her car for a moment, trying to figure out what she was doing. She had no idea where to go or what to do when she got there. There was no destination, no direction, and no reason to bother with any of it. She had to know where she was going, or she wouldn't be able to move.

She started thinking back to when she was a teenager: sixteen years old, in her first car, driving along back roads in the fall, scattering leaves like little chunks of flame in all directions. She'd needed no destination then. The drive was enough, just to be able to drive, and to feel the movement and smell the air swirling through the car. Laura reached up hesitantly, unpinned her hair, and let it spill over her shoulders. She shook her head, ruffled her hair, and slipped on her sunglasses. She started the car, but before she put it into gear, she rolled down the window. The air was lukewarm and smelled sweet. Laura carefully backed out of her parking spot and left the garage.

Unlike the day before, Laura traveled through rural neighborhoods and past farms. The air was gentle on her face—and cleansing. The classical music on the radio felt out of place. She worked the dial, searching for an alternative. Within moments of her selecting a classic rock station, "Stone in Love" by Journey came on.

Laura still knew the words and the time in her life they marked so well: dancing in the moonlight, reckless laughter, and young love. She'd been a blue-jean girl herself, and at the time, the magic of those years had felt as if it would last forever. She wondered how she could have forgotten the way music could absorb the air where memories form, allowing them to live on forever.

There was a kind of surrender in what she was doing. Along the gray road that weaved in between emerald fields, she acknowledged dusty memories she had all but forsaken. Her head swam from the perfume of healthy cut grass. Then, to her right…horses! She eased off the accelerator and watched two of them galloping side by side. The muscles of their mighty legs and chests flexed and bulged as they ran. Laura almost had to stop when her eyes filled with tears, the same way they always had.

She went by Laurie back then and spent a lot of time taking care of horses on a huge ranch in the country. It was hard work, but she likened it to standing at the threshold of heaven.

Her favorite was a spotted mare named Valkyrie. She was white and gray, peppered with darker shades, with huge eyes and a calm demeanor that always put Laurie at ease. Valkyrie was unshakable and courageous, powerful and swift. Whenever Laurie climbed onto her back, she could feel the massive animal tensing up in anticipation, because more than any of the other horses she cared for, Valkyrie *loved* to run. So Laurie would hold on tight and yell, "Heeya!" There was no need whatsoever to kick at her flanks because Valkyrie knew what to do. They thundered across the hundred fifty acres with Laurie holding on tightly and howling with unbridled exhilaration, Valkyrie's hooves shredding the earth until she could run no faster.

Only when Valkyrie had her fill of tearing across the fields did Laurie lead her to a nearby stream and dismount so the horse could drink and rest. As Laurie stroked Valkyrie's healthy coat, she swore before God and everyone that one day, she would have a ranch of her own. And if they ever decided to breed Valkyrie, Laurie would be the first in line for a foal.

"You're gonna be a mama someday, and I'll be there to take care of your little ones." She stroked Valkyrie's nose and softly butted heads with her.

Back at the stable, Laurie brushed and fed Valkyrie and the others. And at the end of the day, there was Jimmy, a muscular boy with silky brown hair and no shoes. He appeared in the doorway behind her. His shadow slinked up the walls and dusted the hay. He always came at the same time, to walk her to her car, or carry her, if she'd worked too hard.

"You earn your money today?" Jimmy asked playfully. Laura ignored him until he walked up and wrapped himself around her. He gently pressed something smooth and made of wood into her hand. When she looked down, she saw a perfect little hand-carved wooden horse. The likeness to Valkyrie was so amazing that her jaw fell open, and she stared at it in silence.

"Like it?" he whispered. There was no one in the world like Jimmy, and no one would ever be able to match such a gift. Not in this lifetime.

Laura drove far and away that morning, all the windows down, air rushing in on her like the embrace of an excited old friend. Several times, she felt as if she were driving her old '79 Firebird with the T-top, rust spots, and chipped windshield, and only when she allowed herself to come down from that serenity did she realize that her old car was nothing but a memory, too. A casual glance at her reflection in the rearview—when the wind tossed her hair aside just so—revealed a thin, three-inch scar that ran almost parallel to her scalp. That image was like punctuation to it all—a mark left by a distant, more painful reality. A *reminder* from a reckless past.

After an hour of driving, Laura pulled out on a side street near Julian's restaurant, where she'd seen the stranger for the second time. She peered across the road, but of course, he wasn't there. Once again, she questioned the motives behind her curiosity. The subtle trace of disappointment she felt when she didn't see him there left her confused and anxious.

The little farmer's produce stand was still there, indicating that she wasn't completely crazy. At least she wasn't seeing things. She drove across the road and pulled into the dirt lot. She looked and felt terribly out of place among the old pickups and ragged sedans. There was a man and woman, both in their fifties, a younger woman with three restless children, and a silver-haired man in his sixties who smiled and tipped his straw hat to her.

"Ma'am." The man smiled, exposing an incomplete row of teeth.

"Go on now, Aaron. You're about to scare away all my customers," an old man behind the booth said. Aaron tipped his hat and chuckled before retreating to his old truck and leaving.

"Can I help you?" The man in the booth was in his sixties, had a gentle face and watery green eyes.

"Oh, I don't know." Laura had absolutely no idea why she'd stopped.

"Well, I've got the best produce you've ever had. It's grown right, not like that plastic stuff in the grocery stores. No chemicals and no preservatives, all fresh from the garden." His voice was steady and deep, and when he smiled, Laura felt at ease for the first time. "I'm not into high-pressure selling, so if you see anything you like, just let me know. I'm Duncan." He extended his hand, and Laura shook it.

"Laura. Nice to meet you." She turned away and started browsing.

Used to purchasing dull-orange tomatoes at the local grocery, Laura was amazed by the bright-red color of the ones Duncan had on display. Likewise, the zucchini, pears, and apples all looked unique and crisp, bright and colorful. *Healthy.*

Laura carefully selected half a dozen large tomatoes, four

cucumbers, a head of lettuce, two green peppers, and one apple.

"Just *one* apple?" Duncan asked.

"I'm going to eat it now, I think. How much for everything?"

"Five dollars. The apple's free," Duncan said through a smile.

"Five dollars? That's all?"

"Yep. Something wrong?"

"No, nothing, I just…thought it would be more." Laura handed him a ten.

He gave her back a five and winked. "Enjoy your apple."

Laura sought out a place to eat her apple—doing so while driving didn't seem too practical or appealing. She wanted to enjoy the fruit. After driving for several minutes, she turned in to a park. She hopped out of the car and walked along a gravel path, which proved a bit tricky in her low heels. Making sure no one was looking, she removed her shoes, walked across the grass to a large tree, and sat beneath it.

The park was almost deserted given the time of day. But people began walking or jogging by as noon rolled around. Some rode bicycles, and others walked their dogs. Like a mirror under the sun, the pond looked still, except for a pair of rowboats gliding past. And it was quiet. The only sounds that reached her ears were natural ones: water slapping the shore, wind tossing the trees, and the erratic chirping of little birds. Sometimes, she would catch a whisper of conversation, just enough to remind her that she wasn't the last woman on Earth.

The apple was delicious—as crisp and ripe as it looked. The sweet juice ran down her throat, making her smile and sigh through her nose. When she closed her eyes, she imagined being on a farm somewhere, enjoying fruit she'd just plucked from a gnarled apple tree. Her head swam in the illusion, where she remained until she'd finished eating.

She took a deep, long breath and exhaled, feeling better. Laura really didn't want to go back to work, but she didn't have much choice. The last thing she wanted was to have Kate looking for her, or even worse, calling her on her cell. So she reluctantly returned to her car and headed back, savoring the warmth and serenity of her hour in the park.

She was still lost in a hazy fog of bittersweet euphoria when Kate met her outside her office and cornered her before she could duck inside. Kate shamelessly inquired about where Laura had been and the nature of her appointment.

"And what happened to your hair? Is that a *leaf*? Here, let me..." Kate plucked the small leaf from Laura's hair.

When Laura chuckled carelessly about how unkempt she must look, Kate's expression clouded. "Are you cheating on Don? Where were you? Come on, tell me." She kept her voice to a whisper, and her eyes gleamed with anticipation.

Laura squeezed Kate's shoulder and smiled. "I just took a break. That's all."

She offered nothing more, knowing that trying to explain would only be a waste of time.

The break Laura had awarded herself was more than enough to get her through the entire weekend, but what she really wanted was to tell someone about how good it felt to be alone like that—in the absence of depression or anxiety. The only problem was her inability to describe those feelings effectively. And she wasn't sure Don would understand. Kate? Nope. She couldn't possibly comprehend what Laura's little excursion had meant to her. Besides, if Kate learned that Laura had been skipping out of work to sit under a tree in a park and eat apples, she might drag her into the huge office so they could have a "discussion."

That was where she started off on Monday—concealing her whereabouts on the Thursday before from everyone as if she were an international spy. She even declined to have lunch with Kate, explaining that she had errands to run.

"What? Is it because we always take your car? We can take mine if you like," Kate offered.

Kate had a brand-new BMW she never drove unless she absolutely had to—she normally expected her subordinates to chauffeur her around.

"No, don't be silly," Laura said. "I've just got this thing to do."

"What is it?" Kate flashed a smile, the one she used when teetering on the edge of getting upset.

"It's personal. I'll be back in an hour or two." Laura slipped away before Kate could detain her any longer.

Lunch beneath her tree quickly became a daily routine, and Laura continued to jealously guard the location of her retreat from others. She also began taking a small blanket to keep her clothes from getting dirty, and before long, she was removing her shoes and soaking her feet in the cool pond while she ate. Sometimes, she would take a little nap and dream of soft colors and fragrant plants while the birds sang and darted through the air.

Laura settled into a groove of the trunk of her old maple tree. She bit into her apple and stared out at the rippling pond, mesmerized by its calm and sleepy gestures. She longed to be one with the pond, to drink in all the liquid serenity it promised and to remain as clear for all time.

As the water-kissed breezes tossed her hair and swept across her face, Laura heard voices tickling the air—voices she knew. When she glanced around the tree to her right, her eyes widened, and her thoughts scattered in all directions. What she was seeing couldn't be real.

An older woman in her seventies and a teenaged girl who looked to be about fifteen were strolling up the path. The teen held a little two-year-old girl in her arms, and the child busied herself with a doll sitting on a small horse.

Laura stared at them with a sour mix of astonishment and horror. *They can't be real.*

But they looked so real that Laura slowly stood up and took a timid step toward them as they walked away from her. She stopped and pinched her eyes closed. The voices changed and started to fade. When Laura opened her eyes again, she saw a woman in her fifties and another in her twenties. A small girl of maybe three or four walked beside them, tugging at a green balloon on a string. Puzzled and relieved, Laura sat down and leaned back against her tree.

What the hell was that?

Her eyes bobbed along the surface of the water, to her left and right, searching for an explanation that did not exist. Her heart was still pounding in her chest, but a deep, soothing breath steadied it. Even though she realized she wasn't seeing ghosts, a door had been opened, and a few old memories had escaped. And when Laura closed her eyes again, those memories embraced her with vivid color and magical clarity. It felt like being immersed in the gentle currents of a long-forgotten river intent on carrying her away…

Laurie explored the enchanting new world of the old house with the careful determination of any two-year-old. The house belonged to an old woman she knew as "Meme," a kind lady who possessed the spirit of someone much younger, and it was cluttered with so many wonderful things: statues carved out of driftwood, seashells, and a wide range of antiques and odd devices that frightened and intrigued Laura at the same time. A dozen pots hung from the ceiling, little plants filling each, and vintage bottles sat in the windows, painting the sunlight with a rainbow of colors.

"How's my little darling today?" Meme asked, her eyes fixed on Laurie.

Laurie was at that age where she loved to explore, and the moment the grownups' backs were turned, she toddled away, weaving among piles of knick-knacks and boxes stacked against the walls. She stumbled on the carpet, landed with a soft thud, and looked around to find herself in the doll room. There were so many new ones that she gasped with delight.

"More dollies! Ma-ma! Ma-ma, look! More dollies!"

Her excited cry brought Sarah and Meme, who both pretended to be as surprised as she was by the discovery. Laurie felt safe when Meme scooped her up, and she found the kindness in her sparkling blue eyes hypnotizing. Normally, Sarah was the only one Laurie permitted to hold her. Anyone else would suffer a pummeling by her swift little legs and small arms, not to mention the glass-shattering shrieks she would unleash. But Laurie allowed Meme to hold her for a long time while she busied her small hands with a silver necklace around the old woman's neck.

"We have the same eyes," Meme said.

Laurie blinked at her for a moment before going back to the necklace.

Meme carried her on a tour of the room, which housed several dozen antique dolls. Laurie abandoned Meme's charm necklace with its many odd shapes and figures to focus on the bright, lifelike faces of the many girls all around her. Laurie reached out toward one doll in particular. She was dressed in jeans and a flannel shirt. Sitting on a small pony, she wore a cowboy hat and a red scarf.

"*This* one?" Meme chuckled and took the doll and her pony down from the shelf. She turned to Sarah, who nodded her consent.

"I think you're old enough now. She likes you. I'll let her go home with you, if you promise to take good care of her."

Laurie nodded eagerly. Her small arms invited the gift, which Meme delivered with a raspy laugh. Laurie embraced the girl and her pony. They were both soft, but the doll's face was made from porcelain and felt cool against her lips when Laurie kissed her.

"They're inseparable," Meme said to Sarah, who smiled as Laurie cuddled the little pony and its rider.

"What do you say, baby girl?" Sarah said to Laurie.

"Thank you, May-May."

After a short lunch, Laurie occupied herself with stroking the pony's hair and talking to the doll, asking what her name was, what the pony's name was, and so on. A brief discussion with the doll revealed that her name was Jill, and her pony's name was Biscuit.

As Laurie played, Meme and Sarah went on talking. Then Sarah made a noise—a sad noise—and put a hand over her mouth. Laurie's head snapped in the direction of the sound, and she looked up into her mother's eyes. Then she glanced at Meme. Back and forth she went, her eyes looking from one to the other, trying to understand what was going on.

"I thought I raised her better than that," Meme said. "I ought to go over there and… Jesus Christ…turning away her own daughter…"

Sarah started crying, and before Meme could cross the room, Laurie abandoned Jill and Biscuit and ran to her mother's side. Sarah scooped up Laurie, who twisted her head around and glared at Meme, as if *she* were the one responsible for Sarah's fit of sadness. Laurie patted her mother's head and peppered her cheek with quick little kisses.

"I'm okay, baby girl." Sarah sniffled and reciprocated her daughter's affection. "It's not Meme's fault," she said, reading Laurie's mind.

Sarah began to translate Laurie's misunderstanding, but Meme wouldn't hear it. She held up her hands and said, "I know. You were the exact same way with Nancy."

Once Laurie had been effectively reassured that Meme was still their friend, she walked over to her and sat in her lap.

"Mommy's having a tough time," Meme explained. "But she's going to be okay. I promise."

Laurie stared into her rich-blue eyes for a few seconds before reaching for the charm necklace again. But Meme set her down and said, "Go to Momma now. Go on."

Laurie stood where she was for a moment, looking over at Sarah—her mother, who had just turned fifteen—before trotting over to enjoy the comfort of her affection. Sarah was trembling. She clung to Laurie as if something were trying to pull them apart. Calm followed—deep, steady breaths and a series of light kisses.

"Mommy's okay, baby girl. Go on and play. Go visit with Jill and Biscuit. I'll bet they've missed you."

Laurie studied Sarah suspiciously. She kissed her on the cheek and warily returned to her place on the area rug. She started talking to Jill about what she fed Biscuit but kept looking up at Sarah and Meme from time to time to make sure everything was okay.

A burst of laughter from a pair of joggers snapped Laura back to the present. With a quick breath and a series of blinks, she regained her bearings. But the trip to her childhood left her tingling, as if she'd stumbled and fallen into a frigid lake.

Laura was walking back to her car when saw him again. He climbed into his Jeep, and before she could take three steps, he was gone. Laura's reaction bordered on pissed off. Her face crumpled, and she grunted in frustration. Three times she'd seen him, and three times she'd been unable to follow him.

"Dammit," she muttered. "Who the hell does he think he is?"

A young couple turned to look at her, but Laura paid them no mind. She went on staring at the place where she'd seen him, then she followed an imaginary trail left by his Jeep. Even though he was long gone by the time she reached the road, Laura leaned around the parked cars and squinted in anger at nothing at all.

That evening, Laura was brooding and detached throughout dinner. Images of the stranger grew like weeds in her mind, crowding out more important thoughts and concerns. During the past few years, Laura had come to detest mysteries in all forms. She had no patience for such things and wanted only the answers without having to ponder the evidence for days or weeks at a time. She was also becoming suspicious of this man, who seemed to be following her for some reason. Her eyes widened a little. It was suddenly clear to her what was going on: Kate had hired a private detective.

"So *that's* it, you tricky bitch," she muttered. The first two sightings, she decided, were of little consequence. Whatever reasons Kate might have had for them were not important. But the *third*—the one that happened so soon after she had rejected Kate's company— *that* was the one that made it all come together.

"*What's* it?" Don asked from across the table.

"What?"

"You said, 'So that's it,' or something. What are you talking about?"

"Oh, nothing. Work. I was just thinking aloud."

Laura wondered why Kate would do such a thing. Then it started to seem improbable. Kate was a nosy woman, but Laura doubted she would hire a private investigator to spy on her.

She looked up at Don, who was busy wolfing down his salmon, and wondered if perhaps he had hired the man. No, Don was more trusting than that. Laura's eyes shifted about as she chewed slowly. The stranger didn't look like a PI, but Laura supposed that was the whole point—to be invisible. Annoyed by the whole thing, she growled like an irritable alley cat.

"You say something?" Don asked.

"What? Oh, no. Just thinking again."

That night, she lay awake and thought even more. She wondered if he wasn't a PI, but rather some kind of pervert who was stalking her. It didn't seem too far-fetched in today's world. But it didn't seem to fit quite right—even though seeing the same stranger three times strained the probability of coincidence. He was distracting her. Once again, the steady drumming began inside her head: *Is it me, or is it something else that's driving me crazy?* When she finally fell asleep, he floated in and out of her dreams like an irritating mosquito.

When Laura arrived at the office the next morning, Kate practically knocked her over the moment she walked through the door.

"You'll never guess what's happened!" Kate smiled like a lunatic, and she kept pressing a hand to her own face, to check her temperature, presumably.

"What is it?" Laura asked.

"Mr. Kessel was so impressed, he's thinking about hiring us to represent the other three firms he's affiliated with! Do you know what this means? It's incredible, Laura! *This* is the break we've been waiting for!"

As Kate tried in vain to contain herself, Laura only smiled, as if the news were business as usual—which it was.

A few hours later, Laura realized exactly what the "break" would mean to her: She was assigned four times her usual workload and was expected to work until seven o'clock three nights a week. Lunches would be eaten inside while she and her team analyzed the backgrounds of the additional companies.

On several occasions over the next two weeks, Laura noticed Kate escorting Bob Rutherford, one of the legal executives, to lunch to enjoy a little pre-celebration of the accounts they would soon acquire. They always took the legal exec's car.

So on a beautiful Thursday, after two weeks of Chinese and pizza delivery, Laura threw down her pen and picked up her phone and laptop.

"Where are *you* going?" Phyllis Minter asked. She appraised Laura over her gold bifocals. The woman happened to be an assistant to Kate, but Laura outranked her.

"*I* am going to lunch." Laura continued toward the door.

"We've got sixteen more pages to review, the accountant's assessment has to be filed, and then—"

"I'm going to lunch." Laura glanced about the room. "The rest of you have my permission to do the same. If Kate and Bob can take a lunch, then so can we."

Laura left the boardroom. In her wake, she could hear the rustling of papers and people laughing as they got up to go to lunch. The only person who *wasn't* laughing was Phyllis.

That bright afternoon, Laura went to her spot in the park and enjoyed an apple she'd bought from the fruit stand. As much as she tried, relaxation eluded her, and she was only mildly relieved by the natural symphony around her.

At one o'clock, she went back to the office and found Kate waiting for her outside the boardroom, arms folded in front, wearing an indifferent expression.

"Where have you been?" Kate's eyes bored into her.

Laura knew that look: she was standing before Kate the powder keg. "I went out." Laura walked past her into the boardroom and settled into her chair. The others had returned before her, which was good. She hoped no one else would be spoken to. When Laura looked toward Phyllis, the woman kept her beady eyes on the papers in front of her.

"Well, everyone else stayed," Kate announced.

Laura turned to face Kate without having the first clue as to why she was so brave all of a sudden. "*You* didn't."

Kate's face contorted into a mask of rage. "I don't answer to you. You understand that? If I have a business lunch with prospective clients that *you* are supposed to convince, it's none of your goddamned business! We're pressed tight enough as it is without the interference of your selfish whims, and I promised Mr. Kessel we'd come through for his associates the same way we came through for him. That means everyone puts in a hundred and ten percent. Is that clear?"

Laura looked up from her briefcase into Kate's eyes. They were like two little pilot lights, flickering with malevolence and venom. Laura knew what Kate was capable of. She could end a career with the snap of her fingers, take away everything Laura had worked for over the past ten years. And she loved to put people in their place in front of others. It wasn't tactful, but she didn't have to do it very often—people knew better than to cross her.

Laura nodded submissively. "Yes, I understand. I apologize."

The words smoothed out Kate's wrinkled brow and her curled lip. She raised her chin and breathed deeply through her nose. "Good. There'll be time to rest when this is over. Until then"—Kate looked around at the entire group—"let's get this done right and on schedule." Kate glanced at Laura, narrowed her eyes in silent warning, and left.

Laura was hoping to visit the park on Saturday while Don was off mountain biking with his friends, but her work schedule had been shifted to accommodate a few Saturdays so the project would be completed ahead of time. Kate had explained that this would provide Laura with ample time for final revisions and so forth. So instead of relaxing for most of the day beneath her shady tree, Laura went to work. Kate proved she had a heart by allowing everyone to dress casually, although unsurprisingly, she herself was not in attendance.

Laura might have gone to the park on Sunday, but it rained. Don wanted to meet with some friends at a sports bar and implored Laura to join them. Their wives would be along, and it would do her some good to get out, he insisted. The idea conjured images of the same conversations and observations she'd heard a million times at a million other lame social gatherings. Barbecues, birthday parties for one VP or another, a wedding here and there—they were all the same to her, so Laura faked a twenty-four-hour bug and told Don, "I'd rather not spread it around if I can help it." Don chose to go without her rather than miss out on any valuable sales tips or office gossip.

He kissed her on the forehead and left her on the couch in the living room, a knit throw draped over her and the television on. Once he left, Laura clicked off the TV and started searching the house for a book to read. In an old box of papers and junk in her closet, she found one, *Unanswered Prayers* by Truman Capote. Her mother, Sarah, had given it to her years ago as a peace offering. Laura had actually refused the book, but Sarah had snuck it into a box of Laura's things when she wasn't looking. Laura didn't remember reading it before, so she took it back to the living room.

She settled in on the couch and opened the book. A small photograph fell out, and Laura set the book down and stared at the picture. It was taken when she was just a child, four or so. Sarah was holding her in her lap, arms clasped around her, a smile on her face. In the picture, Sarah was barely an adult—seventeen or eighteen.

Laura studied every detail of the photograph until she could almost feel Sarah's arms around her. The natural perfume of her mother's skin wafted through her memory. The scent had always calmed her as a baby. The image blurred. Laura felt as if she were falling, sinking into the abyss of days gone by.

She shook her head, fighting the hypnotic spell. She stuffed the picture into the back of the book, out of sight, and started reading, but the daydream she'd had at the park resurfaced. Even though the old photograph was tucked away, every time she blinked, it was right there in front of her. Her eyes traced the sentences, the paragraphs, but at the end of the page, she had no idea what she'd read.

"Shit." She started the page over.

She read one paragraph and had to start over again. Then she did the same thing again.

The same strange idea kept fluttering through her head, refusing to be ignored.

"There's no way in hell I'm calling her." She spoke as if someone else were in the room with her, making suggestions. She tried to read some more without success.

It had been at least five years since they'd spoken to each other. The conversation hadn't lasted five minutes, and she vaguely remembered slamming the phone down.

Laura stared warily at the phone for several seconds then looked away. The thought of her last call made her feel sick with guilt and helpless at the same time. She set the book on the end table and stared at the phone again.

Just call her. No big deal.

Laura analyzed her motives and expectations. She failed to see what could be gained from calling, and had no idea what she could possibly say. She wondered if she still blamed Sarah.

That was the big question, if she still blamed her. When she considered it, she didn't know how *not* to blame her. Even still, she found herself reaching for the phone with a numb hand. It was Sunday. She would be home. Laura curled her fingers into a fist and grunted.

"Why?" she asked the ceiling. "Why the fuck do I have to call her?"

There was no answer. The only thing she knew for sure was that a meddlesome voice within her would not be silent until she called. It was probably guilt. *What if she dies? Today. What if she dies, and you never get another chance?*

"Goddammit." Laura grunted and snatched up the phone.

The cordless handset felt heavy in her hand—like an anchor. She had to think for a minute about what the number was before pressing the soft little buttons. Her head swam as it rang.

A raspy female voice on the other end said, "Hello?"

Laura was struck dumb for a few long seconds.

"Hello?" the voice said a second time.

Laura cleared her throat. "Hi, Sarah."

The ensuing silence was heavy and awkward.

"Laurie?"

Laura nodded stupidly. "Who'd you think?"

At that, Sarah laughed a little. "Well, I wasn't sure. Other people call me Sarah, you know? Jesus, kid, how are you? It's been a while."

Again, Laura nodded before speaking. "It has."

Each of them seemed to be waiting for the other one to continue the conversation. Finally, Sarah went on. "I've missed you. Talking with you, you know?"

"Yeah." Laura poked her thumbnail into her mouth.

Silence again.

"Honey, are you still mad at me?"

Laura said nothing.

"God, I worry so much about—"

"*Worry?* You *worry* about me?" Laura screamed. It happened like that—she just started screaming at her.

"Laurie, please…don't do this."

"You *worry* about me?" Laura chuckled spitefully.

"Yes, I *do*. Okay? Fuck, Laurie, what the hell do you want me to say to you?"

"Nothing, I shouldn't have called." Laura squeezed the phone as if to choke it silent.

"Right. Well, I'll talk to you again in, say, five more years? Maybe ten," Sarah snapped.

Laura wanted so much to slam the phone down. But she couldn't.

"Laurie? You still there?"

"Yes."

Silence. Sarah sighed, and Laura heard her sniffling.

"I love you more than anything in the world. That's never changed, and it never will. I wanted you to know that…before you hang up. So there, it's been said."

Laura began twisting a lock of hair around in her fingers. She wanted to say something, but she didn't know how without screaming.

Sarah exhaled and sniffled. "You know, since you were old enough to talk, I thought of you as a little sister."

"Jesus, Sarah. Don't start. Just don't fucking start that shit with me. Not now."

"Then when? Huh? In five more years?"

"Stop it."

Laura shook her head, hating herself. Part of her wanted to forgive Sarah and be done with it. But she couldn't do it.

"I wasn't the perfect mother."

"Oh, Christ," Laura moaned.

"Listen to me. I know I wasn't perfect, but I tried. Okay? I really did. I just…made a mistake." Sarah started crying. She hardly ever cried.

"Don't cry, Sarah. Please." Laura bit at her bottom lip. "Let's not talk about it now."

Sarah sounded as if she were regaining control. In the background, Laura could hear voices, men and women in the throes of a mellow social gathering if she had to guess. "You have company. I should let you go."

"No. Please don't. Talk to me some more."

Laura's lip trembled. "I don't know what else to say."

Silence again, long and as tight as a piano string.

"You don't have to say anything. Just don't hang up," Sarah pleaded.

"No, I should really go. I have things to do. I just wanted to…" The thought petered out.

"I love you, baby girl," Sarah whispered.

Laura said nothing. Her eyes brimmed with tears.

"Can I call you later? Please?" Sarah asked.

Laura shook her head and sucked in a shaky breath. "No. I'll call you, some other time. I promise I won't wait five years."

Sarah laughed, and Laura smiled at the familiar tickle of it.

"Okay," Sarah said. "Call me again soon. Please call me again soon."

Laura swallowed noisily and bit at her bottom lip. "I will. Soon."

"Okay. Bye for now. I love you," Sarah said.

Laura started to say something but returned the phone to its cradle instead. She sucked in a breath, pressed her face into her hands, and wept.

By late Sunday afternoon, Laura had reburied the emotional turbulence drawn out of her by the brief phone conversation with Sarah. This skill, though surely detrimental to her mental health, was something she'd perfected over the years. One minute, she felt suffocated by a merciless tidal wave of grief and guilt, and the next, she was able to smile and wipe away all visible traces of sadness and self-doubt.

Don returned home at about the time she was discarding the last few used tissues into the wicker wastebasket by the sofa. He asked her how she was feeling, and Laura smiled up at him and said, "Never better."

He mentioned a thing or two about what to do for a stuffy nose before retreating to the kitchen to prepare dinner.

On Monday, Laura discovered that despite all her team's foresight and the extra hours they had put in, the associate firms of the Kessel Group had decided to look elsewhere before coming to a decision. The deal was still on the table, of course, but their pitch was no longer exclusive. Such a development wasn't uncommon, but it always put Kate in a volatile mood. She became a walking landmine when deals weren't closed quickly and to her satisfaction. Laura wondered if anyone else was aware of Kate's other side, expressed by the wringing of her hands and the way she zoned out for minutes at a time. The vacancy in her eyes spoke volumes to Laura. Most of the time, Kate elected to be alone when things appeared to be "on the rocks," as she often said. So Laura was surprised when Kate approached her and asked her out to lunch.

"We'll take my car." She offered Laura a faint, troubled smile.

Kate drove them to Whitley's Bar and Grill, an upscale place disguised as one that wasn't. There was a television and a pool table, but neither served much purpose. A hamburger was twelve dollars, and a beer was five. Though it pretended to be a hole-in-the-wall, there wasn't a broken bottle or a stray cigarette butt to be seen.

"How have you been?" Kate asked.

Laura almost looked behind her. "Uh… Fine, I guess." She nibbled on her ten-dollar turkey sandwich.

Looking at Kate, Laura had an idea that maybe *she* wasn't fine. Her hands were shaking just enough for Laura to notice, and her eyes kept shifting restlessly from left to right.

"How are *you* doing, Kate?"

Kate laughed. "I'm up to my neck! *That's* how I am. I need that bonus."

Laura didn't want to say anything. She *really* didn't.

"Hal and I bought a cute little place near Lake Tahoe, and…I just *really* need that bonus."

Laura was clearly being drafted as a counselor again. It had been a while, but there had been many other times. The first was when Kate was worried about her promotion, which she'd ended up getting, but not before charging almost twenty thousand dollars in furniture and accessories for her new house. Then it was the bonus she'd needed to pay for the addition to her five-thousand-square-foot house—that bonus had saved her at the last minute—followed by the brand-new BMW 850 she'd sold her late parents' house to acquire. There were other instances, of course: real estate purchases in Idaho and Cape Cod, antiques from auctions, trips to Greece, and cruises on chartered yachts. This was merely the latest hurdle for Kate, one she seemed nervous about presently, and with good reason—the affiliates of the

Kessel Group could easily afford to take their sizable business elsewhere.

"You'll get it." Laura smiled with forced confidence. She honestly had no idea what would happen in the next few days or weeks.

"You think so? I mean, we're very competitive, and Mr. Kessel seems to like our work the best. They'll side with us, won't they?" Kate licked her lips and clenched her fists, as if Laura had any say in the matter.

She nodded again and sipped her sweet tea. "Sure, they will."

Kate looked relieved at last, and from then on, she talked as if she'd already been awarded the bonus. She went on and on about the little place on Lake Tahoe, the potential necessity for four-wheel drive—BMW had a spectacular line of SUVs—and the excruciating task of furnishing the little getaway with only the best items money could buy.

"And," Kate whispered, "I've been looking at several plans for a guest house and a deck. This place is just what I need. To relax, you know? Just get away from it all and really *relax*."

Laura was reasonably attentive, but her thoughts drifted at the idea of "just getting away from it all." She and Don were due for a vacation, and hers would be coming up soon. They hadn't even made plans about where they would go yet. Laura hardly cared, as long as they did *something*.

"That reminds me." Kate reached across the table and touched Laura's arm. "The corporate party is in a couple weeks. I just bought this incredible dress. Expensive as hell, but I consider it an investment. With all the existing and potential clients we've invited, it's in everyone's best interest to shine. Have you picked out a dress yet?"

Laura shrugged and confessed she hadn't given it much thought.

"Well, you should. Don't wait until the day before. Please don't do that," Kate pleaded. "In this world, you're either the best...or you're *nothing*. There's the top of the pile, and then there's everything else." She punctuated her hollow sentiments with a sharp little nod and sipped her wine.

Laura did what she felt was the safest thing: she nodded and said, "Mm-hm."

As Laura prepared dinner that evening, Don expressed his desire to buy a boat, and he refused to allow the conversation to stray from the subject.

"Nate just bought a real beauty. It's a twenty-six-footer with a two-hundred-horsepower motor. You ought to come see it with me tomorrow. It's silver and blue. You like blue. I think maybe Thursday I'll go and talk to the dealer." Don was like a little boy—huge smile, eyes sparkling with wonder. He had obviously already made up his mind and was completely thrilled about the new addition to his toybox. "It'll be fun. We'll drive out, and maybe the dealer will let us test one on the lake. You'll love it."

Laura smiled and shrugged. "You go ahead. I think I'll just hang around here, maybe go for a drive if it's nice."

Don stopped chewing and studied her. Laura tried to smile, but her gaze drifted then sank back to her plate. With an absent stare, she studied the silver fork in her hand, the cloth napkin, the grilled chicken on her plate… She had prepared the meal and presented it just so, with a cute little portion of vegetables and seasoned bowtie pasta. The plates were garnished with purple kale and sliced apples, dipped in lemon juice so they wouldn't turn brown. For a few seconds, Laura imagined that she could have been anywhere, with anyone. Don could easily have been a business contact and her surroundings a fancy restaurant. The thought scared the hell out of her.

She didn't want to look up and see his smiling face, though she knew it was free of sorrow or concern. It might have been his perpetual happiness alone that depressed her, but somehow, she knew there was more to it than that.

Absence was the only thing that followed her words. She knew he was thinking about what she'd said, wondering why she didn't want to accompany him. And as he thought about it, he was probably filtering out any negative possibility for her decision, selecting only the reasons he could live with. Laura suspected this was his way of ensuring his idealistic perception of their relationship would not be disrupted.

"That's okay," he said. "I understand how hard you've been working. You need time to relax on your own. I won't *make* you go if you don't want to."

There was a trace of disappointment in his words, but Don didn't argue or get upset. Laura sighed, wishing to God he would.

That night, Don wanted to make love, and Laura assumed it was his way of trying to fix a problem he dared not inquire about. Or it might have been his way of trying to enhance their joy over the new boat he would soon purchase for *them*. She couldn't be sure. Whatever the case, she welcomed it and even enjoyed it for a little while. Laura didn't subscribe to the myth of women having sex for intimacy alone, as she, too, enjoyed the drug-like shockwave of her orgasms, when she had them. But she wasn't able to achieve that sensation as easily as she used to. Sex with Don wasn't terrible. She had once formed an analogy to describe it to herself. It was like a seesaw. He would perform in a certain way, then she would perform in a certain way. The exchange felt awkward and unnatural, much too difficult and forced. With Don, she felt as if kissing and sex never blended smoothly, and nothing could pass between them without a serious amount of thought beforehand. They often had to speak to each other, which was all right sometimes and downright unnerving at others.

When they were finished and Don had fallen asleep, another

analogy sprang to mind, one to describe how she felt making love should be: like a carousel. She pictured that as the ideal symbol of perfect lovemaking, spinning evenly and without any abrupt disturbances or conclusions. It went around and around, until both lovers were dizzy and had to close their eyes. One turn blended evenly with another until there were no turns at all. And when it was finally over, it slowly came to a stop. Naturally, its momentum would fade, until she and her lover came to rest in the warmth of motion ended, relaxed and spellbound.

Laura frowned. With her hands propped behind her head, she thought about the carousel, knowing she never could have formed such an analogy had she not experienced it firsthand. Those years were so distant now, the years when she was a teenage girl with an attitude and no money, with no knowledge of the world but knew everything. She *had* known everything that mattered, though. The freedom she enjoyed with her midnight-blue '79 Firebird, the finger-like wind caressing her short hair…and the carousel.

"I love you, Laurie Alman." Jimmy's whisper in her ear felt as soft as the nighttime summer breezes tickling her naked body. Laurie's head swam as she straddled him on the soft blanket spread out on the grass. Jimmy sat up and tucked her legs behind him so that she was seated in his lap. He kissed her deeply, and the darkness behind her closed lids exploded with color. Her body trembled when her second orgasm hit. She exhaled and clung to him, and her head swam as he lowered her onto her back. He nibbled gently at her neck as he made love to her, leading her once again toward an explosive rush that left her feeling as fluid as a mountain stream warmed by the sun.

It never felt as though it ended. There was no abruptness to it, no definitive line that separated the deep connection of making love from what came afterward. Jimmy never let go of her, and Laurie rested with her head on his chest. When she got chilly, Jimmy grabbed a sheet from her car and covered them with it.

"We could sleep out here tonight," he said.

Laurie kissed him. "We could stay out here forever." She rolled to one side so they could both look up at the stars. "I'll bet it's like this in heaven. We get to stay outside all the time, never have to worry about food or rain or cold weather."

"Or your snoring." Jimmy glanced at her and smiled.

Laurie slapped his chest. "I don't *snore*. Asshole."

"The hell you don't. You sound like a tractor needs a motor job." Jimmy laughed.

Laurie stared at him, her mouth agape. She rolled on top of him and started tickling him. "That's a lie! Take it back, liar!"

Jimmy tickled her back, and because she was more ticklish, he ended up winning, as he always did.

The battle quickly wore them down, and they rested again, Laurie on top of him, his arms around her waist. He kissed her neck.

"I'll never find another girl like you." Jimmy held her head in his hands so he could look her in the eyes. "You're as much as my heart can handle, and you're more than I ever thought I'd deserve in this world."

Laurie kissed him. "You won't have to find another girl, baby. And if I ever catch you so much as looking at one, I'll kick both your asses."

Jimmy laughed. Laurie clung to him, and they stayed that way until dawn.

Laura's nose stung, and her eyes filled to the edges. Tears ran down the sides of her face and into her ears. She sniffled and wiped her nose. After a short battle, she forced her memories back into the closet of her mind and locked the door.

It was becoming more difficult, the selective recall of the few times that brought her joy. The other memories always pushed their way in, until she had no choice but to turn her back on all of them and embrace the sterility she had come to both accept and despise. She opted for sterility because it felt safe; there were no surprises there. In safety, she convinced herself that she'd found peace, though the two were not as alike as she pretended. At the very least, there weren't many nightmares. But she dearly missed the caress of her dreams.

Don went to see his friend's boat the next morning. It was a clear Saturday, and Laura informed him that she would rather work in the yard. When he was gone, she did just that, pruning the bushes and weeding the flowerbeds. The simple routine enabled her time think, to have silent little conversations with herself that made her both pensive and hopeful. For the most part, she regarded each of her ideas as nothing more than a harmless fantasy. Imagine, for example, Laura Alman, Director of Marketing Development, buying an old, run-down farmhouse somewhere in Franklin or Johnston County, and… She laughed at herself and shook her head.

Another fantasy emerged, and Laura began to think about her car, shining like a polished gemstone in the driveway. It was a light, metallic-blue color with gray leather. She stopped to stare at the car as if it had appeared there by accident. After a while, with a thoughtful frown and a little harrumph, she went back to work.

Her thoughts went in all directions as she pruned, like so many leaves caught in a playful vortex of wind. She breathed in a scent in the air, something unique to the Southeast. When she closed her eyes and breathed deeply enough, she could smell Savannah. A crisp wind danced through her hair, and she smiled at the sensation, so much like gentle fingers…like Sarah's fingers.

Laurie always felt at home on the busy streets of Savannah, amid the colorful people and their many odd ways. Bag ladies on the corner, scraggly-looking men trying to sell things no one could possibly want, children whizzing past on bicycles—they were all part of the erratic heartbeat she'd come to love. And whenever she and Sarah ventured into the city, both of them would marvel at the old houses and the canopy of trees overhead adorned with streamers of Spanish moss waving in the wind like feathery tentacles.

On a crisp March afternoon, they dressed up in vintage thrift-store clothes before venturing out to enjoy the sun. Sarah forced a wide-brimmed hat onto Laurie's head. "It looks *sooo* good on you!" she announced in a stuffy accent and capped it with a volley of raspy laughter.

They were cheap things, the hats and clothes, even the jewelry, but Sarah had some magical ability to transform them into articles reserved specifically for the wealthy elite. Laurie laughed so easily with Sarah, her foolish mother, strutting around like a peacock and maintaining a straight face through it all.

They walked for miles, pretending and laughing most of the way. Sarah played up the masquerade by pausing in mid-step. "Oh, gracious darling, I do hope you realize how dreadful that scarf is behaving." She snatched the silk scarf away from Laurie's neck and added it to her collection.

"Hey! That's *mine!*" Laurie protested then laughed as Sarah started off again.

"Hush hush, bunny. You couldn't *possibly.*" Sarah looked about the open street. She wrinkled her face and burst into a carefree laugh. Leaning against Laurie, she returned the scarf and kissed her on the cheek three times. "I love you so much, baby girl."

Whatever they lacked, Sarah convinced Laurie they had in abundance, if only for a little while, all so they could "try it on for size," as she often said. Fancy clothes were a biggie. They played a lot at this game, leaving the house in extravagant costumes as if it were Halloween. Most people who didn't know them—along with many who *did*—believed that both were completely crazy. They would don fancy silk dresses over cut-offs and T-shirts and drape imitation feather boas over their shoulders. No ensemble was complete without a pound of fake jewelry cluttering their wrists, necks, and fingers—strings of glass beads and fake pearls, which Sarah had acquired at flea markets and thrift stores for next to nothing.

In particular, Sarah enjoyed her little parasol with the purple butterflies fluttering on an off-white cotton fabric. Sunglasses were another of Sarah's fetishes, one that Laurie adopted immediately.

Once they were in disguise, the world became their oyster. At a private beach on Hilton Head Island, Sarah found a way to sneak the two of them in, and they pranced out onto the sand with a picnic basket and proceeded to strip in front of everyone, revealing their vile cut-offs and T-shirts for all to see. They managed to have a nice lunch and a quick dip before being asked to leave.

"Oh, what's the harm?" Sarah pinched the hotel clerk's cheek. Later, she referred to him as a member of the Elitist Gestapo.

Never one to be dissuaded from showing her baby girl a happy time, Sarah set off for a different part of the island, carrying Laurie through the woods on her back.

"If they see us sneaking through the woods like this, they'll automatically know we're filthy imposters," Sarah whispered.

Laurie held on as Sarah shuffled through the fallen palm debris, assuring Sarah that she was *not* the least bit filthy. "I've *seen* filthy. Scabby Abby at school is *filthy*."

"Well then, maybe you should invite her over for a bath," Sarah said.

"What? Are you sick, Mom? She's got the cooties!"

Sarah gave her a sour look. "Don't be so mean, kid. I'll drop you right here and let *you* get the cooties."

"There ain't no *cooties* here."

Sarah hefted Laurie up higher on her back. "Are, too. They live in the sand sometimes. And they bite little girls' toes."

"I don't believe you for a minute."

"Okay then, let's just set you down here—"

Laurie clung to Sarah. "No! No, no, no! I believe you! I believe you."

They crept out onto a secluded part of the private beach, and Sarah located a couple of chairs someone had left behind—compliments of the local hotel.

"Well, I'll be damned." Sarah put Laurie down, rested her hands on her hips, and chuckled.

Laurie playfully slapped Sarah's arm. "Don't cuss, Sarah."

"Laurie, honey, you've got a lot to learn about what cussin' is. Here, you're a big girl. Grab your own chair."

"I'm not *that* big!" Laurie pouted.

"C'mon now, your poor old mother's worn out from luggin' your carcass around."

Laurie grabbed a chair, grunting as if the chore were too much for her to bear. It wasn't, of course, but thanks to Sarah, Laurie loved to pretend.

The salty air wafted past and around them, gusty ocean breezes threatening to toss their hats into the air and out to sea. They relaxed into their chairs, and Sarah dug some fruit out of her bag: a banana and dried pineapple with a little sugar on it.

"Paradise." Sarah leaned back in her chair.

Laurie replied with a little sigh, adjusting her hat to shield her face from the sun.

Sarah turned toward Laurie. "Who gave anyone the right to buy this land? You hear what I'm saying, baby girl? From *whom* exactly did they buy it? And how did *they* get it?"

"Maybe it belongs to a prince or a queen," Laurie said.

"Maybe. I dunno." Sarah let out a heavy sigh. "Seems like all the good places were taken long before the rest of us even *got* here."

Laurie leaned forward. A man wearing a tight little suit approached from the nearby hotel, trudging awkwardly through the dry sand.

Sarah turned to Laurie and gave her a little smile. "Well, kid, I think we'd better call it a day, don't you?"

Laurie stood up and dusted herself off. "Okay."

"I was gettin' sick of this place anyway. A little too quiet for me. You feel like some ice cream?"

"Yeah!"

Sarah picked up her bag and took Laurie's hand. "Let's go, before the stiff in the suit makes a fuss about us."

Where the beach met the woods, Sarah stopped to comb her fingers through Laurie's hair, smiling and blinking her brown eyes. "Maybe we can come back tomorrow."

Sarah turned and bent her knees. Laurie hopped onto her back, and Sarah carried her through the woods. By the roadside, Sarah set Laurie down, and they climbed into the faded red Ford Falcon station wagon with the yellow driver's-side door.

Laurie hopped in on Sarah's side and scooted over into the passenger seat. "I wish we could've gone for a swim."

"Yeah, me, too." Sarah closed the door and rolled down the window. "I'll turn on the sprinkler when we get home."

Laurie made a face. "That's okay. I don't wanna get grass all over my feet."

"Suit yourself." Sarah pointed at Laurie's waist. "Seatbelt, sweetie. We don't want any giant cooties pulling you out the window."

Laurie chuckled as she pulled the belt across her lap.

Sarah fired up the puttering engine, and off they went to discover a new adventure.

A gust of wind swept past, whisking Savannah from Laura's memory before she could grab hold of it. A muscle car drove by, smearing the quiet with its growling engine. Laura's attention fell on her car again. She let her eyes go out of focus, imagining her old Firebird in its place—another harmless, short-lived fantasy.

Maybe I can pretend.

Laura smiled. She checked her watch. It was close to noon, and she suspected that Don had gone to the boat dealer.

While she needed no excuse to take a drive, she planned a trip to the farmer's produce stand to pick up some fresh vegetables for dinner that evening. She took the long way, tuning in to the classic rock station just in time to catch the last part of Aerosmith's "Back in the Saddle." Listening to an excitable, shrieking Steven Tyler took her back to her high school days and smoking behind the building when class was over.

The distance between the school and her house was more than two miles, and she'd been forced to walk due to some ambiguous boundary for public bus services. She didn't mind, nor did her wild friends. It gave them time to talk and think and dream about what the future held for them. They could also smoke, swear, listen to music, and act like fools.

On occasion, one of her girlfriends would bring a radio with a tape deck, and they would listen to Aerosmith, Journey, or AC/DC on the way home. Sometimes, Jimmy carried Laura on his back until she became too heavy, at which point he would walk onto the grass and collapse so she landed on top of him. Laura's friends would join the pile until they formed a little mound of arms, legs, and laughing heads. Their collective laughter and hysterical shrieking had attracted the police on at least two occasions.

Laura's smile came and faded. She watched the road as the ghosts exited her mind. She wasn't appreciating the landscape the way she'd intended. The flowering pear trees and fragrant violets painted the air with color and perfume. The greens all seemed much greener, having awakened from a short winter slumber. Laura drank in the beauty all around her, marveling at it as if for the first time. In a way, she felt that she, too, was awakening from a slumber.

After driving around for half an hour, she cut across town and headed for the produce stand. She came out directly across from it as she had before, and when she stopped for the light, her heart jumped.

The white Jeep was parked in front. The stranger was talking to Duncan behind the counter. He wore jeans, a loose T-shirt with some kind of picture on the front, and black sneakers.

Laura squinted at him and cocked her head to one side. Her instincts told her he wasn't a PI or a pervert, but she knew there was really no way to tell for sure.

If she had been involved with a brokerage firm that acquired businesses and that sort of thing, she wouldn't have ruled him out as an agent working with the Securities and Exchange Commission. But she had nothing at all to do with high-dollar acquisitions and liquidation, and so she remained confused as ever.

A horn blast from an angry-looking fool in his twenties with a crew cut and sunglasses prodded her from behind. Laura passed through the intersection just as the stranger hopped into his Jeep and pulled out onto the road. Her heart pounded, and she was seized by an irresistible sense of curiosity.

She didn't stop at the produce stand. Instead, she casually fell in behind the white Jeep and followed it. He didn't drive too fast for her to keep up. In fact, he kept his speed just a hair over the legal limit.

"What the hell am I doing?" She suddenly became aware that *she* was the pervert, stalking *him*.

Nevertheless, Laura couldn't give up her pursuit any more than she could explain why she was following him. She'd seen him too many times before, so he must be following her. That alone entitled her to know who he was. It was a thin and twisted sliver of logic, but it was all she had.

She followed him out of town, onto a winding road in the country. By her estimation they couldn't have gone more than six or seven miles before his left turn signal came on. He turned onto a narrower road that headed west. Laura hesitated, stopping by the edge of the road. She wondered if he was luring her to his house, where he would have the opportunity to attack her. The idea was ludicrous. She pulled out onto the road again and made the left.

She could still see his Jeep when she made the turn, driving down a road flanked with young trees and abandoned old tobacco sheds. She maintained a distance of more than a hundred yards—just enough so that making out her license plate would be impossible. And if he turned around and tried to chase her, her car would easily leave him in the dust. Laura laughed and shook her head shamefully.

You're really crackin' up now, woman.

As much as she half-believed she was going crazy, she couldn't deny the exhilarating sense of adventure. The Jeep rounded a bend and vanished from sight. Laura maintained her speed and kept on the alert. He might have spotted her and could be waiting around the next bend. She slowed down and cautiously approached the curve. Through the young trees, she saw only gray pavement and large boulders by the roadside. Anything as obvious as a white Jeep would have been easy to spot, and sure enough, when she rounded the bend, the Jeep was gone. She looked around everywhere. The road stretched out for more than a mile and was devoid of any vehicles.

"Damn. I lost him."

She continued driving slowly down the road, glancing left and right at the gravel driveways that branched off on either side. There was no way to tell which one he'd taken, and choosing one at random felt terribly risky. People out in the country kept guns, ferocious dogs, and such. Admitting defeat, Laura finally turned around and went back the way she'd come.

At the very least, she knew the road he lived on. Then she wondered if he even lived on this road or if he was merely visiting somebody.

Frustrated and more curious than ever, Laura drove back to the produce stand and began selecting vegetables. She smiled at Duncan, who remembered her, and went back to browsing. The questions running through her head continued to pester her for answers. *Could the Jeep driver be married or involved with someone? What does he do for a living?*

What kinds of music does he listen to? They were date questions that no self-respecting bride-to-be had any business asking, and yet there they were.

Speculations started taking shape, all equally inappropriate and senseless. She suspected that he was working-class, with mechanical aptitude, and that he loved nature. She further assumed that he was active and enjoyed long walks in the woods, that he was caring and considerate, and that he was easy-going—an adult.

"Stop it!" she hissed at herself.

A woman with pink curlers and sea-green eyes looked up at Laura, who smiled with embarrassment.

At the counter, still burdened by so many questions, Laura wondered if Duncan knew anything about the stranger. An idea popped into her head, a plot to obtain the information she sought. She'd seen it in movies before.

"Um, I was wondering," she said. "Do you know anything about the man who stops by here driving a white Jeep?"

Duncan grinned and nodded. "Why, sure I do. Those are his tomatoes you've got."

His response threw off Laura's timing. She looked down at the healthy, ripe tomatoes and touched one of them. It was strange inanimate connection. She cleared her throat.

"Well, I was wondering…if you knew anything. I mean…" Her concentration was completely blown. She had worked out all the words in her head, then he'd mentioned the tomatoes. "He sort of cut me off in traffic and…" She couldn't finish. The idea had fled.

"He did? Really? Hmm. That's not like him. Was there any damage?" Duncan asked.

"No! No, no. Never mind. It's nothing. I was just concerned. I mean… I wanted to give him a piece of my mind." Laura forced a crooked smile and laughed.

"Hmm. Well, if it's that important to you, I could give you his number. You're not a lawyer or a cop, are you?"

"What? No. God no."

"Salesman?"

"Uh-uh. No."

"Religious fanatic, member of a blood drive? He hates to be reminded about donating, you know."

"I'm…I'm none of those things." Laura's heart swelled with anxiety as Duncan wrote down a number on a slip of paper.

"I was only kidding." He winked at her. "Don't you go telling him I gave you this—he's apt to be a little annoyed if he finds out."

"I won't. I won't." Laura took the piece of paper and tucked it away.

Duncan raised his eyebrows and shook his head. "Go easy on him. He's a nice guy." He smiled at her.

"Oh, I just wanted to…" Her voice snagged in her throat.

"Give him a piece of your mind, I know." He flashed a wry smile at her. "It'll be seven dollars for the produce. Number's free, since you're not the police."

Laura laughed and handed over the money, embarrassed that her hands were shaking. She thanked him and returned to her car.

She dug the scrap of paper out of her pocket and looked down at it. The paper contained only a number, no name.

Now that she had his number, she couldn't decide what to do with it. She considered all the possible avenues. She could call and hope for a voicemail message that might reveal something about him, but many people just repeated the number and instructed the caller to speak after the tone, offering nothing about their lives. The next option would be to call and speak directly to him, asking questions as if his life were any of her business. She shied away from this approach, considering how badly she'd almost botched her attempt at lying to Duncan. There was always the possibility of trying for the machine and actually getting *him* instead. She could hang up, but calling him would give away her number. Unless she could find a pay phone somewhere.

"God, this is getting ridiculous." She rubbed her temples.

Dizzy from the anxious whirlwind of possible success and failure, Laura sighed with despair and shook her head. "What the hell am I doing?"

Upon speaking and hearing her sobering words, she crumpled up the phone number and tossed it out the window. She started the car and pulled away from her parking space, driving in silence until she was at the edge of the lot. She was about to pull out into traffic again, but she hesitated, thoughts and possibilities dancing through her head. Laura's gaze darted about as she thought.

"Goddammit." She put the car in reverse, backed up to where she'd parked, opened the door, and snatched the little ball of paper off the pavement. After tucking it back into her pocket, she slammed the door and drove away.

Back at the house, Laura made an early dinner. Don returned with a beaming grin and stories of the boat he'd driven on the lake.

"You should have been there, babe!" He kissed her on the lips so hard, she worried about him bruising her.

The whole idea of having a boat had utterly consumed his every thought—the same way having a motorcycle had consumed him a year before. Whatever shame she might have exhibited regarding her cloak-and-dagger activities went unnoticed as they ate and he talked.

"I made a wake three feet high. The dealer said he's never seen a guy pilot a boat like me on his first run." Don beamed with pride.

Laura couldn't help but wonder how Don, a salesman himself, could be taken in so easily by the boat dealer's sycophantic sales pitch. After a moment or two, she didn't care. Her thoughts remained focused on matters of a different nature, leaving no room for anything else.

That night, she claimed to be too tired for sex, and Don agreed to being exhausted, as well, having wrestled the monstrous boat on the water for hours that afternoon.

Laura dreamed of open fields and the thundering gallop of well-groomed horses. In her dreams, she ran alongside them, sharing the soft plains and cool water from the intersecting streams dividing her own private horse ranch. She couldn't recall the sky ever being so blue.

At that moment, the sky was blue, clear, and open, affording a view too broad and too deep for her to fathom entirely.

To be on that ranch with the earth rumbling beneath her as the horses raced by was to indulge in a kind of meditation. In the presence of that thunder, Laura understood what clarity was. Rolling in the knee-high grass, running about, or riding Valkyrie, she also knew freedom.

A woman appeared in the distance. A little older than Laura, she had darker hair, a smaller nose, and kind brown eyes. Smiling, the woman approached, and Laura wanted so much to hold her…to be *held* by her. But she backed away, and the woman's smile faded, right before she vanished from sight. Laura blinked and said, "Sarah?" but the vision was gone.

She closed her eyes, and when she reopened them, she was walking beneath the lamps lining Main Street early in the morning, sometime before dawn. The hazy yellow light was mechanical and surreal. It was only light, but light in and of itself could be such a wonderful thing, splitting the darkness and chasing away the shadows where doubts are born.

Someone else was there with her. She was leaning against him and stroking his firm upper arm as they walked. Jimmy. He was more than a masculine, beautiful memory drifting through her dreams. His smiling face, soulful eyes, and soft words gave her warmth. She stood up on her bare toes and kissed his lips, drinking in the bliss she always felt in his arms. Then she closed her eyes and slept soundly in a quiet ocean of warm darkness.

15

On her way to work on Monday, Laura passed the same Mercedes dealership she had done business with two years ago. She looked at all the luxury sedans, colorful gems on shiny wheels, all lined up in neat little rows. She tilted her head slightly to one side, drumming her fingers on the wheel until the light changed, and she drove on.

At work, she found Kate in a neutral mood, preoccupied with a number of dilemmas. And that was bad. That immediately put Laura on high alert. Kate was a powder keg when she was like this, and a collective anxiety grew in those beneath her. They didn't know exactly how big the keg was. Finding Kate screaming in a rage was always better. When she was brooding quietly over something, there was no way to gauge the potential damage if and when she finally went off, which normally resulted in many more casualties.

When a young man with thin hair and glasses named Garrison Hobart misplaced six pages of accounting information, he became the spark.

"How the hell could you *lose* six pages of crucial data? Huh? How are we supposed to know how much to bill those clients? Well? You don't have an answer, do you? Find those pages in the next hour, or so help me God, you're done. Get away from me. Go!" Kate pinched her eyes closed in disgust.

Garrison's face paled, and he looked sickly and worn as he walked away, trembling. His expression was understandable. Kate roared like a lion, and Laura had always known Garrison to be a gentle, soft-spoken man. When he passed Laura, he smiled at her weakly, and she forced a smile back.

"Don't let it bother you, kid. Happens to all of us." She patted him on the arm.

At eleven o'clock, Laura took an early lunch, ducking out of the office before Kate could find her. The last thing she wanted was to dine with Kate when she was prone to explosive outbursts. Obviously, something pretty serious was bothering her, and Laura wanted absolutely nothing to do with it.

She drove to a fairly secluded part of the park she'd walked through before. There was a pay phone there—one of very few left in the world, she suspected. Feeling like a spy in the movies, she left her car with the stranger's phone number and some change to make the call. She was hesitant at first but decided that there was really nothing to worry about. If the stranger answered, she would simply hang up. If he traced the number, he would only be tracing a pay phone.

Laura slipped the coins into the slot and dialed. The little purr of his phone ringing made her stomach flip. It rang four times before a click came on, followed by a message.

"Hi. If you know my voice, and you're calling intentionally, leave a message after the beep. If you're a salesman or a lawyer or someone who dialed this number by accident, hang up now. Better luck next time. Bye."

His voice was clear and smooth, deep and wise. For a few moments after the beep, Laura kept the phone pressed to her cheek. He sounded like a kind person, someone who was sensitive about what he said to others.

Laura hung up the phone and dialed the number a second time so she could listen to it again. The four rings passed, and the message came on. She would have sworn he'd been smiling when he recorded it. His voice had a slight hint of laughter in it. She imagined his mouth bent into a grin, the way she'd seen it that day in the rain. But there was something else. Something about it made her want to hear it over and over again. It was just the right octave, the perfect tone. He spoke as if he'd chosen his words with care and was in no hurry at all. The sound of his voice soothed her in ways she couldn't explain.

She hung up just before the beep and paused for a moment, savoring the echo of his words. It was so pleasing that she dialed a third time, smiling in anticipation of the sound of his soothing voice. It rang once…twice. She could hardly wait for the message to—

"Hello?"

Laura's eyes flew open, and her first instinct was to slam the phone into its cradle. But she didn't do that. It was the same voice, somewhat clearer than what she'd heard coming from the machine.

"Hello?" he said again.

"Um…ahem! Yes, um…" Laura lost all sense of direction, time, place, and purpose.

"Yes?" the stranger's voice inquired patiently.

That might have been what threw her off: She didn't want to *say* anything. She just wanted to listen to him talk.

"I'm sorry to bother you. I…" Laura struggled. "I'm calling because…you cut me off the other day. In traffic." She grimaced from the lie.

"Really? God, I'm sorry. You weren't injured, were you?"

"No! No. Um, I was just…" She fought to get past the concern in his voice, for *her*—a woman he didn't even know. A woman who'd called him to tell lies. The pause dragged out for several seconds.

"Miss? Are you still there?"

"Yes, yes, I'm here. I was just wondering…" She paused again.

"Was there any damage? Was anyone hurt?"

"No, no one was hurt. There's no damage."

"That isn't like me. I'm usually an exceptional driver. I haven't received a ticket since I was eighteen." He let out a soft laugh.

Laura closed her eyes and laughed with him.

"Should we notify the police?" he asked.

Laura's eyes snapped open. "No! I mean, no, that's not

necessary."

"Oh. Okay." A touch of confusion arose in his voice. "Miss?"

"Yes?"

"If you don't mind my asking, how did you happen to get my number?"

A coldness seized Laura's entire body. If she told him the truth, Duncan might be able to offer a description of her vehicle, of *her*, and the stranger might call the police.

"Miss?" He chuckled again.

"That's okay. I just wanted to let you know…to be more careful," she said, pretending not to hear his question.

"I certainly will. I'm glad you brought it to my attention. Thank you."

Laura swallowed nervously. All she could think of to say was, "You're welcome."

"Goodbye?" he said, as if asking.

Laura would have sworn that, once again, he was smiling, amused by the whole thing—a woman calling to scold him about his driving. At last, Laura found her voice. "Yes. Goodbye."

She slowly hung up the phone. Her hand fell to her side. She raised it again, to reach for the phone. Then she started to walk away but went back to the phone again. She stopped, turned back around, and walked away.

Tuesday went by in much the same way—at a crawl, with Laura's thoughts drifting elsewhere. Aside from a gentle reminder from Kate about the upcoming presentation for the associate companies of the Kessel Group, no one interrupted her daydreaming. The usual meetings took place, at which she viewed the same presentations she swore she'd witnessed a hundred times that month alone. Kate would tug on her sleeve now and then, to inform her about one damn thing or another, usually something obvious or unrelated to work.

"Sometimes I wonder if Simone honestly believes anyone is fooled by that cheap necklace of hers." Kate laughed, nudging Laura. When Kate wasn't looking, Laura studied her carefully, wearing an expression somewhere between perplexity and disgust.

After a grueling, hour-long projections meeting—during which Laura mostly daydreamed—the room emptied out into the corridor.

Kate sidled up to Laura. "Hey. I wanted to congratulate you on landing the Gibbons account. Nice work."

Laura acknowledged her for a moment. "Oh. Thanks."

Kate's brow wrinkled, and she asked Laura why she was so *lethargic* lately.

"I'm not lethargic. I've just… got a lot on my mind." Laura knew instantly that she'd made a mistake.

"Like what?" Kate said.

"Nothing too exciting. The Kessel accounts, the corporate party coming up—you know, the usual stuff."

"Oh. Well, listen…" Kate grabbed Laura by the arm and squeezed a little too hard. "You need any help with the Kessel accounts, you let me know, okay? I could very easily assign some of Donna's team to lend a hand."

Laura shrugged and assured Kate that her team was more than up to the task. As it turned out, that admission soured Kate's expression. "Don't try to be a hero on this, Laura. You hear me? We all need to pull together. If you need a hand, you be sure and say so."

"You're right. I sure will." Laura forced a smile and nodded.

Kate stepped closer to her. "What's the matter with you? C'mon, tell me. You're not yourself."

Laura smiled wider and explained that she was simply working through some complex strategies she had planned for the acquisition of the Kessel Group's business. And like the professional that she was, Laura went so far as to run a few of them past Kate, who stared at her with wide eyes, mouth ajar.

"That sounds pretty damn good," Kate said.

Laura nodded in agreement, and they started walking again. It was an effective smoke screen. Diverting Kate's attention back to business made her lose all interest in Laura's personal affairs.

"You think you can have all of that ready by the deadline? It sounds pretty complex."

Laura responded carefully. She assured Kate that, one way or the other, they would acquire the associates of the Kessel Group as clients. Kate nodded stiffly, donning her professional façade again, as if she'd just remembered she was the boss.

"I certainly hope so. I want this thing to go without a hitch, so you polish it up until it glows, okay?"

Laura nodded and wandered off to her office, praying that Kate wouldn't follow.

"I'm trusting you on this!" Kate called out before Laura could close the door.

Inside her office, Laura fought off the urge to call the stranger's number. After the inquisition she'd endured in the hallway, hearing his voice would be so therapeutic. She only wanted to hear the message a few times, but he might answer again, and that would be too embarrassing. Not to mention the fact that he would have her office number if she called from her desk.

On the way home that afternoon, Laura intentionally missed the right that led to her subdivision and followed a main road that weaved its way into the country. After six miles or so, she casually made a left and headed west on the narrow road she'd been down once before. She pretended that the excursion was planned, until she rounded the bend…and saw a white Jeep leaving one of the gravel driveways.

She gasped and almost flew into a panic before realizing that the stranger had no idea she had been the one who'd called him the day before. Trying to look as casual as possible, Laura kept her eyes forward. She glanced to her left as he drove past her. The sunglasses she wore concealed her line of sight, but she noticed him glance in her direction for a second. She quivered at the improbable thought of him recognizing her somehow.

"Oh, God!" She pressed a hand to her chest and kept driving, making a mental note of the exact driveway from which he'd emerged. There was a small, gnarled little tree and a boulder the size of a beach ball beside it. Like the phone number, she had no idea what to do with the information. But whether she liked it or not, the details of where he lived instantly took up residence inside her head, right alongside every other detail she'd collected about the man, whose name she still didn't know.

Wednesday was hectic, and despite her near miss with the stranger, Laura was miraculously able to perform her duties in a manner befitting her reputation. But on Thursday, she skipped out again before Kate could latch on to her, and she changed into jeans, a loose cotton pullover, and sneakers. Attired for comfort, she ate her lunch by the water while considering her plans.

After eating, she hopped back into her car and headed for the country. She made a left and headed west, on what she now recognized as Thompson Road. She continued around the bend, passing the stranger's driveway and continuing on for about a half mile before turning around to make another pass. She passed the driveway again, trying in vain to see through the young trees and down the gravel road.

Even driving by at a crawl did not offer her a clear view. All she could see was the road, no house, barn, or vehicle. So she turned around and drove past again, repeating the bizarre charade half a dozen times before she decided to quit after one more pass. *Just one final look, then I'll leave.*

She drove west once again, intent on turning around down the road and heading back to work. But on the last pass, the sun broke out from behind the clouds, and she thought she saw something silver shining back there through the trees. As the stranger's driveway came up again on her right, her Check Engine light came on, and the car died.

"What? Oh, shit." She pulled off to the side of the road, stopping not more than twenty-five feet from his driveway. "Damn it! You've gotta be kidding me."

She tried to restart the car several times.

Luckily, she had her cell phone in the car with her. She reached for her briefcase and tipped it off the back seat, spilling the contents all over the floor.

"Rrgh!" She wedged herself between the driver and passenger seats, groping for her papers and looking for her cell phone. While she was occupied with collecting her things, a sound arose toward the front of the car—a wheel splashing through water. An engine hummed along nearby.

When Laura turned around, her eyes widened in horror. The white Jeep was parked at the end of the driveway, and the stranger was looking right at her.

"Oh no…" she whispered.

He parked just off the road, exited his vehicle, then sauntered up to her car and removed his sunglasses. "Hi. Having some trouble?"

"This isn't happening. This *can't* be happening," Laura muttered as she smiled at him. The electric windows wouldn't even roll down. She had to exit the car to speak to him. She stepped out, cell phone in hand. "Um, hi. I…yeah, I had a meltdown. It just stopped."

Up close, she could see the alternating shades of green and gold in his eyes. They were bright eyes—a lively green that captured her attention and wouldn't let go. She couldn't look away from him. A faint dusting of stubble covered the lower part of his face, and when he smiled or squinted, little creases appeared at the corners of his eyes.

"Here, let me have a look. May I?"

Laura nodded and opened the driver's-side door for him.

He stepped around her, popped the hood, and raised it. After a moment, he leaned in and poked at something.

"I'm sorry, miss, but your engine's one big computer. If it were like that old horse I drive, I might be able to patch it up well enough to get you home." He turned and smiled at her.

Laura kept staring at him shamelessly. Wherever the fascination came from, she was almost certain it extended beyond physical attraction. She could detect his unique scent, some blend of cologne and fresh air that mingled perfectly with his skin. His hair was fine and silky, the color of autumn oak leaves and straw.

The unlikely meeting was so difficult for her to grasp, and the strain of seeing him, smelling him, and hearing his voice robbed her of any and all attempts at logical thought or casual conversation. Each response she gave felt thin and shaky and came only after several seconds of draining effort.

"Do you need a ride somewhere?" he asked.

Laura took five seconds to process the question. "Um…no, I… I've got a phone." She smiled awkwardly and held up her phone in front of her. "The garage will come and get it. They'll…they'll give me a ride…I think."

"Should I wait with you? This road's pretty safe, but if it'll make you feel better…"

"Oh…no, that's…that's okay. I'll, um, I'll be fine."

The stranger's lips curled into a grin. He turned his head a little sideways. "Have we met before?"

Laura shook her head.

"Hm. Something's familiar about you. I can't place it."

"I…I get that quite a bit. I've got a familiar face," she lied through a tight smile.

The stranger nodded and extended his hand, gesturing to his left.

"Okay then. Well, if you need anything, I'm just up this driveway here." He held up his right hand in farewell before retreating to his Jeep. Laura realized after he'd vanished from sight that she still had no idea who he was—she hadn't even thought to introduce herself.

"What a day." She looked up and down the road and saw no one. She grabbed the customer service number from her glove box and dialed. The signal was very weak. Before anyone could pick up, her phone went dead. Once again, she'd neglected to charge it the night before.

"Ugh! I don't believe this." Her gaze settled on the gravel driveway leading to the stranger's house.

The driveway was longer than she'd expected, winding up a small hill and through trees that grew steadily taller as she went. She negotiated another slight grade, and the driveway opened into an elevated clearing. A golden wheat field sprawled out to her right, and thick pines covered the other side.

Nestled beneath a large oak, with its back to the wheat field, was a long, blue-and-silver…bus? It looked like an old Greyhound from the fifties or sixties, and it appeared to be well maintained from the outside, the silver skin shimmering in the sunlight that spilled into the quiet space. The giant vehicle was slightly elevated and made level by jacks. A power pole had been stabbed into the ground a dozen feet away. Power and phone cables hung between it and the bus. The Jeep was parked beside it, resting beside a little mound of rich-looking soil.

Laura crept closer toward the makeshift motorhome.

"Hello?" she called out.

The gravel gave way to grass, and trees surrounded her on all sides, closing off the road and whatever houses stood nearby. It wasn't completely quiet, though. Birds sang and darted in and out of the high branches, and little red squirrels and chipmunks were busy raiding a bird feeder that hung from a gray limb.

"Hello? Are you there?" Laura's voice cracked.

The stranger appeared from around the back of the long bus, with gardening gloves on his hands.

"Yes, what can I do for you?" He removed his gloves.

"Um…" Laura held up her phone. "My phone's dead. I was wondering if I could use yours?"

The stranger chuckled. "Not your day, is it?"

Laura laughed as if his remark were the funniest thing she'd ever heard. "That it's not."

"Come on in." He waved his arm toward the door.

Laura felt the pestering notion of danger brush her senses. But even though she didn't know the man, she felt strangely at ease in his company.

Laura followed him up the little handmade wooden steps and into the bus. It was clean and orderly inside and much larger than she'd assumed. Hardwood planks covered the floor, and the walls and ceilings were painted pale gray. Laura smiled at the adorable little kitchenette along one wall. A tiny woodstove sat on a slab of granite toward the middle, and a comfy-looking futon rested against the opposite wall. Long curtains in the back hung in front of what looked like a bedroom. A few clear plastic bubbles in the roof invited the sunlight, which shone down on several unique treasures posed or hung throughout the small home.

One was a pastel drawing of St. Peter's Basilica in Rome, done by an exquisite hand in remarkable detail with rich shades of pewter and bronze. Beside it was a colored drawing similar to what might be seen on the walls of a pyramid in Egypt, with two figures drawn explicitly in two dimensions.

More decorations sat neatly on shelves or dangled from the concave walls by bits of string. There was a little skeleton marionette with a sombrero and a poncho, a small painting of a Scottish man playing the bagpipes on a foggy moor, and a remarkably detailed, foot-tall Samurai warrior statue with leather armor and helmet.

"It's over here." The stranger picked up a cordless handset and handed it to her.

"Thank you." Laura's eyes continued to wander about the place. "You don't have a cell phone?"

The stranger shook his head. "Nah. Don't need one. Though getting a phone line hooked up was no picnic."

Laura dialed the service number. As she waited, she looked toward the back, where the bed sat—a large mattress covered with a burgundy comforter—then to the kitchen, which featured a small sink, a little stove, and a tiny refrigerator.

Someone came on the line, and Laura gave the serviceman directions.

"I'll be just up the driveway, the one on the right, if I'm not by the car. Just honk when you get here. Thanks." She hung up and handed the phone back. "I appreciate your help."

The stranger removed a glass from a little cupboard. "Not at all. Would you like a drink while you wait? Sweet tea? It's good. I make it myself."

"Yes, that'd be nice. Thank you."

He poured a glass and handed it to her. It was sweetened just right.

"I'm sorry, but I don't know your name," Laura said.

"James," he said.

Laura's fingers went limp, and the glass slid right out of her hand. It shattered noisily on the wood floor, throwing amber tea everywhere. She cupped her hands over her mouth and gasped. The shock from the breaking glass snapped her back to reality. But a thorny nest of conflicting emotions swelled in the back of her mind. She couldn't ignore the obvious anymore. The reason for her tracking him down could no longer be denied or dismissed.

Laura peeled her hands away from her mouth. "I'm sorry! Oh God, I'm so sorry!"

"It's all right. I've got five more just like it. Don't move. Let me pick it up. I don't want you to cut yourself. Not with the kind of luck you're having today." He looked up at her and grinned as he started to clean up the mess. "If you cut yourself, you could sue me. By the way, you're not a *lawyer*, are you?"

"No! Oh no, not me."

"Good. You can stay then."

Laura laughed. In under a minute, he had disposed of the glass she'd broken and cleaned up the mess. He filled a new glass and handed it to her.

"If you drop that one, I'm afraid you'll have to go outside. I've only got so many glasses. Maybe I should have given you a tumbler." He furrowed his brow and looked thoughtful, though a faint grin betrayed his sarcasm.

He began opening and closing the small cupboards, pretending to search for a plastic cup. Laura couldn't keep from laughing. In fact, the laughter came so easily and she enjoyed it so much that she gave little thought to how at ease she felt around him.

"Tumblers were made for people like you." He raised his eyebrows and nodded.

It wasn't so much what he said, but how he said it. It was the way he suddenly made his face very serious despite her reckless laughter.

"Stop it, my jaw hurts." Laura's eyes watered. Once she got laughing, it was all but impossible to control.

"Okay then. Just hold on to it. That's it, not *too* tight. You might bust it in your hand. That wouldn't be very funny. I'd have to drive you to the damn emergency room and answer a bunch of questions."

"Stop it! Please," she begged through her laughter, her eyes blurring.

Finally, he did stop, and she wiped her eyes.

"I'm sorry. I shouldn't do that. I hardly know you," he said.

"No, you *shouldn't*." She smirked at him. "Do you always torment your guests by making them laugh until it hurts?" Laura took another gulp of tea.

His face molded into a pensive, scolding expression. "Do you always use people's phones and then thank them by breaking their shit?"

The tea erupted from Laura's nose, and she burst into a coughing fit. As embarrassing as it might have been in any other situation, strangely, she didn't mind so much.

"Whoops. Now I've done it. Here, take this napkin. Give me the glass before you drop it. Jesus Christ, you're a mess. There you go."

He wouldn't shut up. Laura knew that no matter what he said at that point, she would find it hysterical. She went on coughing, trying to rid her windpipe of sweet tea.

"Here. Don't be stubborn now. Let me have the glass before you…that's it. Is there any medication I need to get for you? You can't seem to hold on to anything."

"Shut up!" she cried. But she was actually enjoying the laughter more than she would ever admit. She'd been in his home for five minutes, and already, she was laughing harder than she had in ten years. Or was it twenty?

Thirty. It's been about thirty years.

The thought stifled her instantly. She allowed herself a smile and a quiet little chuckle, but the great tidal wave of laughter and all the joy it carried was gone.

"Feel better now?" he asked.

"Yeah. Just don't get me going again," she said, even though she knew it was impossible.

Thirty years. The words kept flashing through her mind, as steady as a heartbeat. Her smile faded altogether.

"You're not upset, are you?" he asked.

"What? Oh, no. No I was just…worrying about how much my damn car's going to cost this time," she lied.

As quickly and surely as joy had enveloped her seconds ago, she retreated to what was familiar. Even the honest and harmless notion that she'd felt comfortable around her new acquaintance fled from her mind, crowded out by impending obligations and the footsteps of sound reasoning. And something else. Something much darker.

He's not Jimmy.

She regained her balance, and it was safe there. Her job, goals she had, things she would do, her future marriage to Don… None could be replaced by a fleeting sensation of spontaneous joy. Such a thing wasn't to be trusted. It never lasted.

Laura acknowledged how odd it was for her to be thinking that way. James was just a man who'd allowed her to use his phone. But her aggressive need to defend what she knew and understood effectively stifled any chance of her enjoying his company any further. She needed stability and suspected that everyone did on some level.

After the brief introspection, she looked around again and saw the trappings of a selfish man. His home defined and represented everything she'd come to hate about single men. It was mobile, so he could move it whenever he got bored. It was too small for a couple. Most women would adore the little bits of attractive art on display, but he didn't fool her. She knew the type, had seen it a million times.

He was the sort of man who loathed routine and obligation, more of a child than an adult. The way he lived was proof of that—in the woods, by himself, where it was quiet, where he could hide from the world instead of facing it.

"I should go." Laura set her glass down on the narrow counter.

"Did I say something wrong?"

"No, I just…want to be there when the mechanic arrives." She bent her lips into an icy smile.

"You seem upset all of a sudden." James set his glass down beside hers.

"Why would I be upset? I'm not upset. I just…need to go now. Thank you again for everything." Laura turned swiftly toward the door and stepped out the door.

She strode across the grass and onto the gravel driveway. Before she was concealed by the canopy of trees on either side, she heard the very faint sound of the bus's door closing behind her.

The computer in her car would cost close to fifteen hundred dollars, but her warranty covered ninety percent of it. The garage informed her that it would take a few days to get the part and install it, and in the meantime, she was issued a loaner—a two-year-old white convertible.

At work the following day, she was forced to explain to half a dozen people that no, she *hadn't* bought a new car.

"I like it. Let's take it to lunch," Kate said, and Laura agreed.

At Grisby's, a classy place with terrific shrimp scampi and linguini, Laura was the more talkative of the two. Kate listened as well as she was able—that was not and had never been her specialty.

Laura had drank a large glass of wine in just a few minutes and was speaking louder than usual. Her encounter with James was still fresh in her mind, and the more she thought about how selfish he was, the madder she got. Before she knew it, her frustration was pouring out of her mouth as fast as the wine flowed in.

"I mean… I just don't see where some people get off acting like they have no responsibilities, no obligation to the world they live in. I *worked* for everything I have, and it just pisses me off to see other people who look down upon the way I live because I have nice things. You know?" Laura grumbled.

"Yes. Just the other day—"

"And it's none of their goddamned business what I do anyway, is it? No. I have nice things because I earned them! Nobody ever gave me anything. I *worked* to get through college, I *worked* to get where I am right now, and it annoys me that some people can be so at peace without having any ambition at all!"

Laura paused to sneer at a busboy clearing an opposite table. "Like *him*. How old is he? Thirty? Cleaning off fucking tables for a living. Isn't that sickening?"

"Laura, what's wrong? Who are you talking about? It's not Justine, is it? She wants to be a vet. That's why she's—"

"I just really hate people who think life is one big fucking game!"

"Lower your voice, Laura, for God's sake."

Laura swallowed the last of her second glass of wine and was pouring a third.

"Shouldn't you eat something? You'll get sick."

"I'm fine. But listen—ahem! My point is…why the hell shouldn't everyone work as hard as I do? Huh? I mean, Christ! You got people who, well, like that busboy there. Hmph, bus*man* is more like it. The world would be a better place if we all did our part. That's all I'm saying."

"Laura, you're drunk."

"I am not. I'm just a bit upset about…people who don't obey the rules. You know what I mean?"

"Not really, no."

"Well, I'll *tell* you!"

"Laura, please, you've had enough wine. What's the matter with you?"

"I'm getting to that. Leave the bottle where it is. It'll be okay. All I'm saying is some people just sort of…*drift* through life as if it was all supposed to be fun and games, and it's not!" Laura pounded her fist on the table for emphasis.

"Okay, we're leaving."

"I'm not through yet!"

"You're making a scene. Get ahold of yourself." Kate glanced around the restaurant.

"Okay, okay. Just listen to what I say. Just *listen*…okay? *Listen*…"

Laura hadn't consumed so much alcohol for more than four years, and whatever tolerance she'd had before those four years was long gone. Two and a half large glasses of wine sloshed about in her mostly empty stomach. Her eyelids drooped, and her attempts at whispering failed as the shrill hissing of her voice sent the syllables through the air with sharper clarity.

Kate, of course, was more concerned about Laura making a scene in a respectable place than anything else. There was a time and a place for yelling, and Laura suspected that, as far as Kate was concerned, yelling at an inebriated colleague in a fancy restaurant fell just outside those borders.

So Laura took advantage of the situation and went on, leaning over the table and trying to whisper, which only made her louder than she was before.

"I'm just saying that there's got to be rules. *Rules*! You hear what I'm saying? And people…*some* people, ignore 'em. See? I hate that. Makes me so goddamned sick, I wanna kick someone! Are you even *listening* to me?"

In any other state of mind, Laura might have refrained from snapping at Kate, who was, luckily for her, a good sport about the whole thing.

"Yes, honey, I'm listening." Kate laughed softly, her gaze darting about the room. She glanced at some of the other patrons and smiled apologetically.

"Good. *You* know what I'm talking about. I'm sure as hell glad *someone* does!" Laura blew out a heavy sigh, relieved of her great burden.

Kate finally convinced her to eat a little something and lay off the wine. When they left the restaurant, Kate took Laura's keys and drove them back. She guided Laura to her office and laid her down on the couch.

"I hope to God you don't make a habit of this. Laura? Are you asleep?"

"Nope."

"I want you to be at your best next week. You hear me? None of this foolishness like we had today. If you need to talk to me, I'm right down the hall. You don't have to…wait until we're in public to unload on me."

"Gotcha."

"I mean it! No more of this. I'm going to look over a few reports in Libby's office. You stay here until you sober up. I don't want a client to come in and find a drunk lunatic walking around. You hear me? Laura?"

Laura waved Kate off and closed her eyes. In a few seconds Laura was fast asleep.

Soon after her tirade, Laura discontinued her private lunches at the park, deciding that they served no useful purpose. They were nothing but distractions that interfered with her work and made her unproductive.

Laura began to dine with Kate and Libby Rollins. During these lunches, she did her best to engage in conversation with as much interest and concern as the others. All the while, she kept reminding herself where she belonged, of the road ahead of her, of her obligations, her responsibilities, and all the things that separated the adults from the children.

As the days passed, Laura focused on what had helped her earn the life she had. She worked harder than ever, stuffing all doubt into the deepest recesses of her mind. Everything she'd been questioning made perfect sense again, while her recent distractions hardly seemed worth her time. She laughed at the idea that she'd actually been *stalking* a complete stranger and hoped to God no one ever found out about it.

One evening after work, Laura returned home to find Don talking on the phone. She kissed her smiling man and proceeded to get undressed. From the bedroom, she could hear his high-pitched voice through the walls and caught small pieces of the conversation.

"…if that's what he wants. I'm sure I can make it. No, two weeks isn't that long."

Laura walked into the kitchen again, her face wrinkled inquisitively.

"No, next week is fine. Right. Listen, I gotta go. I'll call you later tonight. Good. All right, bye."

Don seemed ready to burst with joy, but she'd gotten used to that.

"I'm going to Chicago. There's a private convention in three days. I need to be there."

Laura blinked at him. "What? In three days? Honey, the corporate party's in less than a week." Laura stared at him, her mouth agape. By her reaction, he might have told her he was quitting his job to join the circus.

"I know, I'm sorry about that. But with the commission I'm going to get from this, I plan to buy you—"

"Jesus, Don! I have to go to that party on Friday! Kate is insisting all of her *girls* are present. How's it going to look if I'm alone? Did you ever think of that?"

"It'll be okay. Don't worry about it."

"I *am* worried about it! This is how rumors get started. Someone sees me there alone, and all of a sudden, you and I are having *problems*. You think I don't know how damaging rumors can be?"

Laura stormed back into the bedroom in a huff. She unzipped her skirt and threw it on the floor.

Don followed her, his hands out to his sides. "It's only for two weeks."

Laura spun around and scowled at him. "Oh, is that all? Why not run off for two *months*, really give 'em something to talk about!"

"You're not being reasonable."

"*I'm* not being reasonable? Listen to yourself. My god, you're on the phone for five minutes, and you've already made up your mind, without discussing it with me for even a second."

"Honey, come on. You're overreacting. I've done this a hundred times. I can't expect the clients to come to me the way you do. I have to go to market, just like in the old days. What I do is international business."

"Right, good for you. Just fucking go. I'll go to this stupid party by myself, so I can be subjected to all sorts of revolting accusations on Monday."

"I can't believe people would speculate about us just because I'm not with you at a party. Heck, most of them know what I do for a living."

"It doesn't matter. Just go." Laura sat on the bed, fuming with disgust.

"We need the commission, Laura. You know very well that—"

"No, Don, *you* need the commission. So you can buy your stupid boat. Right?"

"It's not just for me. I know you don't think I'm that selfish."

Laura looked at him and huffed a short laugh. "You're right. I am being silly. Everything's great. You go ahead to your meeting, and I'll tell everyone you were abducted by aliens or eaten by a shark or something."

Don sat on the bed next to her. He embraced her from behind and kissed her neck.

Laura was rigid in his arms. "What about our vacation?"

He didn't say anything for a moment. But aside from the party, Laura had arranged to take vacation a week later. "You promised me you'd arrange yours for the same time, remember? I guess it just slipped your mind."

"So that's why you're so mad. Damn, I forgot all about that. I'm sorry."

"Sorry doesn't help." Laura pulled away from him and stood up. "We'll just have to reschedule it."

Laura scowled. "I can't *reschedule* it. Remember what I told you? The way it works at my office is, you have to put in for vacation almost two months in advance. Maybe *you* could reschedule your meeting."

Don laughed. "Listen, when I get the boat, we'll have a good vacation. We'll go to the sound for a week in May before it gets too hot. How's that?"

Laura wondered what she was supposed to do by herself while he was gone. The idea of asking him crossed her mind, but she didn't speak. He would have a solution for that, too. He had one for everything. It was clear, however, that they would not be traveling anywhere together in April, like they usually did. Other, more important plans had surfaced.

"Sure," Laura said. "That'll be fun."

Her voice was flat and emotionless, but as it had so many times before, everything that her bothered tone implied escaped him. She'd wondered countless times if there were men in the world whose intuition was deep enough to recognize the sadness in her voice, even without her expressing it. The notion was nothing but a remote fantasy in Don's presence.

Everything she'd convinced herself of over the past few days began to unravel, leaving her with the sensation of falling. Unlike every other time she'd been was seized by the sensation, she lacked the strength to stop the descent.

Her head ached from thinking about everything so much. Little chunks of self-doubt and misery tumbled down on her head, and Laura was finding it more and more difficult to protect herself from the blows.

Three days later, Don left for Chicago, and two days after that was the big corporate party. Laura's aloofness about the event went unnoticed by her colleagues, including Kate. Laura got her car back from the shop, and only when she stepped out of the convertible for the last time before turning it in did she realize that she hadn't put the top down once.

On the evening of the party, Laura slipped into her cream-colored dress. She accented her ensemble with a pair of diamond earrings in silver settings and a matching pendant on a thin chain.

As darkness smothered the vibrant pink of early evening, she put on her low heels and stood before a tall mirror, where she inspected herself with numb scrutiny. She was indeed an image of beauty, having set her hair just so, allowing a few thick strands to spiral down each side of her face. The rest of her wavy locks, she had folded and pinned up with a shiny silver clip. A wild-looking tail fell between the tops of her shoulder blades and brushed at her neck. She applied only a little makeup, tastefully where it suited her, and she'd redone her nails. Everything about her was perfect.

The only thing she couldn't find was her smile. It, she reasoned, would emerge naturally when the time came—when she was approached by all the clients they were trying to retain or impress. She would smile for them. It was part of the job.

The prestigious event was of the highest caliber in terms of decor and the radiance of those who attended. Kate wore a lovely green dress that set off her reddish hair. She wore golden hoops in her ears and a stunning necklace trimmed with small diamonds and emeralds, which she'd probably rented for the occasion. Although in Laura's opinion, Kate was not above using the party as an excuse to justify such an expensive purchase.

Libby wore a light-blue gown that went well with her blond hair and blue eyes, and the dark-red shade of lipstick drew attention to her bee-stung lips.

The men all looked the same in their black tuxedos, with one or two non-conformists wearing gray or white. The oddballs reminded Laura of something she'd seen at a funeral and a circus respectively— the men in gray resembling pallbearers, the few in white, animal tamers.

And Laura, bored and depressed the moment she entered the dull but colorful circle, found the special smile she reserved for such occasions—the one she didn't have to feel to wear effectively. Looking around, she wasn't at all shocked to see the same expression on so many other faces.

Kate and Libby, among many others, inquired about Don's absence. Laura offered the truth, which wasn't well received, she suspected. There was some unnamable trace of empathy in Kate's and Libby's eyes, and the truth became quite obvious to her all of a sudden. Laura didn't want people to suspect there was trouble between her and Don, because there *was*.

As the evening dragged on, Laura mingled among the guests, as was expected of her, shaking the right hands and ignoring the rest. She finally wandered over to the champagne table and picked up a glass.

Watching people dance in slow, lazy circles or chatting and laughing in strained, awful tones, she came to hate them. An older gentleman with a hairpiece and maroon-framed glasses was dancing with Kate. The man's name was Carl Nicholas, and he was the president of Nytec Incorporated. Kate absolutely despised the man. She'd made herself very clear to Laura on that point, and yet, there she was. Carl would be a billionaire in a few years, and he would be looking toward more aggressive global diversity and expansion. So naturally, Kate wanted his business, and there wasn't much she wouldn't do to get it.

The way Kate danced and flirted with Carl wasn't the least bit extraordinary. Indeed, it was more the norm than an exception. *Ah yes, this room is alive with the stench of infidelity.*

She knew that many of the higher-ups had, in one way or another, talked their husbands or wives into leaving early after making an appearance. Men like Kate's husband never put up much of a fight, but she was mildly surprised to see many of the other husbands and wives absent, as well.

Laura finished one glass of champagne and picked up another, pausing mid-sip when she saw two colleagues, Donna Price and Vicky Adams, sauntering toward her. Although they didn't look much alike—Donna was a short and buxom brunette, while Vicky was a tall, slim blonde—the two were seldom apart, and they reminded Laura of evil sisters from a horror movie.

"Shit. Vampires at twelve o'clock," Laura muttered. She started to make her escape when—

"Laura! Wait!" Vicky's shrill voice was like an ice pick in her ear.

Donna clomped up, her cleavage sloshing about in her dress. "Hey, Laura. Where have you been hiding all night?" She smiled, revealing bright-red lipstick on her teeth.

Laura stepped away from her, trying not to stare. "Uh…behind the ice sculpture…until it melted."

Donna laughed with all the charm of a donkey. She and Vicky had been pestering Laura for weeks about helping them with a project, and Laura had been doing so well avoiding them.

"Doesn't Kate look fabulous? I hope I look that good in my fifties." Vicky smiled brightly.

"She does look great," Laura admitted. "How does she do it?"

"I heard she's had some work done, but who can blame her?"

Donna chimed in.

"What's it like working for her? I hear she can be a real *snake*." Vicky whispered the last word.

The champagne was kicking in, so Laura felt like having some fun with them. Her jaw dropped, and she looked at Vicky in mock disbelief. "Kate is an absolute saint. She tried to donate one of her kidneys to a carnival barker in Kansas a few years ago. She didn't even know him. Poor old man got trampled by a blind elephant the day before the surgery." Laura dropped her gaze to the floor and shook her head. She looked back up at Donna and Vicky. "She hasn't been the same since."

Donna and Vicky glanced at each other.

"You're kidding, right?" Donna said.

"Nope. But don't let that get around. She's very sensitive about missed opportunities." Laura tossed back her remaining half glass and grabbed another flute.

Donna smiled again, and Laura's eyes widened. She pointed at Donna's mouth. "I hate to tell you this, Donna, but it looks like you've been biting the heads off chickens."

"Excuse me?" Donna frowned at her.

Laura smiled and pointed at her own teeth. "Lipstick on your teeth."

Donna looked horrified. She fumbled for a mirror and looked at herself. After softly cursing, she wiped off the lipstick then turned toward Vicky, who looked guilty.

Laura pointed to her right. "I gotta go over here. Excuse me."

She walked away smiling, glancing back as Donna and Vicky bickered.

"Why didn't you say something?" Donna asked.

Vicky's mouth worked in silence. "I...I didn't notice—"

"Liar! I was just over there talking with Sam Lowenstein. Damn it!" Donna inspected her teeth again, her face as red as a baboon's ass.

Laura turned back around and nearly collided with a short man with wiry black hair and a round face.

"Would you like to dance?" he asked.

Laura nearly coughed from the liquor fumes he breathed at her. "Uh, no, thank you. I haven't been feeling well lately."

"Oh!" the little man cried, seemingly delighted by the news. "I'm a doctor. What's the trouble?" He leaned in close and whispered, "I promise to maintain patient-client confidentiality."

His little beady eyes wandered shamelessly across Laura's chest, and his words drifted to her nose long before reaching her ears. The distinct, offensive odor of strong liquor on his breath made her eyes water. Clearly, the doctor was the type who required a bucket full of social lubricant before he could bring himself to approach a woman, much less speak to her.

Laura would sooner frolic around naked in a pit of angry vipers than dance with him. The repugnant bite of liquor on his breath caused Laura to draw her head back, a gesture to which he seemed oblivious.

"I'm Todd Price. *Dr.* Price to most." He smiled in a way he probably thought was charming.

Laura realized she was smiling back at him—a reflexive action she'd mastered over the past hour or so. She stopped smiling when she realized she might be inadvertently leading him on. The idea of engaging him in conversation was unsettling, so she leaned toward him, widening her eyes. "I hear voices."

Dr. Price's smile fell, and his eyebrows bunched together. "I'm sorry, what was that?"

"I hear *voices.*" Laura looked around for eavesdroppers. She nodded emphatically. "Shhh. Did you hear that? Someone just said, 'Drown the baby.' You didn't hear it?"

Dr. Price looked disturbed. Laura maintained a serious expression throughout the long silence that fell between them.

"I, uh, I'm not that kind of doctor. Excuse me." Dr. Price turned and scurried away.

Laura grinned with satisfaction and drained her glass. She selected another and drank it. When she noticed Dr. Price speaking with someone she knew, Laura quickly moved behind a deformed ice sculpture that used to be a dolphin but had melted into what looked like a fat banana.

Dr. Price had started to point in Laura's direction just before she ducked out of sight. It had never occurred to her that her clever lie might cause her problems.

Midnight inched closer, and many people, the ones Kate didn't consider crucial, had left already, a few of them with people they weren't married to.

Laura realized by the way her thoughts moved sluggishly through her head that she was drunk for the second time in a month.

"Uh oh, I'm making a habit of it, Kate." She giggled with a hand over her mouth.

Peeking around the sad ice sculpture, she saw Dr. Price walking over to yet another single woman, whom he would no doubt assault with his breath before calling it a night.

Laura snatched an open bottle of champagne from an ice bucket on the table. With the bottle and her glass in hand, she crept quietly out the back.

As soon as the door closed, Laura realized she had no idea where the parking lot was. Not that driving was an option, but that seemed like the best place from which to call an Uber. She tried to get back inside, but the door was locked. "Ah, shit." She poured herself a little more champagne, took a sip, and wobbled toward the sidewalk.

Walking down the empty street, Laura looked like an abandoned prom queen. She strolled along, talking to herself, pausing now and then to carefully refill her glass.

"They have no damn *right* to act like children." She blinked and smacked her lips. "No, no, no, no, no. They don't. He should know better than to act that ways. That *ways?* That *way!* Hoof. I'm drunk. Ohh! Hah-hah! It doesn't matter. I'm still right!"

She stopped to pour a few more inches of champagne into her

flute, pressed it to her numb lips, and tilted her head back, allowing the bubbly golden liquid to trickle down her throat. She lost her balance, wobbling on her low heels a moment before regaining control.

"Mm hm. Come to think of it, what right does he have to act like a baby? Huh? None! That's what rights he had."

After a few minutes of staggering down the sidewalk, Laura decided she was lost.

"Oh no. I…where the hell…? Oh, damn." She looked about in a daze. "Someone could come along…uh, oh…the police could come along, and… I should really just go. Yes, I should go now."

She quickened her pace, the glass in one hand, the bottle in the other.

After almost fifteen minutes of walking, she reached a busier road.

"Okay, act natural. Police could be anywhere…anywhere and everywhere in between. What time is… My watch is gone! Oh, God. I need my watch. Phew. I'm so thirsty from walking all this time. I just need to have a little sip here…"

Laura stumbled along the sidewalk, making a sincere attempt to appear sober. She found the many colors of the city enchanting: the amber streetlights, the flashing traffic signals, and the glowing reds and whites as cars raced by in opposite directions.

Several people tooted at her as they passed, and Laura saluted them by holding up her glass and bottle, a goofy smile on her face. When she came upon a car resting by the curb, an Uber badge in the windshield, she stopped and stared at it with wonder. She laughed in triumph and set down her glass and bottle on the sidewalk.

Groping at a small tan purse she'd forgotten was there, she located the zipper, opened the tiny bag, and took out her phone. She poked at her phone's screen, located the Uber parked a few feet away, and booked a ride.

Moments later, a chime rang inside the car. The driver picked up his phone, and Laura saw him look around. "What the hell…"

Laura wobbled up to the car. "Hey, you… Hey…listen to me, you, driver…" She crept closer to the car, turned back, and grabbed her bottle, forgetting the glass. She stopped by the open passenger-side window and leaned in to be heard. "Hey!"

"What! Jesus Christ!" The Uber driver was Hispanic, about twenty-five, with a smooth, clean-shaven face and dark-brown hair. His eyes were wide with confusion and shock.

"You're my Uber." She held up her phone as evidence. "Just booked it. S'okay, right? Open the door back here…please, sir."

The driver stared at her, perplexed. Laura's eyelids drooped, and she kept tugging at the door handle in vain.

The driver reluctantly reached for the lock. Every time he tried to unlock it, Laura would tug on the handle, blocking his effort.

"Okay, open the…damn door." Laura kept grunting and tugging.

"Lady, let go of the handle," the driver snapped.

"What? I said—ungh! Open the fricken door. Whew! I'm tired of all this."

"Let go of the damn—I can't open it if you keep tugging on it!"

Finally, the driver managed to time his attempt between hers. When the door gave way, Laura nearly fell to the ground.

"Whoooa! What the *hell* are you trying to do?" The champagne sloshed and spilled on Laura's dress. She crawled into the back seat and molded herself into a sitting position.

"Close the door?" the driver said.

Laura ignored him. He sighed with disgust, got out, and closed it himself.

"I swear to God, the moment you yack on my floor, the ride ends and I bill you for the trouble. Got it? Now where to?"

Laura smacked her lips together and snorted. "You, hey, *listen* to me for a minute."

"Oh, Christ, not one of these."

"Shhh! Shut up and *listen* for a second. Do you just happen to know where…oh, damn. What's the name of it?"

"C'mon lady, it's late."

"Forget it, just start down this road here. It'll come to me in a second."

After a moment, they pulled into traffic. The young driver watched Laura through his rearview as they headed toward the country.

"Don't pass out on me. Hey! Wake up back there!"

"Will you… Jesus! Just be quiet. All the yelling… Oh! Okay, this is familiar now. Keep going like this. I'm awake now. I plan to give that little bastard a piece of my mind and…yeah…"

They drove past Thompson Road, and Laura looked about in confusion as they passed houses she didn't remember.

"Hold it. One…nope. It's the other way now."

The driver shook his head and turned the car around. They traveled in the other direction for a half a minute before Laura reached over and tapped him on the shoulder.

"Slow, slow, slow… Look. Slower…real slooow. That's it. Shhh! Be real quiet. Okay, make a right…right there. See it? Thompsum's Road. Okay. Shh…drive real quiet. Turn off the headlights."

"Are you crazy?"

"Shhh! Don't yell! It's coming up…on the right."

Laura remained silent as the car rolled up along the edge of the road, stopping a little ahead of where her car had died.

"This it?" the driver asked.

"Yeah. I got a few…words to say to this baby in there. You have to wait for me…okay?"

The driver sighed and nodded. "Yeah, sure, lady. I'll wait right here."

Laura stepped out of the car and saw a bright light trickling through the trees. It was like a streetlight, only brighter, and she could see the gravel driveway almost all the way up to the motorhome bus.

She grabbed her bottle, which was all but empty, and wobbled backward on shaky legs.

"Okay, God…damn it! This won't take but a few. You wait here for me. Right *here*. Don't you dare move or anything! You hear me?"

"Whatever you say, lady."

Laura started toward the gravel drive. Before she had taken five steps, the Uber raced off into the night.

"Hey! Hey, you little bastard! Come back here!" Laura took off one of her shoes and threw it at the car. It clattered on the pavement somewhere in the dark. A small dog started barking in the distance.

Laura turned back around and took a few awkward steps with her one remaining shoe. She yanked it off and hurled it into the woods. Pebbles and bits of wood jabbed at the soles of her bare feet as she inched forward. "Ow! Son of a bitch."

She finally entered the clearing, where the white light shone against the bus's silver walls. The Jeep and the skinny branches all around her painted the ground with crooked shadows.

"Okay, *mister.*"

She walked on, not the least bit concerned about her own safety, about being mistaken for an intruder and getting shot. When she reached the steep little stairs, she decided she would be unable to negotiate them effectively and stood back a few feet. "All right! I know you're in there! Get…get out here! God *damn* you!"

A yellow light came on in the bus. A small crash rang out as something fell over. Then a shadow moved around inside. Laura watched the shadow move past the small windows near the entrance.

The narrow door opened, and James appeared. He combed a hand though his unkempt hair, squinting out at the night. His eyes widened when he saw Laura standing there barefoot with a champagne bottle in her hand. She snickered at him, drained the bottle, and tossed it behind her. It thumped on the grass with a hollow *thoom* sound and rolled noisily across the gravel.

"Listen to me, you. Just who the hell do you think you are? Huh?"

James looked perplexed by the question. He didn't seem to have the foggiest idea how to respond. "I don't know who you are, but I think you've got the wrong house." His tone sounded confused and annoyed.

"Oh, no! This is the right goddamned *house* or whatever the hell it is. *Bus.* I should know. I was here to use your phone a while ago."

James's eyes narrowed then widened again with recognition. "Dear God."

"Yeah! Well, I think you owe me an explanation, buddy. You think you could do that? Hmm? Who the hell do you… Listen to me, okay? I am really bothered by you and your lack of maturity. Running all over in your little *truck.* Ahum! And it's a little hard for people like *me*, okay, to…concentrate on my life. Do you understand that? Answer me!"

James blinked a few moments and shook his head. "I have no idea what you're talking about."

"Well, that's just fine for you, isn't it! You don't even—*listen* to me! You don't even…*look* at me half the time! You never even ask me if something's wrong! And I'm just really tired of…" Laura's head swam when she closed her eyes. Her face suddenly felt very warm. Then her stomach churned in the worst way. "I'm just… I think… I think I'm going…to be sick." She fell to her hands and knees.

James came out of his bus and hurried over to her. "Jesus, are you okay?"

Laura heaved twice, ejecting the champagne and the small amount of food she'd eaten onto the grass. Only then did she wonder what she was doing. She was so drunk, she couldn't remember where she was or how she'd gotten there.

The words that had flowed out of her mouth—all the things she'd said to a man she didn't really know—came from somewhere outside of her. Remorse set in, followed by fear and uncertainty, and finally, utter confusion and helplessness. Her emotions gave way to embarrassment once she realized, however vaguely, where she had ended up. She curled into a little ball and started crying.

"Hey. It's okay, come on." James lifted her effortlessly from the ground.

Laura made no protest when he carried her not to the Jeep, but to the stairs of his home. On the way there, he said, "I wouldn't have minded another visit, but you could have at least waited until sometime after dawn."

The light and easy way he spoke elicited a soft laugh from her.

Inside the bus, he set her down on the couch and went to the bathroom. She heard water running. He returned with a warm, damp cloth and gently wiped off her chin and lips. Then he folded the cloth over once and told her to close her eyes. She did so, and he wiped her eyelids in the same gentle manner.

As if that sort of thing happened to him all the time, James lifted her from the couch and carried her to his bed. Alarm bells went off in her head. Her heart thumped in a panic. *Is he going to…?*

No.

James laid her down and pulled a single sheet over her. The vague but noticeable scent of him radiated from the cotton—a scent she was unable to fully appreciate in her present condition. She was too tired to move very much, and the warm, soft mattress felt like a smooth hand that embraced her entire body.

The last thing she felt was a hand brushing the hair from her eyes. She heard him laugh a little by exhaling through his nose. "Goodnight, whoever you are." He walked over to the couch and settled himself in before turning off the light.

Laura found something eerily familiar about the whole thing: the pounding in her temples, the God-awful taste in her mouth, the way the room wouldn't stop spinning… She didn't concern herself with where she had ended up or how. The jagged and surreal voices and visions from her past had a way of drowning out the present.

Exhaustion hit her with the force of a mallet, knocking her out. She always tried to be selective about where she ventured in her dreams, keeping close to the flowers while avoiding the thorns.

The late spring of Laurie's sixteenth year was a flowing river of bliss and freedom. Standing in her small room in Savannah, she slipped into her torn-up jeans to get ready for the party of the century.

There was something electric and irresistible in the air on Friday nights. The sun's inevitable surrender to encroaching darkness was her cue that night had arrived, and the stage belonged to the young and reckless.

A week's worth of anticipation always came to the same conclusion: rippling fingers of excitement, phone calls to friends, shiny muscle cars gargling by, and radios blaring Van Halen or Bad Company. Sparks were already flying, just a half hour after dusk.

Almost no one was immune to the subtle beckoning of what the night promised. But Laurie's friends were notorious for igniting whatever room they entered, pushing the volume higher than anyone, bleeding every ounce of fire from their youth, and transforming the night into a timeless fabric that would never tear or fade.

At sixteen, Laurie had the attitude of one who would never age and would live for centuries. Each night was an opportunity to forge another timeless memory, and she always took full advantage.

"Sarah, where's Meme's charm necklace? You borrow it again?" Laurie hollered through the wall.

"It's on the counter!" Sarah hollered back.

Laurie strutted into the kitchen, wearing her low-heeled leather boots. Her shirt was torn at the midriff, and her denim jacket was stylishly peppered with holes and bleach stains.

"Thanks, love." She kissed Sarah on the head. The phone rang, and Laurie walked over to pick it up. "Hello?"

"Hey, kitten! You ready?" It was her friend, June, a comical, bubbly blonde who looked and sounded a bit like Kathleen Turner in her younger days.

Laurie's face lit up. "You fuckin' betcha! You gonna be ready this time, or am I gonna have to break in and yank you out of the bathroom again?"

"Don't be stupid. That was a one-time thing. I'll be ready to go in about twenty."

"The clock's ticking. Don't piss me off again." Laurie tapped her boot on the floor.

"Oh, fuck you, Laurie. You'd be lost without me."

"Being lost couldn't be any worse than this."

"You adore me."

"Just be ready, or I'll make you walk. I mean it this time."

Laurie hung up and turned to face Sarah, who was sitting at the table with a book in her hands. That single image crowded out everything else in Laurie's mind. She walked over to the table, her head cocked to one side. She was about to attend an out-of-control party, and she would probably stumble home drunk and stoned at four o'clock in the morning, if she came home at all. And Sarah was reading a book.

Laurie stared at Sarah for what felt like ten minutes, watching her turn pages. Sarah's mouth was shaped into her little trademark smile that Laurie both loved and wondered about. It seemed so goddamned tragic, Sarah sitting there reading.

She sidled up to Sarah and placed her hand on her shoulder. "What the hell are you doing?"

"Reading." Sarah didn't bother to look up.

"At the *table*? That's weird. Why not in the living room? Or even the bedroom?"

Sarah sighed, shook her head, and turned the page without answering.

Laurie walked her hand up the back of Sarah's neck like a spider, making her giggle.

"Quit! You know I hate that—gives me the creeps."

Laurie walked her hand onto the side of Sarah's head and stuck a finger in her ear.

Sarah slapped her hand away. "Will you stop! What's the matter with you?"

"You're scaring me," Laurie said.

Sarah squinted at her and shook her head. "I have no idea what you're talking about."

Laurie stroked Sarah's hair lovingly and smiled at her. Their eyes locked, and without words, Laurie knew what she was thinking. At sixteen, Sarah had been raising a three-year-old daughter.

Even though Laurie had no choice about being born, she was suddenly overcome with guilt. And when she tried to imagine herself in a similar position—a mother at thirteen—she had no choice but to force the terrifying thought out of her mind. Quickly.

Laurie took the book from Sarah's hands, laid it on the table, helped her up, and hugged her. She hummed a melody to Sarah, and they danced around slowly in the kitchen.

"My friends all love you, you know? No one would give it a second thought if you came out with me," Laurie whispered.

Sarah giggled. "Yeah right. I'm sure all the kids are inviting their mothers to parties these days."

"You don't look a day over twenty-one." Laurie pulled back and cocked her head to the side. "Other than June and a few others you've met, I'll bet you ten bucks no one would ever know I'm your daughter."

She knew Sarah could have rejected the idea. She could have fought it, and she might have even won, despite how tenacious Laurie was. Instead, Sarah shook her head and said nothing, and Laurie took her silence as an invitation to continue.

"We wear the same size clothes," Laurie went on. "A little makeup, and you're nineteen again, I swear to God."

Twenty minutes later, Sarah stood by Laurie's side, tastefully dressed and made up. The two of them burst out of the house and ran to Laurie's old Firebird as they always did, looking more like sisters than ever.

Laurie hopped into the driver's seat, and Sarah sat beside her. Before Laurie could turn the key, Sarah touched her on the arm.

"Buckle up, sweetie." She pulled her belt across her chest and clicked it into place.

Laurie glanced at her with a loving smirk and reached for her seatbelt. Sarah had always been particular about wearing them. Laurie had originally wanted an older car—a '67 Chevy Chevelle—but Sarah wouldn't let her have it because it lacked three-point seatbelts in front.

"Yes, ma'am," Laurie muttered, strapping herself in.

They pulled up to the house, where the remainder of the night would burn brightly at both ends. The windows were aglow with lamplight and busy with dancing silhouettes. The music of Ozzy Osbourne was a demonic lullaby, luring teens inside five at a time. Something shattering inside the house was applauded by reckless laughter.

"Welcome back to the madness, Sarah darling." Laurie kissed her on the cheek.

"Jesus, what am I doing here?" Sarah whispered. The delicate application of makeup had turned back the clock just enough. Sarah *was* nineteen again. No one could argue that.

A sultry teen girl greeted Laurie at the door, handed her a beer, and asked about her friend, whom Laurie introduced as "my cousin from South Carolina. She's at USC in Columbia!"

Laurie's yelling drew the attention of several pairs of curious eyes, most of them belonging to boys. Hands clamped onto Laurie's waist from behind, and she turned to see Jimmy.

There was a long pause suddenly, as if the film of her life had become stuck in the projector. Laurie reached up and touched Jimmy's smiling face.

So beautiful. So fragile.

Laurie forgot everything for a while, lost in the action of rubbing his cheek with her thumb. "Hey, baby."

"I've missed you."

Jimmy pressed his lips to hers. Laurie closed her eyes and saw the explosive birth of the universe. Jimmy pulled her close, and they swayed like tall grass in a lazy summer breeze, despite the thunderous classic rock shaking the walls.

Someone else spun Laurie around. It was June, complaining about not being able to find her shoes and having to walk. People laughed, and when Laurie turned around again, Jimmy was gone. The longing she felt for him went deeper than what was normal. Laurie looked all around the room for him, but she couldn't find him anywhere. She wept into her hands, and no one seemed to notice.

When delivered on a carpet of dreams, memories could skip like a record, or a flat stone bouncing along the water. They became distorted and surreal. A ripple in Laurie's dream passed, and she was in a different room, maybe a different house. It might have been the first night Sarah came out with Laurie, or it might have been one of the many similar nights that followed. Regardless of which night it was, the next moment, Laurie was tossing back drinks to help dull the pain. One after the other, she poured the burning elixir down her throat until it felt like water going down.

Suddenly, the room went into a spin. The sting of Jimmy's absence was gone. Laurie had a good buzz going, dancing alongside six or eight others in a flurry of swinging arms and hips. And the only one in the entire room capable of showing her up was Sarah.

Sarah had taken ballet and tap as a small child, and she had always possessed a natural, fluid ability. Laurie found herself howling and clapping alongside her friends as Sarah and Luke Crawford, the best dancer at Laurie's school, dazzled everyone with their moves.

When the dance ended, Laurie stumbled over to Sarah, hopelessly drunk.

"You're so wonderful, Sarah. Do you know you are? I forgot how wonderful a dancer you are, and I love you so much." Laurie latched on to Sarah and started crying. "I love you so much, Sarah. I love you," she sobbed.

Sarah laughed and held her. "I love you, too, baby girl. It's three in the morning. We should get home, okay? I'm driving. You're pretty wrecked. C'mon now."

No one else would have dared trying to take Laurie home. It was a well-known fact that she was a hitter when she was drunk. But that night, Laurie went without a fight. Sarah led Laurie to the old Firebird and helped her into the passenger seat.

"Here. Buckle up, sweetie." Sarah leaned over and strapped Laurie in.

Laurie leaned back in her seat, staring off at the starry night sky through the open T-top roof. "Jimmy's gone. Where did he go? Where did he go?"

When tears began streaming down her face, it felt as natural to her as breathing.

The next morning, Laura woke to the sound of rustling paper—someone turning pages.

When she cracked her eyelids, she saw the concave ceiling and the warm rays of sunlight leaking in through the skylights. She didn't have the slightest idea where she was at first. Finally, she remembered where she'd seen the place before but was still at a loss to explain how she'd ended up there a second time.

Her throat felt dry and sore, as if she'd been yelling a lot recently. That only added to the swirling mess of confusion in her head. And when she tried to sit up, the movement had the impact of someone kicking her in the head with a lead shoe.

"Oooh," she moaned.

As soon as Laura realized she was in James's bed, her eyes popped open, and she lifted the sheet to see what she had on. She still wore her off-white evening gown she'd purchased for the party. Fragments of her memory, brief images of the night before, filtered in. The clues were few: a short man trying to pick her up at the party, a bottle of champagne, and being abandoned by her Uber ride.

She propped herself up on her elbows, much more slowly than the last time, and focused on the man sitting in a chair across the room. James slipped a bookmark into the book he'd been reading. The neutral expression he wore did nothing to vanquish her anxiety, nor did it present her with any significant information. He blinked at her with his green eyes, and his mouth bent into a kind smile.

"Good morn—" He stopped and consulted his watch. "Good afternoon."

"How did I get here?" Laura looked about.

"That's a good question." James walked over to his small refrigerator. He removed a jug of orange juice, glanced at her purposefully when he selected a plastic tumbler from the cupboard, then filled it three quarters of the way up.

Laura responded to the little joke with a weak laugh, one that hovered instead of floating away, casting a shadow of uneasiness and embarrassment over her.

She felt uncomfortable in his bed, but when she tried to move, her head throbbed and swam, and she had to close her eyes.

"Slow down. Relax for a minute. Here." James handed her the juice.

"Thank you." Laura took a sip. It refreshed her, and she drank the whole cup down in a few seconds. James took the cup and refilled it again.

"James, wasn't it?" she asked.

"Yes. James Ameche." He extended his right hand.

Laura did the same and found his grip firm but sensitive. "I'm Laura. Alman."

"Nice to meet you again, Laura. At least, it would have been nice…had you waited until now to start screaming outside my door," he chided her.

Laura's eyes widened in disbelief. "I did what now?"

"Never mind. I'm just glad you didn't hurt yourself walking up the driveway. Do you remember how you got here? Did you walk?" A look of doubt narrowed his eyes.

"I…think I took an Uber."

James was silent for a long time. He looked her over with a concerned expression. His lips twitched thoughtfully. "It might not be my place to ask you this, but are you okay? I mean, last night, it seemed like you had a lot on your mind."

"I'm fine, except for my head." Laura touched her temples. It wasn't an altogether honest reply, and what she followed up with was even worse. "My fiancé would kill me if he knew about this."

James answered without missing a beat, and Laura had to admit that his easy manner stung her in a way she found confusing and shameful.

"It's okay, I won't say anything." He said this as if the mention of a fiancé meant nothing to him.

Laura brooded over his response and grew angry about it. Self-honesty hadn't been one of her stronger attributes in a long time, and it evaded her completely at that moment.

"Well, I should be getting home. Can you give me a ride?" She swung her legs out of bed. Her head throbbed again, but she managed to stay sitting.

"Sure." Only then did he sound a little sad. "You wanna go right now?"

"Yeah, I've got some things to do. Where are my shoes?" Laura looked around on the floor.

"No idea. You weren't wearing any." James shrugged.

Laura bunched her eyebrows together. "I wasn't wearing any?"

"Nope."

Laura glanced up and met his eyes. She saw a concern and wonder she both wanted and was terrified of at the same time. So she looked away.

"Hm. Oh, well." She pushed herself up from the bed.

"Hey?" James said.

Laura kept her eyes closed so she wouldn't have to look into his again. "Yeah?"

James didn't say anything. He waited until she opened her eyes so she had to look at him. Her line of sight fought to remain below his chin.

"Are you okay?" he asked.

Laura couldn't answer. Her bottom lip twitched, but she was suddenly unable to produce one of the quick responses she knew so well. None of those sufficed.

It's been a long time since a man asked me that.

When the silence stretched out for several seconds, she did finally look up. Never before had she felt such tenderness in the absence of words or touch. His expression was all it took, his golden-green eyes tracing the contours of her face as if he were reading everything that was on her mind. When his lips bent into a subtle grin, she experienced a kind of empathy she'd forgotten was possible. Tears came, and she blinked them back. She couldn't look away from his brushing, non-intrusive stare and fluctuating smile. Without words, without a single gesture, she felt as if something horrible were being lifted away.

"It's okay. You don't have to say anything." James reached up and brushed away a thin wet line on her left cheek. "C'mon, I'll take you home." He sounded so casual that Laura suffered no shame or embarrassment. There was a tiny little flicker of happiness in his voice, as if he knew she would be okay. It was almost enough to make her believe it.

They both climbed into his Jeep, and he drove her back to where she'd left her car. Neither of them said much on the way. Soft breezes tossed her hair about, and she didn't mind. The air was warm and sweet, peppered with all the perfumes unique to spring.

At last, they arrived at the parking lot, where her car and only two others remained.

"Thank you." She removed her seatbelt and stepped out of the Jeep.

James smiled and nodded. "Listen, if you ever need someone to talk to, let me know before you go on another tirade like you did last night. Okay?"

Laura smiled and nodded.

Before she could speak, he said, "You've got my number, right?"

Absently, Laura nodded again. "Yup."

James's face bent into a knowing grin, and Laura realized she'd just said something wrong. And it was too late to take it back.

"In the meantime, I'll be sure not to cut anyone off in traffic," he said.

Laura tried in vain to offer an explanation, but James laughed and shook his head.

"I have to tell you, Laura, of all the strange people I've met in my life, you're definitely in the top ten." He paused and squinted at her, tilting his head to one side. "Top *five*." He held up his right hand. "I'll see ya." He shifted into first and drove away.

Laura remained where she stood, barefoot and wearing a marked-up dress. Her hair was a frazzled nest atop her aching head, and her makeup was smudged, streaked, and faded. Despite all this, Laura closed her eyes and smiled. She laughed softly at herself—something she hadn't done in a very long time.

After a long, hot shower, Laura spent the rest of her Saturday replenishing her fluids. The hangover wasn't as bad as it could have been, but it was enough to keep her still for most of the day.

She lounged in her small yard, savoring the air and napping intermittently. A smile graced her face as she played back how foolishly she'd behaved. Her behavior and the hangover made swearing off alcohol again no chore at all.

On Sunday, Laura got it in her head to make James an icebox cake as a token of apology and gratitude. She did this in what was technically Don's kitchen, which again led her to question whether or not she was behaving appropriately. She dismissed her concerns, however, and reasoned that she simply *had* to do something to thank him for his kindness and understanding. It was dishonest, and part of her knew it, but given all the self-defeating lies she'd told herself over the past several years, she allowed it.

After finishing the little cake, she thought for a long time about whether or not to call him. Guilt, her old companion, returned to insist that any relationship with a man like James would prove senseless at best and utterly devastating at worst. Laura paced and thought about it, weighing the consequences differently than she had before. It was always the practical things she placed the most importance on, things like sensibility, moral obligations, pride, maturity…and marriage.

In response to her silent brooding, the lavishly decorated hallways in which she paced, with their echoing hardwood floors, gave voice only to absence. Her drumming footsteps reminded her of how hollow words could be and how empty and damaging ideas of irresponsibility could become.

So she decided, however imprudently, that she would deliver her offering of thanks rather than succumb to the invisible shame. It might have been a nest of lies she was armoring herself with, but she didn't care. Without delay, she snatched up the handset and dialed his number.

It rang twice.

"Hello?" James answered.

"James? It's Laura. Listen, I've made you a cake, and I'm going to bring it over. That okay?"

"A cake? Hmm…"

"Yes, a cake. An icebox cake. You ever have one of those before? It's made with whipped cream and cookies. The cookies get soft after being in the fridge for a while."

She was terribly nervous. It might have been the undeniable feeling that she was setting herself up for something she knew was wrong. Infidelity sounded like such a lovely word until you knew what it meant.

"Okay, sure. You weren't planning on showing up at two in the morning, were you?"

The remark made her laugh, lightening the weight she felt just enough.

"No, I thought maybe the crack of dawn."

"I see."

"How's this evening? It ought to be ready by then."

"Okay. You wanna eat over?"

His offer didn't ring with the usual suspicious overtones. He sounded more like an innocent child than a man with an agenda. She still felt uncomfortable about having dinner with him, fearing that dinner might lead to something she had no business doing.

"I don't know." She poked a thumb in her mouth and nibbled on it.

After a pause, Laura heard soft laughter on the other end.

"What's so funny?" she asked.

"You. You're funny. You make me laugh."

"Why?"

"Well, last night you show up in a stupor, hollering at the top of your lungs. You pass out and end up sleeping in my bed. Have you forgotten that already? It was yesterday morning…*early*."

"Of course I haven't forgotten. Sheesh. What do you think I am?"

"I probably shouldn't say."

"What?"

"Nothing. Look, if I wanted to behave inappropriately with you, don't you think I would have acted that way the other night?"

He had a point. But it only softened her reluctance a degree or two.

"I'm making Cajun chicken tonight. It's a light coating, not too spicy. Rice pilaf and green beans from my garden. And your ice-cake thing for dessert—if you decide to grace me with your presence."

"It's ice*box* cake. Not ice-cake. You're a cynical man, you know that?"

"Of course. What cynical man doesn't know he's cynical?"

"Okay," Laura said. "I'll *eat over*."

"Good, because I'd really like to ask you about some things you said the other night."

Laura winced. "Can't we just forget about it?"

"Maybe. I'll see you at around seven. Okay?"

His voice had softened, making Laura feel relaxed and anxious at the same time. "Seven's fine."

They said their goodbyes and hung up.

Laura stared down at the phone, her lips pursed to one side.

Dusk settled in with the subdued pastel shades common to spring. The sky was painted from one side to the other in peach and blue, with scribbles of light-gray clouds that reminded Laura of smoke from a winter chimney.

When she arrived, James let her in, and she presented him with the cake, a bright smile on her face. "For you."

James cracked the lid of the plastic container and bent his mouth into a frown of approval. "Looks tasty."

Laura had frosted the entire cake with whipped cream then grated chocolate over the top.

James set the cake inside his small fridge and offered her a glass of iced tea. "I didn't figure you'd be in any hurry to drink wine, so I didn't get any."

"You're right. Tea is fine. Just don't make me laugh while I'm drinking it."

"No promises."

Laura sipped her tea and looked around. "Where are we eating?"

"In the living room." James raised his eyebrows and smiled.

He was clearly making a joke that Laura didn't understand. She looked around the small space and didn't see any table or chairs, much less food.

"I don't *see* anything." She fixed her stare on him and smirked.

"Come on, follow me." He nodded to the door.

James exited the bus and led her down the stairs. Laura followed him around to the back, and when she came out on the other side, she smiled widely and laughed.

She stood at the edge of a garden planted in the shape of a horseshoe, with exotic plants and flowers, vegetables, and fruits. A plume of water spilled out the top of a small ceramic fountain, trickling into the reservoir below. The clearing was flat and even, and a small pad had been built with twelve-inch garden stones of gray and purple. On the pad sat a little round table and two chairs. A large charcoal grill stood off to the right. Smoke escaped from the closed-off portion; green beans, onions, and red peppers sizzled in a copper pan.

"Wow." Laura crept slowly onto the patio.

The golden field beyond was tinted with a dull shade of pink from the waning sunlight. In the breeze, she smelled the food cooking, and it made her stomach growl with anticipation.

"This is beautiful," she said. It was the biggest living room she'd ever seen.

James had spoken the truth about the Cajun chicken. It was lightly seasoned and not too spicy. The pilaf was loaded with tomatoes, carrots, onions, and peppers. The green beans were crisp and flavorful, and she didn't find a single string among them.

"So if you're not a lawyer, what do you do?" James asked. Laura told him she worked in marketing and advertising, and was surprised when he asked her where she went to school.

"NC State, right in town."

James nodded. "Good school."

"What about you? What do you do for a living?"

James swallowed and sipped his tea. "I'm living on my savings for the time being." He offered nothing more on the subject.

After dinner, James brought out the dessert and proceeded to cut off a tiny sliver. He tasted it and raised his eyebrows, smiling. "Mmm." He cut the cake in half.

"Jesus, you're gonna eat *all* of that?" Laura stared at him wide-eyed.

"Sure. It's just whipped cream and cookies, right? You want the other half?" He wore a dead-serious expression that made Laura laugh and shake her head.

"Just a sliver's fine for me," she said.

James hacked off a thick slice.

"Not that big!" Laura protested. "Thinner. *Thinner.* Never mind." She took the plate.

James made hazelnut coffee to go with the dessert, and when that was finished, he looked her over the way he had Saturday morning. It wasn't the look of a man after something physical. The empathy and curiosity had returned, and sober, Laura was more nervous than before.

"What happened the other night?" he asked.

Laura laughed and shrugged. "I don't know. I was trying to relieve stress or something. I'm sorry about barging in on you like that."

"That's okay. I mean, I hope you restrict your visits to normal hours from now on, but it's no reason for shame."

Laura glanced up, brushing him with her eyes in silence.

He sipped his coffee. "Do you remember anything you said that night?"

The way he spoke and behaved reminded her of the psychiatrist she used to see, and Laura responded the way a patient might, exhibiting clear signs of nervous anxiety and shyness.

"You said something about me being immature. You also said I was making your life difficult. Do you remember any of that?" he asked.

Laura did remember some of the things she'd said.

"I was just babbling. I don't know what I was saying." She laughed and stared off at the darkening night sky.

"Laura?" James said.

She turned to face him, her smile casual and aloof.

"I'm listening to you."

Her fake smile faded, and she wondered how he could have known what an impact those words would have on her.

"I don't think you were just babbling, any more than I think you ended up here by accident," he said.

She wanted him to keep talking for a while longer, so she could savor the consolation in his voice. Even as her nose began to burn and her eyes blurred, she wanted to hear his voice, those words that extracted her pain like a stinger from beneath her skin. It wasn't forceful, but reassuring and kind.

She wanted so much to speak, but the only expression that came took the form of warm tears on her cheeks and quiet sniffling. It occurred to her briefly how strange it was, a man she hardly knew drawing out the memories she hated so much. For once, she felt safe in that darkness, because his voice was there with her. It was there like a shield when she remembered how drunk she and Sarah had been, the blurry mess of sounds and smells, and the barbs of physical and emotional pain that wrung tears from her eyes. She was scared and alone, and people were grabbing at her, and there was glass shattering like thunder tearing through a bruised, purple sky.

Laura wiped her eyes and nose then looked up at James, her hands out in front of her as if to break a fall. Her lips trembled. "I can't talk about it. Not right now."

James handed her a paper napkin and smiled. "Okay."

That little word alleviated the pressure and the pain, and she was calm again. Yet a presence remained within her, something light and placid that she needed and wanted to protect. It felt as if several pounds of anguish had been removed at once, and the sensation was unlike anything her former shrink had ever been able to do for her. How James did it, Laura couldn't say. She'd ventured into that very same darkness before, both alone and with friends beside her, but never had she experienced such relief afterward.

She stared at James for a long time before allowing a smile to form. "Is this your way of getting back at me for the other night?

Making me cry in front of you?" She laughed.

James smiled and looked away. He rotated his coffee cup in circles. "Would you rather I made you laugh and spurt coffee from your nose? It's not too late, you know."

That got her laughing, and she sighed, inhaled deeply, and exhaled again. "You said you were living off your savings. So what did you *used* to do?"

"Things."

"I'm serious."

"Me, too."

Laura pursed her lips and squinted at him. "I brought you a cake."

"To make up for your criminal trespassing."

"Still, you liked it. Come on, what did you used to do?" she pressed.

"What do you think I used to do?"

"Oh, come on! That's not fair."

"Take a guess."

"Were you a psychologist?"

"Nope. I'm self-taught. Everything I know about psychology I learned from books. No instructors or classes."

"Were you a…farmer?"

James laughed good-naturedly. "No that's what I am now. On good days, when the weather cooperates."

She studied him a while longer. A breeze drifted past, and she felt a pleasant coolness on her damp eyelashes. "A construction worker? A vet? A game show host?"

James consistently shook his head and laughed at her last guess.

He tried to change the subject by asking her about her job, childhood, and so on, but Laura insisted that he go first. After she'd made six more ridiculous guesses, James rose from his chair.

"I might not be as intriguing as you think," he said.

"I'll be the judge of that. C'mon, out with it."

"Okay, come inside, and I'll tell you all about me."

Inside the bus, Laura sat on the small couch and waited while he retrieved a book from a shelf by the bed.

After telling her to make room, he sat beside her and opened the thick photo album. The first photo was of him in his teens, an attractive young man with shoulder-length hair and a silver hoop in his left ear. His muscular arms were folded in front of him, and the shadows of the tree he stood beneath dusted his smiling face. He wore raggedy jeans and a light-blue T-shirt.

"That's me when I was seventeen. It was taken right after I joined a band called Lethal Wisdom."

"You were in a band? Cool."

"I sang, and I wrote most of the lyrics. It was fun."

"What kind of music?"

"Rock and roll, Bad Company, Cheap Trick, that kind of thing."

"Sweet! Does that mean you're gonna sing for me later?" Laura grinned like an imp.

James glanced at her as if she were insane. "Yeah, sure. Right after you make me an ice-cake thing the size of this bus."

"It's ice*box* cake. For the fifth time."

"Whatever. That's the deal: a cake the size of my bus for a song."

Laura chuckled. "That's a pretty shitty deal."

He turned the page to reveal photos of himself a couple years later, standing in front of an old college dormitory. Beside him stood a cluster of obnoxious-looking young men, the shortest of whom was in the process of removing his shirt.

"College days—I took a year off after high school. Note the confused look on my face. I'm wondering what the hell I'm doing there. That's exactly how I felt."

"What was your major?" Laura examined the photo closely, laughing at one skinny fellow holding a ferret.

"Marketing," he said.

Laura laughed and cupped her hands over her mouth. "You're kidding!"

"Wish I was. That was the path that chose me."

"What do you mean you wish you were kidding? I told you earlier that's what I do."

"You did?"

"Yes!"

James glanced at her. "You're in marketing. That explains a lot."

"Wait. What does *that* mean?" Laura asked through a smile.

"Never mind that now. Pay attention. Here I am at my first job."

James had folded the page over to show a photo of him about four years older, more serious, and dressed in a clean navy suit and a white-and-red-striped tie.

"My first year at Lewis and Hennely Incorporated."

"You worked for Lewis and Hennely?"

"Shhh. No interrupting please."

"They're *huge*."

"Please, miss. Pay attention." James spoke with mock seriousness, grinning at her just the same.

"Fine."

He went on to explain that he'd graduated with honors and secured a top position with Lewis and Hennely right out of college. He turned another page. "And this is Jeanie, the love of my life. This is Jeanie and me the day I proposed. Hard to believe that was almost fifteen years ago."

James leaned over and whispered very proudly, "She said *yes*," and flashed a smile.

The woman was tall and slender, with reddish-blond hair and big blue eyes. Her mouth was bent into a wide grin, and James stood behind with his arms folded around her.

"Jeanie was completely outside the loop, you know? She wasn't some hopeless fool doing the same thing I was. She was a teacher at an elementary school—the sweetest woman I've ever met. And then…"

James turned the page again, revealing an adorable little girl of maybe two or three. She had James's golden-green eyes and his small, symmetrical nose. Her hair was reddish like her mother's, streaked with darker shades.

"That's my little girl," he whispered.

Laura looked at the photo in stunned silence. "She's beautiful."

"She was three in this picture. Little Nina. She'll be thirteen pretty soon. Hard to believe." James touched the photo, a flash of longing in his eyes. His voice was distant, and his eyes had gone vacant. Laura waited patiently for him to return.

Finally, he said, "I love them both very much. I miss 'em."

Laura waited for him to go on, frightened that something terrible had happened. When he didn't speak, she asked.

He scratched his head above his right ear. "Well, Jeanie changed. That's how it started. I didn't want to stay on with the company. I felt trapped and overworked, didn't care much about a big salary anymore. When I used to write poems and songs, I was poor, but I was happy. Problem was Jeanie started to develop a taste for the finer things, and of course, many of her friends were enjoying the same. I spoiled her with what I was making at Lewis and Hennely, and the idea of loving a struggling poet-slash-songwriter wasn't all that appealing to her. Then when Nina came along…"

"You *had* to stay," Laura guessed.

James laughed and shook his head. "Yeah. To make sure she was taken care of. Poor thing was caught in the middle whenever we'd argue about new furniture showing up or maxed-out credit cards."

James paused a moment, the vacant look surfacing again. "I didn't even care when I caught her with him. Didn't even get mad, and let me tell you, in those days, you didn't want me to get mad. When I walked in on them, just like in the movies, they were groping for their clothes, and I just walked out. Jeanie had left me long before that. The woman in our bedroom that day was as much of a stranger to me as the man she was with."

His face registered embarrassment, and he tried to laugh it away.

"Jesus, how the hell did I get so far off track? I shouldn't be telling you all this."

"That's okay. Go ahead." Laura prevented him from turning the page.

James cocked one eyebrow. "I did get mad. Later. I grew fond of breaking things. One night, I got drunk and threw a park bench through a storefront window."

"Jesus."

"Yeah, I know." He looked ashamed for a moment. "I was thinking about when Jeanie actually left me. When I told her I was unhappy at work, and all she did was remind me of responsibility and how much my family needed me. As it turned out, my little outburst landed me in jail. And because it wasn't the first time I'd done something like that, Jeanie was awarded full custody of Nina."

Laura looked down at the photo of Nina and blinked a few times. "That must be hard, not seeing her."

"It is. We write each other a lot. I get photos of her, and sometimes, we talk on the phone. It's not the same as being with her, but it's better than nothing."

"Yeah." Laura smiled and exhaled through her nose.

James flipped the page again. There was a photo of him and Nina, about nine years old or so, with her arms wrapped around James's neck.

"Before the paperwork was finalized, I had a chance to talk to her without Jeanie hanging around. You know what she told me? My little nine-year-old said, 'I love you the most, Daddy. But Mommy needs me.' This with tears in her little green eyes."

James closed the book. "I signed over custody to Jeanie. I haven't seen either of them in almost five years."

Laura was speechless for several moments while James returned the book to its place.

"It wasn't my intention to depress you. I just wanted to share that, considering how I forced myself in a little while ago."

"You didn't force anything… Don't be silly."

"Anyway," he said, clapping his hands and rubbing them together. "Jeanie's remarried and found what she wants, I guess. So for some, it's a happy ending. Nina likes the guy at least. I might even get to see her when she starts high school this fall."

"Yeah?"

James nodded. "It was my fault, too, Jeanie and I splitting up. There was more going on inside my head than work and my family. Half the time, even when I was *there*…I was somewhere else."

He walked around for a while before sitting back down in the chair across from her. "I've never been much for company. I've never had many friends, didn't want any. But Jeanie just came along, and things happened. Then Nina, and…I love her so much, but it scared me."

"Why?" Laura asked.

"Because I knew she was innocent. I knew I couldn't blame my claustrophobia on her. I resented Jeanie for the way she changed, and I withdrew. I gave all my love to Nina, and none to her. So maybe I'm to blame after all."

James looked up at her and smiled. He was silent for a long time. "Give me simplicity, and I'm free. Complications and wealth go hand in hand. It's almost as if the more you have, the more you *have* to have just to keep up with everyone else. And I don't want to do that. I'll just ease to the side and let 'em race on by. Anyway, that's enough history for one night, I think. It's getting late."

It was almost a quarter to midnight, and Laura jumped when she noticed the time. "Damn, is it that late?"

"Yes."

"I have to get going." As she rose, she found herself staring at James, wondering what she would be doing presently, had she not seen him on that rainy Monday. Watching something pointless on television or reading a book, she supposed, neither of which could compare with his company.

James followed her out to her car, cautioning her to watch her step as she went. When she was seated in her vehicle, Laura cocked an eyebrow at him, and before her filter could stop her, she asked, "You're not gay, are you?"

James blinked, and his mouth curled at the corners. "Yup. You're definitely in the top five." He started to walk away without answering her question.

"I'm sorry, I didn't mean to offend you," Laura called out.

"You sure pick the damnedest things to say."

"I was just wondering—"

"Goodnight, Laura."

"I mean, it's okay if you're—"

"Good*night*, Laura!" James smiled and shook his head before turning around again.

"Hey!"

"Yeah?" he replied.

"I was wondering about your name."

"James?"

"No, your *last* name—Ameche? What kind of a name is that?" She felt the warmth of embarrassment in her face from asking if he was gay.

James walked backward toward his bus. "It's Italian. It means friend." He waved and retreated into his home on wheels.

Laura had a bad feeling Monday would be hell. After returning to the house on Sunday night, she went straight to bed, where she tossed and turned for more than three hours. Her evening with James bothered her immensely; the details about his life formed a bitter fable that she suddenly wanted no part of. And the way he spoke to her suggested that he understood completely both the presence and the nature of her dark streak. The lingering depth of their time together served as a distraction she both enjoyed and hated. The thoughts were pleasant, but her lack of sleep was not.

She turned the pillow over and hugged it, forcing her eyes to close. They popped open again. He was at least part Italian. She never would have guessed it, but knowing he was made a difference. It accounted for his olive skin, which now seemed more the result of genetics than long days in the sun.

Go to sleep!

She wondered how he was able to see her pain so clearly, and then extract a small but noticeable sliver of it. The analogy of a splinter deeply embedded in her skin came to mind again, though he hadn't dug at it with a needle as her mother used to. He'd drawn it out with his words, carefully and almost painlessly. It was she who had clamped down, snapping it off and trapping most of it inside her. She knew her fear was responsible. Acknowledging that massive shard of pain in its entirety scared her, perhaps even more than the effort required to remove it.

She rolled over and glanced at the green numbers glowing indifferently in the square face of the clock. It was three thirty.

"Shit." She rolled back the other way with a huff.

She had to get up in less than three hours. Doubt and anxiety hung over her like filthy clouds threatening rain. Laura wanted nothing more than to whisk them away, but she went on to consider James's life and how it pertained to her. She had first assumed he was uneducated, immature—and selfish. But every moment she'd spent listening to him produced something revelatory and disturbing, details that both amazed and frightened her. A smile swept across her face as she recalled his "living room."

Glancing up at her twelve-foot ceiling and over at the broad walls adorned with expensive artwork she felt no connection to, Laura considered James's little home on wheels and wondered which was more constricting. Waking up in his bed, staring at the concave ceiling with the sun filtering down through the skylights, she hadn't felt that misplaced suffocation she often felt in the middle of the night in her own bed. It might have been the product of not knowing where she was, but she had to admit the pleasant sensation lingered even after she had realized where she was. Perhaps the silence that embraced his little place accounted for it. Or maybe it was the sense of detachment from her life. She couldn't say. She only knew she wouldn't be feeling it in—

She looked at the clock. *Two and a half hours.*

Maybe on that particular morning she hadn't been plagued by the inevitable dread of another day. Such a brave admission gave her pause.

"I hate my life," she whispered.

Her voice sounded loud in the room. It served as a primer through which other feelings emerged, and Laura was able to speak of them without shame.

"I hate my job. I hate this house. I hate my car. I hate my

clothes…"

She smiled as she spoke, even though tears filled her eyes.

"I hate the way Don doesn't listen to me. I hate being scared all the time. I hate not knowing who I am today. I hate feeling depressed…"

Her smile widened by degrees, so cleansing were the words. The tears spilled from her eyes and flowed down her cheeks. She sniffled and laughed at herself, wondering if her sanity was slipping away. She laughed anyway, welcoming the tears and her newfound willingness to release the dark emptiness in her life so she could embrace something honest.

She spoke with confidence and clarity, working through a long list of all things petty and stifling. And then she fell silent, breathing much more deeply than she was able to before, having verbally acknowledged the presence of so many stale and heavy layers. Her thoughts felt clearer, and as insane and aimless as they seemed, she decided that irrationality might be the only thing that could save her.

The raging sea stilled, and Laura floated peacefully in calm waters. Not once did she jerk herself awake in panic. Not one single jagged nightmare dared intrude. In her sleep, she imagined what it would feel like to be healed completely. James stood near her, smiling with a warm kindness, demonstrating how proud he was of her.

"Freedom always starts from within," he said.

Laura felt safe in his presence, serene in the absence of worry. She felt as if this comfort might simply go on and on, lasting for the rest of eternity.

And then the alarm clock went off an hour and a half later.

Despite how well rested Laura felt, Monday *was* hell. Though she was still in possession of the little epiphany she'd experienced just a few hours before, the forces of evil had gotten more rest, and they attacked her from all sides the moment she walked through the door.

"Laura! I need to see you! Now!" Kate looked panicked as she waved for her to come forward.

She gauged Kate's tone and gesture—*someone* had already pissed her off, though not necessarily Laura.

"We've got until the end of the day to spin this promotional for Lefty Tool Company. Competition beat 'em to the punch. Randy, get your ass moving! What are you doing just standing around?" Kate barked.

Randy, an analyst in the research department, looked disoriented and perhaps a little traumatized by how his day was going so far.

And the fun's just started.

"I want that report in Gil's hands by nine! Move it! Anyway, listen to me, Laura. I need you to go at this all day. I want it done by five so Lefty will be up and running tomorrow. Can you do that?"

Laura's head throbbed from the aftershock of Kate's booming voice. "Well, I've got to—"

"Yes, I know, but you can *do* it! Craig! Get Steve and the others and get in the general meeting room! *Now*! You've got a full day ahead of you!"

Kate spotted Libby rounding the corner and snapped her fingers. "Damn, there's Libby. Laura, get your team in the general meeting room by nine. I have to talk to Libby. I'll see you in a few. Libby!" Kate charged down the hall.

Even though Kate wasn't angry with her, at least not at the moment, Laura still felt as if she'd been mauled by a pit bull. She thought about checking herself for cuts, bruises, and puncture wounds. Instead, she wandered off in daze, her heavy eyelids fighting not to close.

On her way to the meeting room, Laura's phone rang. She checked the number, saw it was Don again, and sent it to voicemail. After a moment of thought, Laura set up her phone to send all calls to voicemail. She stopped off at the break room for a strong cup of coffee. While she was filling her huge mug, she overheard two women talking.

One of them was Irene Hume, a petite accountant with auburn hair and squinty little eyes, and the other was a tall, raven-haired sales manager named Paula Langer. Irene was all smiles, explaining to Paula how she'd recently purchased an expensive new house with her husband and hadn't spent a lot of time furnishing it yet. She laughed, sounding both excited and worried at the same time. She leaned in close to Paula and said, "Everything is so expensive. At this rate, it'll take years to fill that place, and my parents want to come visit in a couple of months."

Laura stopped what she was doing and listened.

"Best thing to do," Paula suggested, "is keep an eye out for the big sales. But do *not* buy any junk. Just be creative until you can furnish it properly, like Tom and I did."

"It's such a big house." Irene's fingers drummed on her coffee mug. "It feels so empty. Whenever I speak, it sounds like I'm in an empty warehouse."

Laura turned to face the two women. She was about to say something to Irene when—

"Laura! Jesus, I've been looking everywhere." Kate hurried up to her. "Here are the most recent files on Lefty Tools—request forms, historical data, and projected sales for the next five years. We can't afford to lose a minute on this. Let's go, go, go!"

Kate ushered Laura down the hall and into the meeting room, which was already filled with most of her team, plus a few deadbeats Kate had assigned for some unknown reason.

Laura set down her briefcase and the files. "Okay people. Today, we're going to part the Red Sea."

Reworking an entire marketing plan was a three-day job, *minimum*. Laura had less than twelve hours. And so began her Monday.

Fortunately, brainstorming new ideas was what Laura did best. By noon, they had a workable set of possibilities. They ordered lunch in, even though Laura noticed Kate stepping out at eleven thirty with one of the VPs.

The senior graphic artist of Laura's team, Craig Sharp, worked on sketches and logo designs while her writers penned out slogans and promotional write-ups. It was a frenzy of scurrying personnel, flying papers, and frantic conversations. Kate, anxious to know how things were going, interrupted the circus half a dozen times. Laura ignored her twice and suffered a barrage of stiff verbal reprimands, which she accepted humbly. She was able to function in the madness because she knew her vacation was less than five days away. She had also quietly retained a sizable portion of the tranquility she'd discovered the night before.

They didn't stop until after eight in the evening, when her team was exhausted and hungry. Laura boosted morale by promising half of them the next day off and the other half the day off on Wednesday. She left it up to her subordinates to decide who took which day off. Lefty Tools was a sizable account, and Laura decided that giving her team a day off from work was cheap compensation for retaining them as a client. The gesture was greatly appreciated and brought cheers of approval from her team.

Laura remained in the general meeting room until eight forty-five, overseeing the final touches of their new strategy. Those who would take Tuesday off stayed and helped with the final polishing. At nine fifteen, Laura and the rest of her crew finally left the building, weary and proud of a successful day's work.

When Laura returned home, she tossed the mail on the table and staggered through the house like a punch-drunk prizefighter. Aimlessly, she wandered to the kitchen, unable to decide if she wanted food or not. When she glanced at her phone, she noticed she had several new messages. She didn't remember missing—or purposely ignoring—that many calls throughout the day, but there they were.

Laura put her phone on speaker and played the messages.

"Hi, Honey, it's me. It's Friday at around…seven thirty. Um, Chicago's great. I'm doing well here. Can't wait to tell you all about it, so give me a call."

The next message began:

"Hi, Honey. It's me again. We're having dinner in town, but I should be back in my room by ten. Okay? Talk to you later. Love you, bye."

And the next.

"Hi, Laura, it's Kate. I just wanted to know if you'd heard anything about Lefty Tool Company. I know it's late, but we've still got a major problem to—"

Laura erased the message.

The next message was Don again.

"Hi, Honey. I guess you're busy. Anyway, give me a call as soon as you can. Love you, bye."

And the next message.

"Hi, Laurie. It's Mom. I know you said you'd call me, but… Anyway, I was just wondering how you were doing. I was thinking of you. Call me if you want, anytime. Love you, baby girl."

The next message was Don again.

"Hellooo! Hah-hah! Hi, Honey. It's me again. God, they must have you working sunup to sundown. Listen, I might be staying here another couple days. Willard Conroy's in town. He's a big-shot venture capitalist who owns a lot of

companies. Could be worth the wait to meet him. Anyway, call me when you have a chance, and I'll explain everything. Love you, bye."

Laura put on her earpiece, picked up her phone, and walked over to the fridge. She paused, closed her eyes, and breathed before dialing.

It rang three times. "Hello?"

Laura was out of breath for a moment, unable to speak. "Hi, Sarah."

The ensuing pause felt like it lasted several seconds. Laura closed her eyes and swayed like a reed in the wind.

"Hi, angel. I…I wasn't expecting you to call me back. I thought you'd be…"

"Thought I'd be *what?*" Laura's eyelids drooped, and the words barely made it out of her mouth.

"Mad at me. For calling."

Laura laughed but said nothing.

"I was just thinking about you the other day and thought I'd call," Sarah said.

Laura smiled faintly but remained silent.

"I went and saw your father Sunday. That's what got me thinking. I mean, you've been on my mind always, but since you called me…" Sarah exhaled loudly and sniffled. "Since you called me, I've been thinking about you all the time."

Laura didn't want to speak. She was so tired, she had to lean against the counter. Finally, she took a deep breath and asked, "How's Dad?"

Sarah cleared her throat. "Resting. There were new flowers when I got there. I think his folks stopped by last week or something. I wrote a poem and left it with some wildflowers. Seems impersonal to buy flowers, don't you think?"

Laura smiled again at Sarah's voice and her perspective of the world. "I guess."

"How are you? You sound tired."

"I am. I can't talk long. Had a long day."

"Oh. Well, maybe we can talk again some other time?"

Laura rested her head against the wall and sighed. "You can keep talking for a little longer. Would you?"

"Sure, baby girl. You wanna hear about what Annie did last week? She got this idea in her head that she was going to make bat houses out of pallets from the warehouse down the road. Annie's mad about bats, has been ever since she was a kid."

Laura smiled, savoring the sound of Sarah's voice. Each word seemed roughened by sandpaper. Sometimes, the raspy edge to Sarah's voice reminded her of all her mother had endured, that even when a person only screams on the inside, their voice changes. And other times, there was nothing else in the entire world that could soothe Laura's nerves as effectively as her mother's voice.

With her head resting against the wall, Laura pretended she was leaning against Sarah as she told the story about Annie. When she closed her eyes, the illusion was almost complete.

"But they let her keep the pallets, even though *technically*, it was stealing. The police showed up and everything. I honestly don't know how she gets away with half of her little schemes."

Laura chuckled. "I guess I should get some sleep."

"Oh. Okay. Goodnight then, baby girl. I'm glad you called. Should I call later this week?"

Laura thought about it. "I'll call you. Maybe this weekend."

Sarah made a sound, something between an affirmation and nothing. "Are you okay?"

Laura looked up at the ceiling and clucked her tongue. *Go ahead and ask her, she'll know the answer.* Laura nibbled at her fingernail. "Can I ask you something?"

"Of course, honey. Anything."

"How do you know when…when someone loves you? I mean, *really* loves you? Not just in the sense that they say it all the time. How do you know if they mean it?"

"Oh boy…" Sarah snatched a breath and let it out.

Laura waited as Sarah made a little humming sound on the other end, something she always did when she thought hard about something.

"Your father's the only man I ever loved," Sarah said. "I knew he loved me, *really* loved me, because I tested him."

Laura perked up. Her eyes opened wider. "You did *what?*"

"I tested him. I was young when we started dating, *very* young, as you know. So was he. Anyway, when I was four months pregnant with you, he was invited to an Aerosmith concert. One of his friends had an extra ticket or something. I didn't want to be selfish. He really wanted to go. It was the chance of a lifetime. But I had to know. So I called him at his friend's house right before they left for the show and told him I needed him. He asked me if I was in any pain, if everything was all right. I told him I felt okay, but that I needed him right then. He was quiet for a moment. Then I heard some talking in the background. He came back on the phone and told me he'd be there in fifteen minutes."

Sarah paused, the way she did when she wanted something she'd said to sink in. "He never mentioned the concert, not one word. That's how I knew he really loved me."

Laura nibbled on her pinky nail. "I'm sorry I hated him, Sarah."

"You were too young to understand. How could you? Don't be sorry, honey. I think we've both had enough of that."

Laura nodded and sniffled. "I have to go now. Before I pass out."

"Okay. Sleep well. I'll talk to you again soon, angel."

"Okay. G'night, Mom."

"Goodnight, baby girl."

Laura ended the call and wiped her eyes. She took three steps, stopped, and looked down at her phone. 11:37 p.m. It was an hour earlier in Chicago. Don would still be up.

"Fuck. I really don't want to do this tonight." Laura shuffled toward the bedroom, stopped again, leaned her head back, and groaned. *But I have to know. If I want to sleep tonight, I have to know right now.*

Laura clicked on her phone contacts and selected Don. She hesitated a moment before hitting the call button. It rang three times.

"Hello?" Don said.

Laura took a breath. "Hi, honey."

"Hey, babe. Where have you been? I've been calling for the last three days."

"Been working late, rising early." Laura closed her eyes and rubbed her temple with her free hand.

Don cleared his throat. "I called earlier today. Did you get my message?"

"I…I think so. Maybe not. I don't know. It's been crazy here."

"Oh. Listen, Chicago's great. I'm cleaning up out here. I made about a dozen new contacts on my first day."

"Wow. That sounds great." Laura cleared her throat and started to say something. She heard the words she wanted to say in her head and imagined them coming out of her mouth. But they didn't.

Don told her how much he missed her and went on more about Chicago, sales he'd made, people he'd met, and places he'd been. Finally, he asked how things were going with her.

"I want you to come home right now," she said.

The air was silent for what felt like minutes. She closed her eyes and held her breath.

"What?" Don sounded perplexed.

"I said I want you to get on a plane and come home right now. Please."

Don made a strange noise, something between a groan of confusion and a laugh. "You're kidding, right?"

"No. I'm not *kidding*. I'm dead fucking serious. If you love me, you'll come home right now. Right this minute."

Her lip quivered. Tears stood in her eyes. She knew she wasn't important enough for him to leave Chicago. She didn't mean enough. Guilt seeped in, and she blamed herself, too. Fear could make a person do the most awful things.

Don sighed. "Honey, I told you I'll be there before you know it. A couple more days. A week, tops."

Don asked her again how things were going, trying to realign a conversation that had gone off track.

Laura wiped her eyes and shook her head. "Everything's great. It's just busy here."

"The busier you are, the faster time will pass, and then I'll be home." Don went on more about all his sales contacts. Laura listened, but she didn't hear him or understand what he was talking about—or give a shit.

That was the conversation. It consisted of *his* work, friends *he'd* made, how much commission *he* was pulling in, and of course, the new boat he was planning to buy on his return.

"As well as I'm doing, I'll be able to get the bigger one. It's gonna be great. We can anchor on the lake and sleep in it!" Don sounded so excited.

Laura laughed dutifully and acted thrilled for him. She did what she had always done when they—or rather *he*—talked: she waited for him to finish.

"Listen, honey, I gotta go. We're going over something for tomorrow. It's a big presentation. But I'll call you in a few days. Okay?"

Laura sniffled. "Sure."

"I love you," Don said.

Laura hesitated, and when the words finally came out, they sounded hollow and felt stale on her tongue. "I love you, too."

Don hung up.

Laura's hand fell to her side. She felt as lost as ever, wandering through the dark, and the only thing she found in the darkness was a blind hatred for all men.

"Fucking bastards," she grumbled.

Don and James started looking a lot alike to her. And then, oddly enough, she lumped her father—a man she hardly even remembered—into the same group.

Lacking the strength to eat, much less cook, Laura undressed and showered, then she collapsed onto her bed in a crooked heap just after midnight. She was asleep in a matter of seconds.

In her dreams, Laura returned to her childhood, and her name was Laurie. She swam through a labyrinth of images and sounds, settling at last on those of her father. Sarah's voice echoed in her troubled mind, trying to explain that she was too young to understand what had happened or why.

It wasn't fair the way Laurie regarded him. She never really knew her father. She recalled Sarah telling her once that she was only a baby when he held her for the last time. And because Laurie had no recollection of such things, Sarah repeated the story over and over, as if to etch the image into her mind, whether she liked it or not.

"You kept playing with his little badge," Sarah's voice explained. "He had this silver badge with his firehouse number on it."

Laurie looked around for the source of the voice as Sarah went on to describe the little silver buttons of his navy-blue dress coat, the shiny buckle, and the sharp creases in his trousers—a fireman's dress uniform. An image of her father in uniform appeared before her eyes and faded away.

"Where did Daddy go? Where is he now?" Laurie asked.

Four yellow walls and a low ceiling closed in around her. When Laurie turned, Sarah was next to her on the bed, holding her small hand.

"He's with God now," Sarah whispered.

Laurie didn't understand. The few photos Sarah kept of him were lifeless and inadequate, and Laurie knew his absence had left a hole in her mother's heart. Sarah was her whole world. Laurie saw the man in the photos as an outsider who was gone forever.

"It's not his fault, baby girl," Sarah explained. "He was trying to help people because their house was on fire."

Laurie studied the wrinkled black-and-white snapshots of men she didn't recognize standing in front of a fire truck. They wore T-shirts, some with caps on, others with helmets.

"This one's your dad." Sarah pointed at a muscular young man to the left. Those men had taken her father away, and they made Sarah hurt. Her father looked like the rest of them. She hated him, too. She hated all of them.

Laurie passed through a billowing curtain. First, she was walking through it then falling. Voices dusted the air. She heard her own voice as a child. She'd become a ghost, revisiting days past.

She witnessed her own behavior as a little girl, how it soured whenever a man entered the picture. When Laurie was six, Sarah met a man named Russell. She and Sarah were walking along when they just *happened* to run into him. Russell was tall and thin, with light-brown hair and brown eyes. He wore glasses with dark rims, and he crouched down and spoke slowly when he addressed Laurie, as if she were mentally handicapped.

Laurie scowled at him. She hadn't agreed to have lunch with this man, but Sarah led her into the restaurant anyway, which she hated. Sarah never held her hand like she was a baby, unless she "bumped into" Russell. Laurie jerked her hand free and crossed her arms.

"C'mon, sweetie, what's the matter?" Sarah touched Laurie's hair. Laurie looked up at her mother and squinted, pouting and refusing to listen to what Russell had to say.

"I've noticed many improvements being made to the parks," Russell commented.

Laurie studied Sarah, who nodded intently as if this tidbit were of some interest to her. Laurie kicked Sarah under the table, making her yelp.

"Ouch! What the hell's the matter with you?" she snapped.

Laurie scowled at Sarah then at Russel. He attempted to smooth over the ripple by trying to entice Laurie with the dessert menu.

Laurie picked up her water glass and threw it at him.

"Jesus!" He jumped up as if the ice water had burned him. Laurie had missed his face, but the water had thoroughly soaked his chest and lap.

"Laurie! What's gotten into you?" Sarah grabbed her by the arm but let her go after a moment. A short conversation followed. Sarah and her would-be boyfriend exposed Laurie to a shallow, panicked variety of psychoanalysis.

"She's not used to strangers," Sarah said.

"I see that. It's okay. I understand. It takes children time to adjust to other people—especially when they know so few adults."

They spoke as if Laurie had been hauled away to the loony bin already, leaving them alone, and it enraged her even more.

Laurie ducked under the table, came out on the other side, and kicked Russell in the shin. He howled and winced in pain. Laurie stormed out of the restaurant and onto the sidewalk. She sat on a bench out front by herself, her arms crossed and her face molded into a tight little ball of anger.

Moments later, she heard Sarah calling her name, asking people outside the restaurant if they'd seen a little girl with short blond hair and blue eyes. When Sarah rounded the corner, Laurie didn't look up at her.

"Little lady, I hope to God you have an explanation for your behavior." Sarah glared down at Laurie with narrowed eyes, her teeth clenched. Her deep-brown eyes were heavy with frustration and disbelief.

Laurie looked up at her and glared back. "You make me ashamed sometimes."

Sarah's face shed its anger, and sadness took its place. Laurie felt bad as soon as it formed.

Sarah sat down and shook her head. "This is the fourth time you've done this."

Laurie leaned over to comfort Sarah, as she always did. And as always, Sarah accepted her.

"Why do you always have to *talk* to them?" Laurie's sharp tone snapped the words out like a whip.

"Because I need someone to talk to. Okay?"

"Well, I don't like them."

"I know." Sarah let out a deep sigh.

Laurie thought for a moment. "You can talk to *me*. Okay? You can always talk to *me*."

"I know I can, baby girl. But it's not the same thing. It's just not the same." Sarah kissed Laurie on the head.

Russell left, and Sarah took Laurie home. Instead of being treated to a fancy lunch that day, they had canned chicken soup and grilled cheese.

When Laurie asked if they would ever have to put up with Russell again, Sarah said that he would call her sometime, so they could go out.

He never did.

The next morning, Laura found herself grasping for the elusive details of her dreams. She'd slept so deeply that recovering even the smallest fragments was futile. Glimpses of a father she never knew reemerged and faded away, like a thin tendril of smoke stolen by the wind.

Despite her puzzling dreams, Laura felt much better than she had the day before. She awoke earlier than usual and remained on her back, staring up at the ceiling, immersed in thought.

A crazy notion stirred inside her head, a frisky idea she wondered and smiled about. She suspected that the idea was a byproduct of the rigorous day before, the night before that, and something else she couldn't put her finger on. The closest thing she could liken it to was a mysterious lack of inhibition. Some might refer to it as *courage*.

Whatever it was, Laura suddenly saw the previous day as a personal assault on her pocket of tranquility, which, more than anything, she wanted to protect and defend. Kate was and always had been the offensive type, but never before had Laura considered the possibility of retaliation. What had happened on Monday was rare, but not unheard of. It was the first assault on her optimism and newfound sense of clarity. So on Tuesday, Laura made secret plans to launch her first counteroffensive during her lunch break.

It was almost as if the invisible forces that comprised her enemy overheard her thoughts, because the day began with Kate summoning Laura to her office.

"What the hell were you *thinking?* You gave four people on your team the day off? Jesus, Laura."

Laura leveled her gaze on Kate. "They worked hard yesterday."

"They get *paid* to work hard. And to work long hours if necessary." Kate crossed her arms.

"I understand that. But these past few months, they've been working overtime more often without being compensated—"

"You can't always reward them for what they get *paid* to do, Laura. You start doing that, and pretty soon, they expect it all the time."

"They can't take off early to balance it out like some of us can. In the long run, many of them end up working a lot of overtime for which they don't get paid."

"Laura, that's not your problem."

"I think it is my problem. They're *my* team. They work better when they're treated fairly."

Kate rubbed her chin and squinted hatefully at Laura. Her eyes shifted from one side to the other, perhaps trying to see what Laura could possibly have been thinking. "Don't *ever* give away days off without checking with me first."

"I believe it says in my contract that I can reward my subordinates as I see fit. I happen to know from working with them that they prefer a day off as opposed to a plaque or certificate saying they did a good job. They also prefer this to money, and it's actually more cost-effective for us this way."

Kate held her hands out to her sides. "Did you hear what I just said?"

"Yes. The other half of my team will be off tomorrow."

Kate's jaw dropped. A splash of color rose to her cheeks, and in the same manner a volcano sucks in air before it blows its top, Kate inhaled a deep breath and let it fly. "Like hell they are! You listen to me and listen very carefully. *I* decide who gets a day off and who doesn't. I don't know where the hell you came up with the idea that you could just turn half of your team loose on a whim, but it stops right now!"

"They *will* have the day off, Kate. It's only fair. They worked until almost nine o'clock last night—"

Kate jabbed a finger at Laura. "If they're not here tomorrow, and I mean your whole team, I'm holding *you* responsible."

"Fine. Half of them won't be here."

Just when Laura thought Kate was going to reach out and strangle her, a soft rapping came at the door. Without waiting for a reply, Mason entered the room. He greeted them both with a warm smile—always a good sign—and was dressed in what Laura recognized as his power suit. Mason only wore his charcoal pin-striped ensemble after a sizable deal had gone through. His gray hair had been trimmed recently, and his gold watch and tie clip had never looked shinier.

"Am I interrupting?" His bluish gray eyes shifted from Kate to Laura.

Kate's mask of rage dissipated into a welcoming smile. "That all depends." She laughed as if the situation were hysterical.

Mason looked at Laura. "Laura, I wanted to offer you my gratitude. Lefty Tools was thoroughly impressed by the swift turnaround you exhibited in managing their account."

"Thank you, Mason. My team worked extremely hard to make it happen." Laura gave him a genuine smile.

Compared to Kate, Mason was a saint. Laura glanced at Kate, who had reined herself in completely. She smiled warmly at Laura as if she were her own beloved child.

"She does good work, doesn't she?" Kate asked. Laura feared that Kate might reach out and pat her on the head.

Mason nodded. "Indeed, she does. They've signed us on for the full five years."

"Great!" Kate beamed and pressed her hands together.

Laura looked at Kate for a moment, and while their eyes were locked she said, "Mason, I was wondering what the policy is for awarding days off."

A deep loathing pulsed in Kate's eyes, which only Laura saw and understood.

"You mean, where *you're* concerned?" Mason straightened his jacket sleeves.

"No, sir. My team. I've awarded half of them the day off today, and the other half the day off tomorrow—as informal compensation for a job well done," Laura said.

Mason nodded and shrugged. "Well, I think the policy entitles you to make your own decisions when it comes to your team. So long as it doesn't affect the work schedule."

"I've reviewed the schedule, and I'm positive that half my team can handle the workload. They've informed me that this type of reward is preferred, whenever practical."

"I see. Well, I suppose it's more cost-effective than monetary rewards, eh, Kate?"

"I would think so, yes," Kate agreed, hatred bubbling beneath the surface.

"Great. As long as there aren't any issues with the current policy, I'm fine with you doling out days off to your team as you see fit." Mason winked at Laura.

She nodded. "Of course. I'm sorry to have bothered you with such a minute detail. I just wanted to make sure I stay within my bounds of authority."

"As long as you and your team keep doing what you're doing, you have my full support and approval." Mason bid them good morning and gave them both a little wave before exiting. He closed the door behind him.

Surprisingly, Kate's smile remained after he had left them alone. "That was *lucky* on your part." She let out a low, malicious laugh.

Kate walked slowly to the door and opened it for Laura, who cautiously made her way toward the opening. Before Laura could enter the hallway, Kate whispered, "Be careful who you fuck with. Hmm?"

Laura paused and met Kate's eyes. "I certainly will."

After her scrape with Kate, Laura was all the more eager to initiate her counteroffensive. She left the office alone, naturally, having been blacklisted by her superior, and drove to the Mercedes dealership she passed every day.

She pulled into the lot and walked into the showroom. The salesmen were as well-dressed as their customers, decked out in sharp navy, black, or charcoal suits. None of them wore brown. She'd been told the color was too dull and passive.

Laura scanned the showroom floor. Not thirty seconds passed before a young man with black hair hurried over to her. His dark eyebrows and lashes made his rich-blue eyes stand out all the more.

"Hello, ma'am. May I help you?"

Laura wondered briefly what the commission was on a car like hers. She supposed that a single sale must net a salesman fifteen hundred to two thousand dollars.

"I'm looking for Brian. Is he in?" Laura asked.

"Sure is. If you'll have a seat, I'll run and get him."

It was part of their training to appear equally as delighted when they lost a sale as when they landed one. A positive attitude was one of the cornerstones at a place like this. Laura knew that as well as anyone.

"Thank you." Laura watched as the junior salesman jogged to Brian's office.

A man in his mid-forties soon emerged, wearing a navy suit and a maroon tie. His bushy brown hair went in all directions, and his light-brown eyes narrowed when he saw her. Brian Nevant had sold her the CLS500 just two years ago. He'd been kind and courteous, and she'd promised any future business to him.

"Miss Alman. Or is it Mrs. Woodruff now? Nope, no wedding ring. How have you been?" He approached her and shook her hand.

"Fine. How are the kids?"

"Well, Julie got suspended for texting answers to a friend during a test. But the rest of them are doing well."

As they spoke, Laura and Brian walked toward the lot.

"How's Anne?" Laura asked.

"Good, good. Finished her master's degree finally, so that's a load off."

"I can imagine."

"So what's on your mind? You're not trading up so soon, are you?" Brian turned to admire Laura's silver-blue CLS500.

"I'm afraid so. I'm in the market for a convertible."

Brian looked at her and nodded. "I can see you in one." He motioned to the right, toward some of the expensive Mercedes convertibles he had on the lot.

"No, no," Laura said before he could lead her toward them. "Not those convertibles." She nodded toward the very back. "*That* one. That's the one I want. Is it for sale?"

She was looking at an earlier model Toyota Celica GT convertible someone had apparently traded in. It was in exceptional shape, with emerald-green paint and a black top. The silver wheels were stock, but it had been equipped with slightly wider tires.

"That one?" Brian's face wrinkled with doubt.

"Yeah. I like it. Reminds me of the MG Midget I had in college. How much?" Laura walked over to it, smiling.

"Well, it says seventy-five hundred on the tag. I could probably knock off two or three hundred, maybe a grand. It's been on the lot for almost three months."

"It looks brand-new."

"Yup. I believe it only has thirty thousand miles on it. It's loaded, I think."

"Let's go for a spin, okay?" Laura said, and Brian went back to get the keys.

With the top down, they raced along a winding country road in the responsive little speedster, taking curves at more than forty miles an hour.

"Woo! This little thing flies!" Laura laughed, as did Brian, who was bracing himself nonetheless.

The seat fit her like a glove, and everything was within easy reach. With the top down, Laura's hair whipped about so frantically that she had to pull over and pin it back out of her way.

They raced around for almost half an hour before returning to the lot, where Laura proclaimed, "I'll take it. This baby's mine."

She noticed that Brian seemed a little uneasy. "Are you, um, trading in the Mercedes?"

Laura laughed as if this were the craziest thing she'd ever heard. "Of course I'm trading. What would I want with two cars?" She gripped the Toyota's wheel, unable to shed her broad smile.

Brian said, "It's none of my business, but may I ask why?"

Laura leaned over as if to reveal a secret. "I'm waking up after a very long sleep."

Brian looked puzzled, but nodded and smiled anyway. "Okay. Let's go run the numbers."

Inside, Brian ran up Laura's account number. His eyes widened. "Wow." He looked over the screen at her.

"What's the matter?" Laura leaned over to try and see his screen.

He shook his head with a smile. "Well, you made one hell of a down payment. Your car will be paid off in less than a year."

"Correction, *would have* been paid off." Laura turned in her chair and looked out the window to make sure no one was molesting her little green sports car.

"Yes, of course. My point is you've got quite a bit of equity in the vehicle. Almost fifty thousand dollars."

"I'll take it in tens and twenties."

They both laughed.

"I'm sure we'd be happy to buy it from you. It's got fewer miles on it than the Toyota." A trace of confusion lingered in his voice.

"I trust you, Brian. Do the best you can for me," Laura said.

The papers were signed within the hour, and minus the sixty-five hundred dollars she ended up paying for the convertible, Laura's personal savings account balance increased by almost thirty-eight thousand dollars.

After transferring the tags and insurance, Laura waved at Brian and the other perplexed salesmen as she fired up the racy engine and took off.

On her way back to work, she stopped off at a local bookstore called Molly's for coffee and a muffin. They had the best hazelnut coffee and blueberry muffins in town. As she was heading out to the patio tables, she stopped at a long magazine rack and stared. Transferring the coffee and muffin to her left hand, she snatched three magazines with horses on the covers.

Laura perused the magazines as she ate, grinning as she turned the pages. She was the only one sitting outside, and the silence refreshed her. From time to time, as she caressed the picture of a stallion or a foal, her eyes drifted away from the page and lost focus. She remained adrift for almost a full minute before pulling herself back down to earth.

Laura sped back to the office in her new car. Zipping through the parking garage, she scared the hell out of a few coworkers before screeching into her parking spot. One of the women she'd frightened—a slender brunette named Rachel—started to explain very pointedly that the spot Laura had pulled into was reserved. The small group reacted with astonishment upon seeing Laura hop out of the little Toyota.

"Thanks for guarding my spot, Rachel. Like my new car? Cute, isn't it?" She gave the fender a little pat and strode toward the entrance.

Kate must have found Laura's behavior suspicious. She kept an eye on her for the rest of the day. Laura engaged in her duties with a carefree smile and floated through the rest of the afternoon high above the senseless clamor of what she had once considered an inescapable reality.

Laura could hardly wait to drive to work Wednesday morning. She'd discovered another way to get there, and while it was a bit longer, the scenery was more beautiful, and the traffic was all but nonexistent before eight o'clock.

She rose a little earlier than usual, allowing ample time for breakfast and the preliminary arrangements of cosmetics and wardrobe. As she applied her makeup that morning, she went lighter than usual and was pleased with the result. She also picked out something less constricting but still fancy: a pair of loose-fitting slacks and a cashmere blouse.

She selected a linen coat and low heels then fixed her hair. When she pinned it up, she didn't pull it as tight as she usually did, instead allowing the long, wavy strands to twirl freely down the sides of her face.

Before she left the bedroom, she grabbed a little red barrette to keep her hair in place as she drove to work with the top down.

Summer was on the way, and the weather enabled her to enjoy her new car. Even with the top up, it was zippy and fun, and she was able to squeeze into places that her large Mercedes had never been able to go. That Wednesday morning, for instance, she managed to ease around a stalled truck in the left lane and make it to work on time. Once there, with the little green racer parked in its place, the fun began.

As Laura had expected, Kate couldn't resist approaching her the minute she came through the door. There was no anger in her expression, but concern and curiosity pulsed and flickered in her blue eyes. "Laura? Did you really trade in the Mercedes?"

When Laura nodded, Kate leaned in and whispered, "Are you in *trouble?*"

This was Kate's way of asking Laura if she were having financial difficulties. Fighting off a grin, Laura shook her head. "Nope." She walked off, offering nothing else.

At lunch, Kate approached Laura again, and she wasn't able to escape in time. Kate suggested that they have lunch together and that they take Laura's new car, naturally.

As Laura drove them to the restaurant with the top down, Kate fussed with her hair, which the wind tossed about incessantly.

"This is cute. Why'd you trade the Mercedes?" Kate had never been the least bit concerned about being intrusive.

"I felt like it." Laura flashed a fake smile.

"I don't get it. With the bonus you'll be getting from the Kessel deal, you could've easily bought a convertible Mercedes."

"Yup. I could have." Laura frowned and nodded.

Kate sized her up. "What's going on with you?"

"What do you mean?"

"I mean you swap your car during lunch yesterday, and when you come back, you're all smiles. Are you having a breakdown or something?"

Laura laughed and shook her head. "You wouldn't understand if I told you."

"Try me." Kate tried in vain to reset her hair.

Laura waited until they were at a stoplight so she could be heard clearly then turned to Kate. "It's none of your business."

The two of them stared at each other, Kate in a state of semi-shock, and Laura with a spark of mild defiance in her eyes.

Kate sighed and waved her hand in a dismissive gesture. "Pardon me for asking."

Laura almost started to feel bad about her response, but was distracted when a pair of teenage boys pulled up beside her in a fast-looking white Mazda. The passenger had an unkempt brown mop that covered his eyes, and the driver had long, greasy black hair. He sneered at her and revved his engine annoyingly.

"Hold on, Kate," Laura muttered through her teeth. "I'm gonna burn this little shit."

"What are you talking about?"

Laura didn't respond—her eyes and mind were on the stoplight in front of her. When the light turned green, Laura dumped the clutch, and the green Toyota took off in a long squeal that made Kate shriek with horror.

Laura shifted through the gears. The Mazda was right beside them. They came into some traffic, and Laura weaved through it, laughing and clenching her teeth. Before she knew it, the little Toyota was racing along at sixty-five miles per hour in a forty-five zone.

The road expanded to three lanes, and Laura's eyes shifted quickly from right to left, watching for the perfect moment to cut over. Up ahead, a garbage truck was just pulling out in the far-left lane. The right lane was blocked, so Laura dropped it into fourth and raced ahead, cutting into the middle lane and passing the Mazda.

She was just ahead of the little white car, and when the greasy driver attempted to overtake her, he came upon the sluggish garbage truck and slammed on his brakes.

"Woo-hoo! Hah hah! Winnnerrr!" Laura pumped her fist in the air.

She cruised beneath the next light just as it was turning yellow, leaving the angry teens stuck behind the red.

"You might have a fancy car, boys, but you got no skills." Laura laughed. She glanced over at Kate, who looked absolutely terrified.

It was a quiet lunch, one that Laura enjoyed as much as Kate didn't, she suspected. For the first time, Kate didn't have anything to say and behaved as if Laura were a complete stranger.

On Thursday, Laura discovered that Kate had juggled the accounts so that three of the more bothersome clients ended up in Laura's lap. It stood to reason that it had something to do with Laura giving her team a day off then clearing her actions with Mason right in front of Kate.

The accounts belonged to semi-profitable clients who were terribly picky about how their affairs were handled, high-maintenance folks with a low return on investment. Apparently, Donna Price, who was *supposed* to be in charge of handling such problem cases, had decided that they were of minimal importance and filed them away.

Because Laura's team had been operating so effectively, all their accounts were up to date, leaving them free to take on maintenance and expansion tasks. So the picky accounts became Laura's problem. She would have fought that, except Kate had insisted they were "everyone's responsibility," and that the company as a whole must "work as a team and assist others who need assistance." Donna was supposedly swamped with clients and saddled with a smaller, less experienced team.

So, faced with a losing battle, Laura reluctantly agreed to lend a hand. Mason assured Laura that it was a one-time thing, and once the cases had been brought up to date, he would not allow that type of reassignment to happen again.

Laura and her team put off their maintenance activities and dug into the mess Donna had left behind. It wasn't as bad as Laura had first thought, but all three needed significant reworking. The marketing schemes were shallow and unimaginative, but easily rectified by her own skilled team.

At eleven thirty that morning, while she was looking over projection reports, Laura did a double take. Kate and Donna were leaving the building. They were going to lunch.

When Laura returned to the meeting room, she said, "Listen up, people. When we finish this mess, everyone gets a day off."

The entire room cheered.

On Friday, Kate summoned Laura to her office once again to complain about the days off she'd awarded her team, half of whom were not in attendance that morning. The other half would be absent Monday, Laura explained. Kate then informed Laura of Mason's absence and reminded her that the VP would also be gone for two weeks. That translated into: "I'm in charge now, so don't fuck with me." But the bombshell was the revelation that followed.

"I'm going to need you here next Wednesday. Donna's got some additional accounts she needs help retooling, and I think you can help her with that."

"I'm on vacation next week," Laura said.

"Except Wednesday. I need you here."

"What? Are you kidding me?"

"No I'm not *kidding* you, and watch how you talk to me."

Laura couldn't believe her ears. She was stunned into silence as Kate went on.

"It has to be Wednesday because Donna and I are attending a meeting in Charlotte Monday and Tuesday. On Wednesday, she'll be available to go over the accounts with you."

"How many accounts are we talking about?"

"About twelve. They're similar to the others, though they might be a little more fragile."

"Meaning what?" Laura fumed.

"Meaning that collectively, they account for a sizable share of next year's revenue on new accounts."

"In Donna's branch, not *mine*. My clients are all happy right now. But if we neglect our maintenance and expansion efforts—"

"This isn't about *you*, Laura, or *your* branch or *your* team. Get it? You remember what Mason said?"

"Yeah, he said the reassignment bullshit that took place yesterday was a one-time thing."

"He said we all have to work together."

"*You* said that. But the only people I see working in my department are *my* team."

"Donna and I—"

"If Donna took care of her goddamned work instead of running off to lunch with you, then maybe my team could focus on its own responsibilities."

"Don't you dare concern yourself with my affairs!"

"Why the hell not? You don't seem to have any problem at all concerning me with *Donna's* affairs. What does her team plan to be doing while my team does their fucking job for them?"

"You watch yourself, Laura. I mean it."

"Or else what? What are you gonna do? Fire me?"

"Nobody wants that, but I'm warning you—"

"I want to talk to Mason about this. *Now.*"

"Forget it, Laura. I'm in charge until he returns, so if you have a problem with any of these arrangements, you'll have to discuss them with me. The last thing you want to do is go over my head on this."

"Jesus Christ, I really don't believe this. Does he know you're shuffling clients around again? Reassigning employees where they don't belong?"

"Of course he knows. And if you keep acting like a goddamned child, I'll make sure he knows about that, too."

Both women were red in the face. Laura found a strange pleasure in the yelling. She enjoyed it even after the yelling had stopped.

Kate had the last word, and Laura was forced to concede the woman another victory. But Laura didn't mind. She simply took some deep breaths and shook her head in silence.

"Are we through with being a child?" Kate asked.

The words would have stung Laura, except that she knew something she hadn't before: Kate was scared of her. If she wasn't, she would still be yelling. Laura had backed her up and had almost beaten her.

"The twelve accounts will be waiting for you on Wednesday. I expect you to give them the same professional attention you would any of your other accounts. Is that clear?"

Laura glared at her. "Yeah. You make yourself very clear."

The way she sneered at Kate should have set her off again, but it didn't. Instead, Kate smiled venomously and uttered a condescending little, "Good."

Laura returned to her office and closed the door. She considered what was happening. Yes, she had succeeded in irritating one of the most influential women in the company, and she was beginning to see the consequences.

How Kate had managed to convince Mason to approve the changes and the reassignment escaped her. But people like Kate had ways. That was her specialty—to manipulate facts, people, and all things in between. Without being able to connect with Mason, Laura's job would become harder and harder. Her team was the most productive in the entire company, and they were being punished for their efficiency.

Laura viewed the circumstances as a direct response to her awarding members of her team time off again. Trading in the Mercedes—and her unwillingness to explain why she did it—probably didn't help Kate's mood, either. It wasn't that she'd traded the car, but what the action stood for: nonconformity. The ball was rolling, and Laura knew there was no stopping it. She didn't *want* to stop it.

As Laura sat behind her desk, flipping nosily through her horse magazines, her anger subsided, and she started thinking more clearly. Her mouth bent into a mischievous smile, and she curled a lock of hair around her finger. She examined it for a moment, and her gaze bobbed about the room.

It seemed like a logical step in her evolution, a way to escape one life and revisit all she had abandoned. The decision came to her as swiftly as the reasoning behind it. All she found stifling yielded before simplicity, and she could breathe again.

While Laura understood that her decision was her own, she had to acknowledge that Kate had given her a little push. Strangely, she found herself thanking Kate for that. Laura might have stalled completely if not for the torment Kate had been dishing out lately.

Motivation and courage aside, Laura felt torn. She wondered if another stunt would only make her feel worse, conjuring pain instead of peace whenever she looked in a mirror. After all, what she was about to do came as close to going back in time as she could imagine.

Laura's hairdresser was a radiant Jamaican woman with a series of thick braids curled around each other and pinned up. Her name was Matilda, but she went by Mattie, and she'd been doing Laura's hair for over five years.

When Laura walked through the door, Mattie stopped what she was doing and smiled. "What are you doin' here? It's only been a week." She went back to styling her client's hair.

"I know. I'm in the market for a change," Laura said.

Mattie stopped again and poked her tongue into her left cheek. "I can help you with that."

When she was finished with the older woman's hair, Mattie handed her off to another hairdresser and faced Laura again. "Now, Miss Alman, tell me what in the world needs changin'. You're makin' me feel self-conscious here." Mattie had a symmetrical face with a button nose and large black eyes. Whenever she smiled her entire face lit up.

She waved Laura forward with welcoming hands. Mattie was tall and solid, with muscular arms and thighs, both of which were mostly exposed. Over the course of many previous visits, Laura had learned that Mattie had participated in triathlons three times and was bothered that she never came in any better than tenth.

She brushed off the chair, and Laura sat. Mattie slipped the vinyl sheet over Laura and started tossing her wavy locks with her fingers. "What'll it be? Hm? I could trim it up, thin it out, and do a real nice braid thing on one side. I've been experimenting with a few designs like the ones on the wall there."

Laura spotted what she wanted almost immediately. The way the model's hair was done reminded her of how she wore hers during her youth. Studying the photograph of the model, she swore that those times were within reach again, that they were returning to her.

Laura pointed at the picture. "*That* one. No, the other one, on the left."

Mattie jabbed her long purple nail at the one Laura had indicated. "This one?"

Laura nodded and smiled.

"Damn," Mattie said. "You weren't kiddin' when you said you wanted a change." She looked back and forth between Laura and the modeling photo then let out a soft laugh. "Honey, I can make this look real good on you."

"One thing." Laura lifted her bangs and turned her head to one side. In the mirror, she could see the three-inch scar running along the hairline. "Don't cut my bangs too short. Okay?"

"I've noticed that before. What happened there?" Mattie gently brushed Laura's hair aside to look at it.

Laura hesitated. "Something when I was a kid. Fell off my bike."

"Don't worry. It won't show. I promise." Mattie squeezed Laura's shoulders affectionately, and Laura smiled with relief.

"I don't want to see it until you're done. I trust you. Do your thing."

Mattie grinned and slowly turned the chair so Laura's back was to the mirror. She went straight to work clipping and shaping with the delicate hands of a master artist.

Laura's wavy locks fell to the floor like silk banners as Mattie's comb and scissors went on sorting through Laura's hair.

"You've got the kind of body most women dream about," Mattie said. She stopped right after she'd said it.

Laura knew what she meant and laughed.

"Wait a minute. That didn't come out right. I meant your *hair*," Mattie clarified. "It behaves so well, I could almost do this with my eyes closed."

"But you won't, right?" Laura joked.

"Nah. I charge extra for parlor tricks."

Twenty minutes later, she led Laura to the sink. Mattie washed and rinsed her hair personally then brought Laura back to the chair, again with her back to the mirror.

"Let me see it," Laura kept saying, but Mattie only shook her head.

"Wait until I get it mostly dry." Mattie blotted Laura's head with a towel. "Close your eyes."

Laura obeyed, and Mattie turned Laura's chair around. "What do you think?"

Laura opened her eyes. She felt as if she'd been transported back to happier times. Her bottom lip quivered, and her eyes filled with tears.

"Shit. What's the matter? You don't like it? 'Cause I can't put it back on." Mattie jammed a thumbnail into her mouth.

Laura shook her head and sniffled. "No. No, no. I love it. It's perfect."

A different woman looked back at her in the mirror. The long, hard-to-manage locks were gone. The short, playful style she'd always loved as a teen had taken their place.

Mattie exhaled with relief. "Thank God. Now look, I want you to see this. Count to fifteen. Go on now, start counting."

As Laura counted, Mattie sprayed and teased her short hair until it looked wild and beautiful. Before she had made it to fifteen, Mattie was finished.

"That's how long it's gonna take you to do your hair once you get out of the shower. You just added about ten years to your life."

Laura played with it and laughed, pushing it down and watching it spring back up again. Looking at herself in the mirror, she saw someone she used to know. The person she saw was Laurie Alman, at the age of forty-five, with the short hair she recognized and adored.

Mattie smiled when tears spilled from Laura's eyes. "Damn, I knew I was good, but I never made anyone cry before."

Laura wiped at her eyes without taking them off the reflection in the mirror. Two words left her mouth in a very slight whisper, and they made Mattie smile.

"It's me." Laura played with her bangs again.

"Yep. It's all you, but with a little less hair." Mattie's gaze dropped to the floor. At the base of the chair was a sizable pile. She wrinkled her brow thoughtfully. "Wow, did I take that much off? You must be three pounds lighter."

Laura glanced down and was equally astonished by the volume of clipped hair. "Hmm. I guess I can go celebrate with some ice cream."

They both laughed as Mattie tousled Laura's hair again.

Laura thanked Mattie seven times before leaving. She handed her a few extra bills, and Mattie looked up with wide eyes. "You sure?" Laura nodded, and Mattie chuckled. "It's nice to be appreciated."

"Thank you so much." Laura hugged her.

"Anytime, darlin'. You keep those clients comin' to see me now, won't cha?"

Laura played with her short hair again. "Well, this masterpiece might keep you busy for quite a while. Don't be surprised if a dozen women with long hair show up here tomorrow."

Before Laura could leave, she heard Mattie jokingly calling out to one of her girls, "Trish! We're gonna need more trash bags!"

The elation Laura experienced inside the salon was magnified a thousand times when she hopped into her convertible and drove down the road. The wind massaged her head with soft hands, and when she arrived back at work, a simple toss with her fingers was enough to reset the few hairs that had blown out of place.

"This is so amazing." She turned her head from side to side to inspect it.

When she stepped from her car and turned around, Kate and Donna were standing there, having just exited Donna's white Lexus. The two women stared at her, blinking in silence as if they had no idea what to make of the odd creature with the short hair.

Laura's mouth bent into a malicious grin. "Afternoon, ladies. Donna, working hard on those problem accounts, I see." Laura walked off, leaving them where they stood.

She entered the building and marched through the office in search of someone in particular. At last, she came upon the person she was after, seated at her desk, talking on the phone. Laura walked into the small windowless office, causing Irene Hume looked up. She squinted at Laura for a moment, not recognizing her. When she realized who Laura was, her eyes widened, and she stuttered into the phone.

"Um, listen, Tracy, I'll call you back, okay?" She hung up. "Miss Alman, what…what can I do for you?"

Irene was almost twenty years younger than Laura and worked as a junior accountant. She got nervous around upper management personnel, hence the formality of how she addressed Laura. Irene's face paled a shade when Laura turned around and closed the door. Irene started to get up from her chair.

"It's okay, Irene. Don't get up."

Irene sat back down.

"Listen," Laura said, "I wanted to congratulate you on becoming a homeowner."

Irene blinked with confusion. Her small mouth curved into an awkward smile. "Oh. Thank you." As if she had no control of herself, Irene went on to describe the place to Laura, the exclusive features, and how perfect the neighborhood was for children.

"That sounds great." Laura bit at her bottom lip. "I overheard you talking with Paula the other day. Rumor has it you're having trouble furnishing the place."

Irene furrowed her brow and shrugged. She seemed a little embarrassed.

"Hey, listen." Laura waited until Irene met her eyes. "You've done very well for yourself at such a young age. You're—what? Twenty-six? You're happily married, and you've got a nice house, right?"

Irene nodded and smiled.

"Well, that's more than *I* can say. Look, the reason I'm bringing this up is I received a lot of stuff from my family that I'm not too crazy about. They got all excited when they heard about the engagement— you know how it is. Anyway, most of it is brand-new. I've got furniture, rugs, even some appliances that I either can't or won't ever use. You hear what I'm saying?"

Irene nodded and giggled.

Laura smiled. "Don't get too excited on me. I'm looking to cut a deal here. I mean, I like you and all, but not enough to give you this stuff."

Irene shook her head. "Oh no! I'd never expect you to do that."

"But I can give you, say…fifty percent off everything. That's a much better deal than you're apt to get anywhere else this time of year."

"Absolutely!" Irene cried.

"I'll be running an ad shortly, but I wanted to give you first dibs. I've got an Italian leather sofa, two matching chairs, a formal oak dinette set for eight, six rugs, and a whole bunch of other stuff."

Irene's eyes looked ready to pop out of her head. "This is *perfect*," she murmured.

"Everything is neutral, so it'll probably go with whatever you already have," Laura said.

"My dad just sent me a little money to help out. When can I come take a look?"

"I'll pick a weekend over the next couple of weeks. That way, I can start the ad on the following Monday—if there's anything left."

"Great!" Irene clasped her hands together and looked up at the ceiling as if she were giving thanks to God.

"Okay then. I'll let you know soon." Laura turned to leave. "Irene? Let's keep this between us. Okay?"

The way Irene nodded, it was clear that the feeling was mutual. She clearly didn't want it getting around that she'd filled her house with used furniture. People would talk.

That evening after work, Laura was feeling especially carefree. After stopping off at home to change her clothes, she headed to the produce stand. She bought some vegetables, including a few of James's tomatoes, and when she paid, the old farmer smiled.

"You cut your hair," he said.

"You like it?" Laura was surprised he recognized her.

He handed over her change. "I'm partial to longer hair, but it looks very nice."

Laura drove with the top down to Thompson Road and made a left. Excitement radiated from her as she approached James's silver bus. She wore a grin that wouldn't go away, and just as she expected, when she left the car and slammed the door so as to be heard, James exited the bus. He squinted at her with a look of confusion. "Can I help you?"

Laura walked up slowly, and James's inquisitive expression faded into a smile.

"Laura?" He looked past her at the little green convertible, pursed his lips, and nodded. "I like your hair. Looks good."

"Thanks." Laura did a little pirouette so he could see the back.

James looked a little uneasy, and she sensed it right away.

"What's the matter?" She walked toward him, noticing that he was dressed a little nicer than usual. His hair was combed neatly, and he wore a pair of loose-fitting khakis and a navy-blue button-up shirt. Then she caught the clean scent of his cologne.

Laura rested her hands on her hips and cocked her head to one side. "What are you all dressed up for?"

James didn't say anything. He smiled at her in a way that bordered on apology. The silence stretched out a few seconds. "I'm going out."

While Laura had been unable to shed her expression of joy moments before, she suddenly found herself fighting to hold on to it. The effort required to maintain a smile was taxing. She wanted to offer a quick response, something casual and dignified, but nothing came to mind.

Instead she said, "On a *date?*" She sounded like a jealous girlfriend, which was completely inappropriate. There was an edge to her voice, a sharpness she regretted the moment it surfaced. By then, it was too late, and he had the upper hand.

James smiled and nodded. "Yeah. On a date."

Laura nodded with gestures too stiff and numerous. She felt like whatever she said or did, her voice and actions would only further expose how hurt she was. At last, she shrugged and laughed. "Well, I should let you go then."

James looked at her with his unique green eyes, with the wisdom and patience of a mind reader. Laura didn't want him seeing what was there, so she waved and walked back to her car.

"Maybe I'll see you around." She got in and started the car.

James remained where he stood and waved at her like he always did, with one hand raised. "Yeah, I'll see ya."

Laura turned her car around and left.

And there it was. James was a player.

Laura felt more rejected at that moment than she ever had before. It was clear what he had told her: "Please don't come around here again. You've got your own life."

All concerns about her own engagement aside, Laura was more than a little upset about his dishonesty. *He should have told me about his little dating affairs. It would have saved me the embarrassment of seeming so desperate.*

"I can't believe I went over there drunk!" she muttered.

She returned to Don's house, where she ate a small salad she couldn't taste, brooding all the while about how James had made her feel so foolish.

It was Friday, and her vacation had begun—and what a beginning. She wasn't sure what she'd expected, but she hadn't wanted it planned out. She had intended to pop in on James, have a nice conversation, maybe cook something in his "living room," and just enjoy his company. And there she was, alone on the couch, staring at one of the long walls.

What the hell did you expect, Laura? He's single, and you're not.

At least not at the moment. She shook her head and laughed at herself. Her conversation with Irene resurfaced, and Laura had to stop and think about what exactly she was doing. She'd sold her car and cut her hair, and she was planning to sell her possessions. When she paused to consider it, the idea of severing all ties to her old life filled her stomach with a wave of cold anxiety.

What are you going to get rid of next? And then what happens? What are you planning to do? Where are you going to go?

Part of her—the irrational, impulsive part—had latched onto the idea that perhaps James could fill in some of the blanks. *And how stupid was that?* She didn't even know him. He'd been patient and courteous toward her on three separate occasions. It was hardly enough to plan a new chapter of her life around.

The sobering reality that James didn't want her stung, but it wasn't all that shocking. *What man in his right mind would want someone like me in his life?* Laura felt herself sinking into the wet cement of reality, and it made her begin to doubt her resolve. All of sudden she didn't know why she'd sold her car—or cut her hair. Worst of all, she wasn't sure why she'd made Kate her enemy.

Because of James?

She pinched her eyes closed and rested her head in her hands. "God, I am so fucking stupid."

Am I really so desperate for a man who will listen to me that I'm willing to abandon everything else in my life?

James did listen to her, probably better than any man ever had. That alone was more than enough to trigger a powerful emotional response. But she recalled what James had said about his last name. *"It's Italian. It means 'friend.'"*

Laura flopped onto her back and rolled halfway off the couch. She let out a self-loathing groan. She wondered what kind of man could be so kind to her without wanting anything in return. "A gay man. He's going on a date with another man." She huffed a bitter laugh at herself.

Her anger changed direction, and she found herself resenting him again. *What kind of show is he putting on anyway? Sure, he acts all understanding and thoughtful, lets me sleep off my drunkenness in his bed, and then casts me aside? He draws out that awful splinter of my past and then goes out on a date?* One thing she knew for sure was that he was doing her no good at all with his kindness. Good intentions be damned.

He might have only wanted to help her, to save her from something. That notion all but made her sick to her stomach. Laura Alman didn't need anybody to save her from anything, least of all some phony man who was only pretending to be her friend, and then only when it suited his interests.

In no time, she was fuming, and the ball of rage was flying in his direction like a cannonball. "I oughta leave a message on his machine, give him a piece of my mind. Son of a bitch."

The more she thought about it, the more sense it made. She would leave a nasty message on his machine while he was away on his date. As soon as she'd worked out what she would say, she picked up the receiver and dialed his number.

"Hello?" James answered.

Laura gasped and sputtered for a moment. She glanced at the clock on the wall and did some calculations in her head. It had only been an hour since she'd left him. That made for a pretty fast date. Unless he hadn't left yet, which seemed odd.

"What the hell are you doing home?" she asked accusingly.

"Laura?"

"Yes, *Laura*." Him picking up the phone had set her off. She was all set to leave a message, and he'd gone and screwed it up. "I was trying for your machine. I didn't expect you to be home so soon."

"Should I hang up and let the machine get it when you call back?"

"Don't be ridiculous."

Silence.

James cycled a soft breath. "So…what's on your mind? You sound upset."

"Why aren't you on your *date*?"

"Why are you being so rude?"

Laura uttered a few sounds that were too small to be words. "I'm not being rude. I just…want to know what you're doing home."

"I don't think that's any of your business."

His voice was even and calm. Laura guessed that he wasn't smiling.

"Maybe not, but I just wanted you to know…"

"Yes?" he said.

Laura's thoughts scattered in a hundred directions. She heard him exhale a low sigh.

"Would you like to come over?" he asked.

Still, she didn't answer. He spoke anyway.

"She stood me up. Okay? Apparently, the friend of hers that introduced us slipped up and told her I live in a bus."

Laura's eyes closed, and she bit at her bottom lip. The depression in his voice completely extinguished the fire she'd stoked up.

"Are you there?" he asked.

"Yeah…yeah, I'm here."

Another pause followed.

"Have you eaten yet?" Laura asked.

"No. I didn't get past the breadsticks."

"Well, I've got some vegetables here. I could bring 'em over, I guess."

James laughed on the other end. "Okay."

Together, they made shrimp-and-chicken kababs, and James boiled pasta in a small kettle. The sky was clear, sprinkled with countless stars, and with the lights off inside the bus, they sparkled all the brighter.

They leaned back in their chairs, each with a glass of cold sweet tea, when James asked, "So are you on the FBI's most-wanted list or something? You're a bank robber, aren't you? Or a car thief."

Laura cocked an eyebrow at him. "What the hell are you talking about?"

"The new car, the hair…is it a disguise? Am I going to see your face in the post office? Are you a secret agent or something?"

She considered this seriously for a few moments. "No, I think what you saw *before* was the disguise."

"Care to elaborate?" James sipped his sweet tea.

Laura thought for a moment. "No, not really."

"Damn. I love philosophical discussions."

"We can still talk, just not about my disguise."

Laura fell quiet and began stealing sideways glances at him. "So tell me about this *woman* you were supposed to date."

James smiled and straightened up in his chair. He took a quick breath. "I could be wrong, Laura, and please tell me if I am, but…you act as if you're jealous."

"What? I am not *jealous*! I'm engaged, remember?" She showed him her ring and snorted as if the idea was preposterous.

"Then how would you explain the little twist you threw on *woman* a moment ago?"

Laura shook her head. "I don't even know what you're talking about."

"I wish I had a tape recorder."

"I was just asking. Maybe I'm mad because she stood you up. That's so cowardly. And if it was because of what you said—that she didn't approve of where you live—well, it's appalling."

James wore a tiny knowing smile. "I agree. So you're angry at her insensitivity, and you're not jealous?"

"No. Don't be stupid."

"Good. Then I might as well tell you, I wasn't totally honest before. This wouldn't have been our first date. Her name is Sophie. We've been seeing each other for almost a month. Last week, I spent the night at her place."

Laura's body stiffened, and she cleared her throat. She stared off at the distant wheat field, where the horizon met the whispering blades of grass. When James didn't go on, she glanced at him. "I'm listening. Go ahead." Even her words had stiffened.

James rubbed his palms on his thighs. "I know it probably sounds pathetic, especially given the circumstances, but I think I'm in love with her."

Laura's face warmed and turned pink. Her breathing grew more labored, and she narrowed her eyes. "Oh really?"

"Yeah. I've never met a woman who was so…I don't even know how to describe her. She's very focused, but sensitive. She makes me laugh, and I love being around her."

"Hm," Laura muttered through pressed lips.

"You listening?"

"Yup."

James fondled his empty glass, rattling the ice cubes around. "I never thought I'd ever find someone who made me feel like Jeanie did. You know, before it all fell apart."

Laura sipped her iced tea. She wanted to spit at him.

"I mean, yes, she did stand me up tonight. But I think she'll have a change of heart soon. I think she'll call me up and apologize."

Laura nodded. Her face was burning up, and she hated him. She swore he was doing it on purpose, playing some kind of game with her emotions. She tried to fight off her anger, but he just kept talking.

"She's got the cutest laugh," James went on, "and the way she holds me makes me feel calm and at peace."

Every word dug into her, and she knew at any minute she'd hurl her sweet tea at his face. She could even hear the smile in his voice; the way it bent his words made her want to scream.

"Last week at her place was the first night we spent together, but it seemed to last forever."

Laura was teetering on the edge.

"And she's such an adult. She's not afraid of saying exactly what's on her mind—"

Laura jumped to her feet before she knew what was happening. She tossed the glass of sweet tea onto the patio stones, shattering it. "You son of a bitch! Who the fuck do you think you are, huh?"

"Whoa. Take it easy."

James was laughing. She couldn't believe it. The smile on his face fueled her rage. She stormed over to him, her hands molded into little balls.

"What are you trying to do? Make me crazy? If she's so perfect, why the hell did she stand you up?" Laura was only a couple feet from his chair.

James stood up and held out his hands, his smile fading. "Laura, listen to me—"

"Why are you telling me all this? To see if I'm as good a listener as you? Well, I'm *not*, okay? I'm not interested in hearing the details of your twisted romantic life!"

"Why are you so mad?" James didn't appear to be surprised—more as if he knew but wanted to see if *she* did.

Laura scowled at him. "Because you're playing games with me, and I don't like it!"

"That's not true."

"You are! This is some game to you, isn't it? You lure women to your little house on wheels and torture them!"

James chuckled. "You know that's not true. Tell me why you're so upset."

"Stop asking me that! If you don't know why I'm mad, then you've got a serious problem!" Laura grabbed her purse and jacket.

"Where are you going?"

"What the hell does it look like? I'm leaving."

James stepped in her way. "Not until you tell me why you're angry."

"Are you crazy? Get out of my way, or I'll scream!"

James widened his eyes theatrically. "Go ahead and scream your head off! We're miles from where anyone can hear you."

Laura couldn't help it. His expression made her laugh in spite of herself, and she almost couldn't regain control of her anger.

"Just tell me why you're mad, and I'll move," he said.

"Move or I'll kick you." She fought off a smile and still couldn't look directly into his eyes without laughing.

"You're so terrified of your feelings." James shook his head.

Laura dropped her stuff and threw a fist at him. He caught her wrist, and she tried to break free. "Let me go."

"You know why you're mad, now say it."

Laura struggled in his grip. "Let me go!"

"Jesus Christ, Laura. Just tell me why you're so mad."

She threw the other fist at him, and he caught her other wrist. She could have easily kneed him in the crotch, but instead, she struggled to free herself until the effort tired her out. James wasn't squeezing her or hurting her. He was just holding her in place.

"Tell me why you're mad."

"Let me go." Laura's voice weakened. She looked at him, into those eyes.

"Tell me. Just be honest."

Her lips moved, and she strained to speak. Then she stopped struggling. "Because…"

James loosened his grip on her.

"Because I'm jealous."

James released her. He took a deep breath and sighed. He gently retook her hand in his. "I made up all that stuff. This would have been our first date." James stroked Laura's hand. "And she didn't stand me up. *I* canceled. Right after you left."

Laura looked up at him. "Why?"

James took another step and brushed at her short hair with his right hand. He came close to moving her bangs aside, and Laura leaned back so he wouldn't see her scar.

"She wasn't my type," he said. "And there was someone else I wanted to be with."

His hands were so light on her that she didn't even feel him pulling her close.

He kissed her on the forehead and touched her cheek. "Of all the stubborn women I've met in my life, you're definitely in the top three."

Whatever could have happened after that didn't. James drew back and kissed her softly on the mouth, and that was all.

"I'm jealous, too." He laughed. "Are you angry at me for lying?"

She shook her head. "No, I'm just…having a hard time with my life right now. I have a lot on my mind. And it's not just the idea of a woman that makes me jealous. It's everything. It's the way you live."

James smiled at her. "You look different."

"What do you mean?"

"Honesty makes you look younger. Your appearance changes when you stop being afraid."

Laura wondered if it was possible to collect fear and internal lies the way the ground collects dead leaves in the fall. It was strange to think that one lie could lead to another and another, that they could eventually build and collect until it became impossible to breathe. Fear was the same, and she decided that it might summon the lies. And it was suddenly clear that the whole cycle had begun with one fear and one lie.

Looking at James, she saw a man who had rid himself of fear and lies a long time ago. She could actually see it in his eyes. And mirrored in his eyes was her own face—a face that still retained some of that poison. Not as much, but some, way down deep. James seated himself on the bench swing, and Laura sat across his lap. In silence, he stroked the back of her neck where her hair tapered to a point. Even though she was engaged, she felt no guilt. Aside from a gentle kiss now and then, James did nothing objectionable. She needed silence to think. Somehow, he knew that. She kept her arms crossed in front of her, legs bent at the knees, and did nothing to return his affection.

She floated in his arms, lost in thought as he touched her as gently as a lazy summer breeze. Even without him speaking, she felt he was listening to her think, and she knew he could see the way she looked without her disguise.

"If there's something on your mind, you can tell me," he whispered.

"There is. Quite a bit, in fact."

She fell silent, and James laughed.

Laura cleared her throat. "I spoke to my mother a few days ago, for the first time in years."

"Your mother? Really?"

Laura sighed and leaned against him. "I love the sound of your voice."

"Thank you. Tell me about her."

"Who?"

"Your mother."

Laura breathed in deeply and said nothing for several seconds. "God, where the hell do I start?"

James waited patiently for her to go on without speaking. He rubbed Laura's shoulders as she thought, and the motion put her mind at ease.

"I guess I can start by saying…" Laura turned to look at him. "She was only thirteen when she had me."

James's eyes were neutral, but he nodded with understanding.

"As hard as it was, she wouldn't let anyone decide what was best for her. I'm grateful for her decision now. I wasn't always."

Laura explained to James all about Sarah. She told him about how, essentially, the two of them had grown up together. Sarah had always insisted that Laura was smarter than her, that she would succeed in all areas where Sarah herself had failed.

"She wanted the best for me, that's all. And that wasn't always easy for her." Laura shook her head and wiped away tears. "It wasn't easy at all. Sarah's family was pretty well off compared to most in the area where I grew up. They disowned her when she refused to terminate the pregnancy or give me up for adoption."

As the words poured out, Laura imagined herself at the age of ten, when she first began to see things in a different light. She resembled her mother a lot, with her high cheeks and small nose. Laura's hair was light, and her eyes were dark blue, like her father's, and Sarah insisted that Laura was all the more attractive as a result.

By the age of twelve, Laura was sexually active, just as her mother had been. It was apparent to Laura, whenever she looked into her mother's eyes, that this behavior worried Sarah. She would mutter prayers to God about keeping history from repeating itself. It didn't, but something else happened. Laura assumed a magnanimous position where her mother's life was concerned, and Sarah began dating again. For Laura, dates turned into parties, and in no time at all, she and many of her friends began indulging in all things forbidden to kids their age, and she welcomed Sarah into that world.

As far as Laura was concerned, Sarah was the best mother a teen could have. She allowed drinking and smoking in her house, sometimes offering Laura's friends some of her own. Weed followed closely behind. Sarah was hip to it, accepting a hit whenever the joint came around. Those were free times to Laura, happy times when she and Sarah would dance slowly about the room in each other's arms, laughing and singing with the music, lost in a daze neither of them ever wanted to end.

There was more to it, though. Laura's teenage years were also littered with wholesome memories of hanging around with Sarah at one shopping mall or another, at the park, having lunch, or feeding birds by the river. Laura's friends at school talked about how strict their mothers could be, telling horror stories of being grounded or denied access to one concert or another. By comparison, Laura's weekend road trips to Atlanta or sleepovers on Hilton Head Island would make the crazy girls she hung around with laugh, and she would give thanks for having the best mother on the planet.

More often than not, Sarah accompanied Laura on her adventures, and as much as Laura adored her friends, none of them held a candle to her mom. Many of the best times were when the two of them were alone, during long drives in the country, afternoons at the stables, and on occasion, a magical Friday or Saturday night by the river or on the back lawn. Times when their only companions were a crackling fire and a bottle of wine, which they passed back and forth between them, would remain sacred in her heart for all time.

Immersed in the warmth of those memories, Laura said nothing for long time. She worried that James might judge her for how she had been in those days, but she dismissed that after meeting his eyes, where she saw nothing but patience and understanding, perhaps a lively flicker of compassion.

"I know how this must sound to you." Laura spoke defensively, even though James hadn't said anything. "It sounds like my mother was a drunk, and she made me one, too, right? But that's not what it was like. I could never explain it without people shaking their heads at me, looking down their noses as if they were so *balanced*. We got drunk once in a while. We smoked pot once in a while. And you know, in a big way, it was *my* fault."

James nodded, his expression not the least bit judgmental.

Laura returned to the warm, rippling waters of what had been. She explained to James how she began to feel guilty about the behavior she'd exhibited as a small child, effectively denying her mother the company of other adults on several occasions, the kind of happiness that she herself was too young to understand.

The guilt went on to encompass the fact that Sarah had been shoved into adulthood at the age of thirteen. She'd sacrificed her youth to raise a child no one thought she was ready to have.

So Laura pulled Sarah into her world, full of young adults without care, late nights, booze, and dope. And Sarah, having indulged in only a taste of such pleasures in her own youth, accepted the invitation with open arms.

The circle of teens would often fall silent as Sarah recounted memories of her past, stories about Laura's grandmother, and how wild *she* had been, the hypocrite! It wasn't always a riot that met the dawn, and the gatherings weren't always marked by overindulgence of illegal substances. Many times, the mind-altering chemicals were used sparingly, *responsibly* one might say. A little wine, a little weed, they were just a little bit of comfort, along with a lot of conversation and plenty of laughter.

Sarah had always been there, with a bright smile, a raspy laugh, and wide brown eyes whenever she told a story. There was no doubt in Laura's mind back then that Sarah was her best friend and always would be.

"But I was wrong."

"Why do you say that?" James asked.

Laura glanced up at him.

"You said you were wrong. About your mom being your best friend. How were you wrong?"

Laura raised her eyebrows and heaved a sigh. "I thought I was wrong. Christ, it's such a screwed up... I shouldn't go into it."

James didn't say anything, and Laura went into it anyway.

"Let's just say something bad happened…and I blamed her for it. I blamed her for not being a good mother, for letting me do all the things a girl my age shouldn't have been doing. I became a real bitch to her."

Then, as if James had tried to coax her into revealing more, which he hadn't, Laura said, "That's all I wanna say for now."

She leaned upward and kissed him on the lips. She trembled in his arms, but the shakiness passed. Soon she was nodding off, grasping at little bits and pieces of happier times, when she used to lounge in her lover's arms, just like this. She might have muttered his name in a sleepy whisper. "Jimmy."

James said nothing. Laura supposed, during the short waking moments that followed, that he knew she wasn't speaking to him, even though their names were the same.

"Where are you taking me? You're gonna get us in trouble again. We're not even supposed to be here." Laurie shined the flashlight on a locked gate between two winding lengths of cyclone fence—the back entrance to Carnelian Park, which was closed for the night.

Jimmy stopped fiddling with the padlock and looked over at her. "Shhh. Keep your voice down. Might be guard dogs around here."

Laurie heard a noise in the woods. She spun around, aiming the light into the black trees.

"A little light, please?" Jimmy said.

Laurie returned the light to where Jimmy poked and prodded the old lock. "Do you even know what you're doing?"

Jimmy frowned and hung his head. "No, not really. It looks so easy in the movies." He took three steps, picked up a rock the size of a cantaloupe, and bashed the old padlock open.

"Are you crazy?" Laurie instantly felt stupid for asking.

Jimmy fluttered his eyebrows at her and pushed open the narrow gate. Laurie followed him down a crooked little trail through the woods. It was a muggy summer night in Georgia. The thick air stuck to her skin and pasted her shirt to her body.

"Where are you taking me?" she whispered.

Jimmy looked over his shoulder at her as he ambled down the trail. "You'll see. Ten minutes. It'll be worth it. Promise."

The trail descended slightly. The buzzing drone of crickets and frogs grew louder as they rounded a bend. A cool breeze sailed past. A three-quarter moon cast a pale glow on the rippling pond just ahead.

"See?" Jimmy said.

"Yes, it's lovely. But what if we get caught?" Laurie glanced about warily, all but certain that park rangers were closing in on them.

Jimmy stepped over to her, took her face in his hands, and kissed her. "They got no right to keep this from us. Not on a night like this." He took a step back and peeled off his shirt. "C'mon." He turned and ran toward the pond. Laurie hurried after him.

Jimmy ditched his cut-offs and stood before her, as naked as he'd ever been. He held his arms out to his sides and looked down at his pride and joy. "Don't leave me hangin' here."

Laurie laughed and peeled off her shirt. She dropped her shorts and approached him. Jimmy kissed her again then scooped her into his arms.

"Don't throw me in!" Laurie pleaded through a laugh.

Jimmy cast a sideways glance. "Would I do that?"

"Hell, yeah. Done it more times than I can count."

But he didn't throw her in. Instead, he carried her until the cool water lapped at her bare skin. He kept walking until she was completely immersed.

"Shit. Water's a bit cold. Not sure I'll be any use to ya tonight," he said.

Laurie laughed. He let her go, and they dove under and splashed around, marveling at the moon and stars.

"This was a nice surprise. Just hope someone doesn't surprise us both," Laurie said.

"Doubt it. Not on a weekday. We'll be all right. 'Less we get bit by a moccasin."

"Fuck! Don't even say that! You just killed the mood." Laurie clutched at herself protectively. She hated snakes more than anything.

"C'mere, I'll protect ya. I was only foolin'." Jimmy laughed and reached out for her.

Laurie stayed where she was, so Jimmy had to swim over to her. She splashed him in the face. He coughed and laughed some more.

"Asshole. You know I hate snakes." Laurie scowled at him.

Jimmy cleared the water out of his windpipe. "Shit, you almost drowned me."

"Mention snakes again, and I'll finish what I started."

He closed in. Laurie splashed him again, but he got ahold of her. He nibbled on her neck, and the fight went right out of her. He lifted her up, and she instinctively wrapped her legs around him. She cried out with surprise and moaned. Apparently, the water wasn't too cold after all.

A half hour later, they crawled out of the water and sprawled out on a big square dock at the center of the pond. They huddled together for warmth against the cool breezes licking at their wet skin.

"It's like we're castaways on a small island," Jimmy said.

"That'd be fine with me." Laurie rubbed his smooth chest. "But we shouldn't stay too long. Don't wanna get busted again. Sarah's about fed up with my shit."

"I don't blame her. You're always fuckin' around, doin' somethin' bad—"

Laurie tickled him. He tickled back and won, as usual. They lay there on the floating dock in silence, the water lapping the sides, stars above like diamonds on black silk.

"Gotta hang on to these moments. You know?" Jimmy said. "At the end of it, that's all anyone really has. Memories."

Laurie nodded. "Don't worry, I won't ever forget this."

Jimmy fell silent for a minute or two.

"I don't think my dad had a lot of good memories," he said. "I think he was…kinda sad most of the time. I guess some people just don't know what to do with life. You know?"

"Yeah. Sometimes I worry about Sarah. I feel like she had to skip bein' a kid because of me."

Jimmy pulled her close. In a tone that sounded much too serious for him, he said, "Don't ever stop livin'. No matter what happens. Okay?"

Laurie didn't know what to say, so she didn't say anything. Jimmy brushed her cheek with his hand, eased away from her, and stood up. "Race ya back!" he cried and dove into the pond.

The cold water splashed her, and she was overcome by a sudden sense of urgency.

"Wait!" she called out, diving in after him.

Laurie swam through the inky water as fast as she could. She paused now and then to see how close she was to catching him, but Jimmy kept getting farther away. Laurie swam faster, finally reaching the shore. She stood, wiped the water from her eyes, and looked around.

The night was silent. The droning of crickets and frogs, the leaves hissing in the cool breezes, the water sloshing against the shore…all of it was gone.

Just like Jimmy.

"Jimmy?" Laurie called out. He was nowhere to be seen. She looked on the ground for their clothes. Gone, as well. She hugged herself against the cold night. "Jimmy!" she screamed. The darkness remained silent. Laurie started down the path, only to find that it had disappeared, as well. Dry branches scraped at her skin and snagged her wet hair.

"Jimmy!" she cried. After a few steps, she felt too weak to go on.

She dropped to her knees and wept.

Laurie stirred and finally broke free of her nightmare. Her body felt heavy and stiff, as if she'd been pumped full of wet sand.

The peace she had savored lying there in James's arms—the gentle, benign presence of his fingers on her cheek and in her hair—quickly dissipated. It wasn't the notion of infidelity, but her bitter-cold nightmare that had drained away her serenity. She found herself caught up in a strange dance, a cadence somewhere between excitement and regret, and she worried that James might misinterpret the latter.

It was a hell of a time to ponder her relationship with Don. Logic told her that the path she'd chosen was the right one, but sensibility argued that she'd commenced this leg of a new journey without considering everything carefully. For example, was she behaving in a manner befitting an adult? Was she being too selfish about Don and what she expected from their relationship? She had to remind herself that, as good as the affection felt to her, the man holding her was not Jimmy.

Jimmy was gone. Forever.

The admission stung. It burned in deep inside her with the sharpness of acid in a fresh wound.

At three in the morning, Laura eased herself away from James. Without words, they parted. Laura offered him a smile as a gesture of gratitude for his compassion before placing another brief kiss on his lips. And James only smiled back in such a way that she didn't feel the least bit distraught or guilty about leaving.

Laura might as well have stayed, and she immediately began wondering why she'd left as she drove home with the top down.

Because he's not Jimmy.

She also suspected that confusion and panic had driven her away, the exact definition of which she could not grasp. Remorse never found a way in, even though her behavior thus far seemed to warrant it. She was using James, in a sense, as a surrogate for a part of her life she could never get back.

I'm an adult, goddamn it. I know quite well who he is, and who he isn't.

Sneaking home at three in the morning reminded her of how she'd greeted the dawn in her youth. She might have been slicing through one of those early summer nights, when the air was forever warm and she'd found comfort in the arms of her lover. The night was like a friend in those months, and she and Jimmy would walk the streets and sing or shout, hiding from the police whenever someone called to complain. At four or five, when the cool air condensed into a film of dew on the grass, Laura would lie in it and smell the divine perfume of newborn innocence there.

She made a turn and headed down a deserted boulevard painted yellow with the hazy light of streetlamps. She longed for things to be as they had been then, when it seemed there was no one else on Earth but her and Jimmy.

Her eyes blurred suddenly, and she let out a heavy sob. The tires squealed as she pulled to the side of the road and stopped. A flood of emotion came without warning. The tears flowed out from between the fingers she had pressed over her face.

She had stopped running just long enough for her thoughts to catch her. She sobbed and wept, wiping her eyes and trying in vain to fight off the anguish. But a mild voice within her kept insisting, *Let it come. It's okay.*

So she started running from it again, perhaps faster than before, terrified that she would soon have to listen to that voice and simply let it come. She collected herself and drove on. The cool air dried her cheeks as the scent of spring calmed her.

At home, she crawled into bed, exhausted and confused, frightened and alone. She slept in the kind of black absence welcomed by the troubled. In that blackness, she concealed herself, pulled it over her eyes so she wouldn't have to face the things she feared. Not seeing didn't silence the voices. She still heard them whispering to her in a fairy-like lullaby.

It's okay, Laurie. Let it come. Just let it come.

The next morning at eleven, Laura stirred herself awake and was greeted by the same concerns that had plagued her hours before. She lay in bed almost a half hour after she'd awakened, sorting through the wreckage of her life. She likened it to a house someone was renovating, with the walls torn down and reduced to a dusty pile in the middle of the room. Clearly, she was responsible for the mess, and it was only with considerable effort that she decided how to begin cleaning it.

Work. The very thud of that single word was like the blow of a mallet to her forehead. Yes, she had successfully torn down the walls making up this sizable part of her world—or had at least made enough of a mess to necessitate a serious change. She wondered how to clean it up, if it *could* be cleaned up. Sometimes the simplest way was to start all over. A new job? The word *new* gave her hope. For the time being, all she had was a plan…a new plan.

Anxiety swelled in the pit of her stomach. It was a good plan; she knew it was. But making plans was easy. Making reality was another matter.

Try as she might to concentrate on this single problem and its solution, the others came crashing in like a noisy drum corps on parade. And she didn't have solutions for all of them, which left her grasping desperately at the absence.

Don. The wedding. James. The annoying voice that repeatedly told her to *Let it come.*

The collective presence of everything made her head swim, and she had to close her eyes again.

Don was a big one. Due to be married in a few months, and she was fucking around. Not literally, but close enough. That was one big, filthy goddamned room—Don. So much was wrong with it, a lot of which she feared was her own fault. *You don't just let something get so bad without saying anything, do you? And how long has it been bad?* Laura couldn't even remember.

On the other hand, she considered the possibility of fixing what was wrong—like one of those once-sad-but-now-happy couples she'd seen on television a few times. *Is it even worth saving? Do I love him? Does he love me? Or does he just love being around me?* She'd heard somewhere that the security of being in a relationship could easily become more important than the relationship itself. Laura believed she was at the crossroads of such a dilemma.

She reasoned that the changes she'd made recently were the product of that realization. Of course, she had to admit that James was one hell of a distraction. She might not have felt the same detachment from Don if she'd never met him.

Finally, she considered James, who still made her mad sometimes. *Where the hell does James get off screwing up my life like this?*

She laughed at herself. James was at the root of it all, and being around him rendered Laura's internal compass all but useless. An explanation started to surface, but she ignored it…because that nagging voice came with it.

James had dredged up something inside of her, and she had reacted to it. Laura exhaled and rolled her head side to side on the pillow.

"You're falling in love with him, you idiot."

Even though she couldn't deny how liberating it felt, as she ran her fingers through her short hair, she wondered silently what other changes she would long to make in the near future. She rolled onto her side. She was anxious all of a sudden, the way she remembered feeling as a little girl when she'd discovered her first loose tooth. She had known quite well that it was only a matter of time before the tooth came out, but she'd always been too terrified to help it along. It would hurt, she would look foolish without it, and people would laugh and make fun of her. But mostly, it was the pain she feared. Having a tooth wiggling around loose wasn't a normal feeling. And neither was the way she felt now.

So went her morning. She ate a muffin for breakfast, showered, then leafed through one of her horse magazines. Anxiety made her squirm, and her mind burdened her with questions only she could answer.

"I don't even see what difference it would make, telling someone." The sound of her voice startled her.

She'd been speaking to that voice again, the one she didn't actually hear in her head, but rather felt somewhere inside.

"What difference would it make?"

The tone in her voice frightened her. There was an unmistakable edge to the question, which meant she was considering it.

In came the afternoon, warm and clear. Laura busied herself with menial tasks she knew were ridiculous, like straightening the refrigerator magnets, wiping down the counter half a dozen times, and skimming the magazine she'd already read front to back.

She walked past the phone several times, eyeing it thoughtfully. *I think I shouldn't call him today. He's probably sick of me by now.* The moment she had the thought, she knew it wasn't really *her*.

Laura pictured herself at Mattie's hair salon, right after her most recent visit. "It's me," she'd said.

That was it, as clear as day. Laurie Alman had smiled back at her in the salon mirror. *Laurie.* Not *Laura.*

"I'm not *Laura*," she said. It was a calm admission, devoid of anger or resentment. But she said it to herself again and again, as if muttering a prayer or a chant. "I'm not Laura. I'm *not* Laura."

The simple three-word prayer became a series of questions she asked herself quietly. "Who is Laura? Who the hell is *Laura?*"

Had anyone been spying on her during this private interrogation, they might have suspected that Laurie had gone a little mad. She turned to inspect her image in the large antique mirror on the wall. Her eyes narrowed suddenly, and she looked at herself for a long time with her head tilted to one side.

"Who the hell is Laura?" She scowled at her reflection. "Laura is a fucking coward."

Laura blames everyone else for her misery. Laura hides behind convention when she's unclear about something. Laura would rather die in a stale routine than change her life.

She approached the mirror and inspected herself a little closer. "I'm not *Laura*. I'm *Laurie*."

Her narrowed eyes lent an edge of malice to her smile, and she chuckled softly. Laurie enjoyed a deep breath and exhaled. At the same time, her smile faded.

"If I want to call him, I'll call him," she said to her reflection. "And if I want to let it come, I will. And *you* will stay the fuck out of it and mind your own business, *Laura*."

Anxiety faded. Confusion and reluctance gave way to conviction—and acceptance.

"It's been too long. *Way* too long." She didn't look away from her reflection, from the dark eyes she recognized so well. Within those pools of blue, she saw a familiar confidence surfacing—the very soul she had turned her back on. In her eyes, she saw everything that Laura wasn't.

Laurie found herself trapped between reluctance and the resolve she'd summoned. The silent battle she waged within herself reminded her of when her mother had offered to pull Laurie's loose tooth once and for all. She wouldn't allow Sarah to help, and when the wiggling tooth became unbearable, Laurie gripped it tightly and yanked it out on her own.

The afternoon grew stale and dry, the sky smoldering in shades of pink and orange. Laurie sat in her yard for a while, wondering if the phone would ring and hoping Don wouldn't be on the other end if it did. But it didn't ring, and she grew impatient with herself.

"Damn it." She rose from the bench swing in the yard and marched into the house.

She picked up the phone, set it back in its cradle, and picked it up again. Her hands were shaking, and she swore there was a tidal wave hovering over her, ready to crash down at any moment. The only thing she knew for certain was that she didn't want it coming down on her when she was alone. Someone else had to be there with her. The alternative was simply too frightening to consider.

So she dialed his number and waited, terrified that she had already passed the point of no return, that he wouldn't be home. But after three rings, he answered, and his voice made her close her eyes with relief.

"James." She sighed.

"You sleep okay?" he asked.

"Yeah. How about you? You sound tired."

"Mm. Well, you had me a little worried."

Her defenses had worn thin. A rip appeared, and a little sliver of emotion slipped by—a tiny sob that James didn't seem to notice.

"I'm fine, but could I talk to you?" she asked.

He laughed softly on the other end. "Sure. If we get started now, maybe I'll get to bed at a decent hour."

Laurie laughed with him.

"You wanna come over?" he asked.

"Yeah. I really do."

"Okay. I'll see you in a little while."

As strange as it seemed, Laurie felt as if James already knew what she wanted to talk about. As she was prone to doing, her intentions began to shift again. She started to plot something altogether different from what she had originally planned. It was a selfish idea, but the decision was made.

When Laurie arrived at James's place, she felt nervous and anxious as she got out of her car, like a mental patient checking into a hospital for a radical new therapy. Looking sleepy, James was waiting for her with a mellow grin. Laurie approached him slowly and cautiously, pushing the frightened part of her along.

She acknowledged how strange it all seemed, inching toward him with the intention of taking that final step. He might have been a therapist, except he didn't behave clinically. He wasn't really a *stranger*, either, but a special acquaintance that she trusted more than those she considered her closest friends.

The silver part of the bus's skin splashed his face with pink and orange as the sun began its quiet retreat. The way his eyes kept blinking, as if he might fall asleep any minute, made her laugh.

"Are you trying to make me feel guilty, letting your eyes droop like that?" she asked.

"If the shoe fits…" He shrugged.

Laurie approached him in a way that felt as natural as his words. Her plan of just talking fell apart the closer she got to him. She wanted to let him in on a deeper level, but that would have to wait. Perhaps she felt the way she did because nothing seemed impossible or off-limits with him, and that single notion gave her the confidence to embrace him eagerly, as if they'd been lovers for years. She pressed her mouth to his with greater intensity than before, without the meddlesome slivers of guilt getting in the way.

His hands wandered slowly over her body, allowing her plenty of time to stop him. She didn't. Not when she felt him caressing the bare skin of her tummy under her shirt. Not when he bowed his head and started kissing her neck. Not even when he pulled back to look her in the eyes before scooping her into his arms and carrying her around to the back.

In a different capacity, Laurie might have taken offense to the blankets and pillows James had placed on the patio, arranged, it would appear, in presupposition of her physical desire. Her breathing was slightly labored, her body spinning out of control, preparing itself for what was about to happen.

James carried her to the blankets and knelt down with her in his arms. He began undressing her with delicate, fluid movements. Warm air, soft hands, and softer lips caressed her body. She lay back, and little by little, James peeled away her clothes.

When he began exploring her body with his mouth, Laurie found it hard to breathe. He made his way toward her lips, pausing to kiss every inch of her along the way. On his back, he eased her left leg across and Laurie guided him in. When she closed her eyes, explosions of light filled the darkness behind her lids. She returned to a place as familiar as it was beautiful. The present melted together with the past. The ground spun slowly at first, but as they rolled around on the blankets, engaging in a timeless exchange without a single corner, one motion melded into the next. She became lost on the carousel for the first time in more than thirty years.

It was dark before the motion slowed to a gradual, unnoticeable stop. Laurie remained draped over him, warm and exhausted, a wisp of a smile shaping her mouth.

Well, shit. I've really done it now.

And she didn't much care. It was exactly what she needed, and she hadn't felt so relaxed in…well, for as long as she could remember.

What *did* bother her was that the carousel ride she'd just enjoyed so immensely was stolen in a sense. She'd paid her fare with little coins of misconception. Once more, she was ashamed. "Honesty makes you appear younger," James had said. Laurie had to face that, to be honest about how she felt and about why she'd done what she had. She had to tell him the truth.

In keeping with his usual disturbing knack for sensing emotional turbulence, James began stroking her shoulder. The contact felt to Laurie like a physical plea for her to be at peace, to stay with him. Whatever reassurances the sweeping of his hand implied, Laurie missed them completely. She became pensive and stiff, and James picked up on it.

"Something the matter?" he asked.

Laurie glanced at him. "Hmm? Oh, no…not really."

"Is it *no*, or *not really*?"

Laurie shrugged and cuddled up to him. "I have to tell you something."

James needlessly told her that he was willing to listen. Laurie suggested that they dress and sit on the swing. Considering what she was about to say, she felt that being naked would leave her feeling too vulnerable.

The moment she suggested getting dressed, she felt terrible. James nodded with a little smile, as if he knew what was on her mind.

Laurie avoided eye contact with him, and once on the swing, she wished they had spoken more as they'd dressed. As she buttoned her blouse and took a deep breath, a single thought occupied her mind. *How can anything good come of this?*

James tugged on the back of her shirt, and when Laurie scooted over to him, he draped his arm around her. Caressed by the relaxing breezes and erratic sounds of nature, she froze.

"You wanted to talk?" He kissed her on the side of the head. "I'm here, whenever you're ready."

Silence stood between them for a long time, while Laurie picked over her memories. Her thoughts were scattered over a thousand miles like pollen dust. Collectively, they would take on a familiar shape, if only she could assemble them.

"I'm sorry about accusing you." She smiled as she glanced at him.

"Accusing me?"

"Of making my life difficult. The night I had a little too much to drink," she said. "I think what I was trying to say was there have to be rules. That's all."

James's stare fell to the ground, and he made a small sound of confusion. "What kinds of rules did you have in mind?"

Laurie's eyes filled with tears. A painful lump grew in her throat. *Oh, Jesus. Here it comes.*

That was what she believed, at least it had been on the night she'd intruded on him. *Rules. You can't live without them. It's not possible, because—*

"There has to be some kind of *order.* You know? You can't just go around doing whatever you want," she told him pointedly. Or rather, *Laura* told him. Laurie allowed it, though, knowing that both of them needed to be present for the revelation. Laura had some explaining to do, and Laurie would hear her speak, even if she didn't necessarily agree with her anymore.

"I used to think the rules were more important than anything," Laurie said. "I don't mean to sound self-righteous. Just bear with me."

"Okay." James blinked at her and waited for her to go on.

Laurie was having trouble expressing her thoughts, even facing them. The words were stubborn in coming because Laurie felt as if she were choking on a baseball that had been jammed down her throat. *Laura* spoke freely, however, and that seemed to ease her pain a little. It got things going—the voice of the woman she wanted so desperately to leave behind.

"You can't just go through life doing whatever the hell you want! You understand what I'm saying? There has to be rules." Laurie blinked away tears. "It's so easy to think you're *above* it. But none of us are. And when you find that out…" Her voice stopped, and she snatched in a breath. She exhaled and closed her eyes.

"I was sixteen when I found out I wasn't above it—just a kid. It was nothing but fun until then. Jimmy and me and a million promising days ahead of us. I didn't tell you about Jimmy, but I think he was the one, you know? Everybody has one love, and Jimmy was mine."

Laurie grew calm. She even smiled as she stared off at the darkening sky. "He used to sing to me and write the weirdest poems. I thought they were beautiful because he wrote them just for me. I felt like there wasn't a single wall or fence in the entire world when I was with him. He took me places we weren't supposed to go, went to great lengths to show me something he thought I should see. We'd drive in my car in the country during the summer months, and he wouldn't wear a shirt. His hair was like silk in the wind. He made me feel so *free*. I never worried, never considered the possibility of anything bad finding us."

Laurie paused to reflect for a moment. "I was so different then. I looked forward to every day without…*expecting* anything." She put a hand to her mouth to hold back a rush of anguish. It passed.

"All of that seems so distant now, too far away to see anymore. I turned away from all the things I enjoyed. How do you remember something wonderful when right in the center of it, there's something…" The sting of the memory stole her breath for several moments. "Something awful."

She waited several seconds before continuing, numbing herself against what was to come. She blinked and sniffled, standing on the threshold of that which was awful.

"Jimmy was my freedom. He protected me from all that's wrong with the world, kept me from getting lost. Without him beside me…I got lost. Sometimes I argue with myself about whether or not he was even real. Running around all summer wearing nothing but cutoffs the way he did, he was like an older version of Tom Sawyer or something, sun-bleached hair and the face of a curious little angel. But he wasn't an angel. He got into more than his share of trouble, usually for accusing one teacher or another of being unqualified to teach or walking out of class before the day was over. He always took me with him."

Laurie smiled. "One night, we went to this bonfire out in the woods. Loud music was playing to celebrate the coming summer. All of my friends were there, and we danced and laughed until just a few hours before dawn. Sarah was there, too. Jimmy and I were the last two standing, and I was pretty wasted. No, I was *really* wasted. He was, too, but not as bad as I was. Sarah was in the best shape…so she drove us home."

Laurie struggled to remember what happened after that. All she remembered was that Sarah had helped her and Jimmy into the car, and the wind was slithering though her short hair as her mother drove them home.

"Jimmy was always so calm. He told me once that he never worried because the river flows as it wants to. I think that was his way of saying he respected time, that he cherished it."

Laurie wrapped her arms around herself, staring off at the horizon. "And he refused to let anyone dictate how he spent his time. I doubt he would have graduated high school, even as smart as he was. You couldn't tie Jimmy down."

It hit her hard at that moment. An explosion echoed inside her head, and she didn't want to open her eyes because she knew what had happened. Her bottom lip quivered when she spoke again.

"He'd never even wear a seatbelt."

She pressed her hands to her mouth, and the tears flowed down her face in warm streams. She felt James's hand on her shoulder, heard his voice trying to calm her, but it was out, and she sobbed in a fit for several seconds. She allowed him to hold her, but she remained stiff with her arms wrapped around herself.

With her eyes pinched tightly closed, she could see the red and blue lights splattering the trees a hundred yards away. Bright lights probed the confines of the battered Firebird. She screamed Jimmy's name over and over as they removed her from the passenger side of the mangled car and set her down on the stretcher. Laurie was bruised, battered, and cut up…just like Sarah. Her mother had a gash on her arm and another above her eye. Laurie would never forget the look on Sarah's face—as if she knew their friendship was over.

As they wheeled Laurie away from the wreck, she realized what had happened. Her car had rolled down a shallow hill, knocking down small trees and flattening the tall grass. Jimmy must have been thrown out of the shattered back window. The car had rolled over him.

Laurie's hysterical screams tore the blurry night to shreds. In her rage, she tried to jump up off the stretcher to charge at Sarah. She cursed at her and swore she would hate her forever.

That was when it all began to change, when her freedom disappeared. Sarah had been just a hair under the legal limit at the time of the accident, but she was still convicted of manslaughter. She was sentenced to a year in prison and ended up serving a total of six months, during which time Laurie had to live with Sarah's close friend, Annie. A few days after turning eighteen, Laurie left town without a word to Sarah, and their relationship had been strained ever since.

Laurie stared straight ahead as James busied himself with stroking her hair. Her eyes filled again, and when she wiped them clear, her words rang like a confession, revealing something she'd known all along.

"Jimmy was the most beautiful person I've ever known," she said, turning to look James in the eyes. "And he looked just like you."

Pressing her head to his chest, she closed her eyes and sighed. The jagged rubble she'd suffered beneath for so many years was dissipating. It felt easy to speak suddenly, and yet all she managed was a soft echo. "He looked just like you."

James listened as she explained how she'd felt that night, and every day thereafter. Admitting how hollow she'd allowed herself to become, how she'd instantly come to hate her best friend in the world, was liberating. Understanding that hatred and allowing it to pass acted like an emotional salve. Every deep breath was followed by a shuddering exhale that felt like another thorn being removed.

An aromatic breeze swept over them, tickling the leaves in the trees. She closed her eyes and breathed it in. She shook her head and grasped his hand. "You know, all these years, I've been telling myself the same thing over and over again. When I have it all figured out, I'll be happy, and when I'm happy, I'll be able to let someone love me. And when I'm able to let someone love me, I won't feel so alone. When I don't feel so alone, I'll be able to make sense of my life. When I'm able to make sense of my life…I'll have it all figured out."

Laurie sniffled. "I keep trying to get started, but I could never figure out how. So I've been standing outside of this unbroken circle of *when*. I could never get inside, and nothing ever changed." She glanced at James and smiled. "Until now. Until *you*. Maybe it was wrong, letting this happen. Not telling you about Jimmy until after. But I fucking *wanted* you. And I'm not sorry. I wanted to feel something beautiful and honest and *real*. I don't expect you to forgive me or to understand why I need a little time to be by myself after this, but…"

Her voice couldn't form the words. In silence, Laurie decided she didn't have to. She could tell by the way he stroked her back and kissed her on the forehead that he did understand. A little time was all she needed, to ease into the idea that contentment was both real and attainable, that she might recover something she'd given up for lost at the age of sixteen.

"I didn't want to tell you before. I wanted to be with you so badly, and I thought if I said anything about Jimmy…" Laurie clung to him. "Please don't hate me."

James smiled. "I don't."

"You've even got the same name, for Christ's sake!"

"I noticed." James exhaled a troubled laugh.

Laurie tilted her head back and admired the stars. She shook her head and felt awful. "Even if there wasn't a Jimmy, I'd still feel the same way. I'd *still* want to be with you—you have to believe that."

James nodded. "I didn't think of this as a consummation. And you don't have to tell me you're not ready." He ran his hand over her head, leaned in, and kissed her on the mouth. His fingers touched her engagement ring. "Technically, you're still engaged. So I'm as guilty as you are."

Laurie tried to laugh, and the effort was too obvious. "I don't know what the hell I'm doing. I mean, all I know for sure is that I'm changing. And you're the reason for it."

"Don't be so sure."

"It's true. If I'd never seen you that day, singing and driving in the rain, I wouldn't be here now."

They sat in silence a while.

"Fuck, I hate this," she said.

"Hate what?"

"Feeling so goddamn selfish that I can't accommodate the most wonderful man I've ever met in my life."

"What about Jimmy?"

Laurie looked him in the eyes. "You've got him beat—you're *alive*." The cool night air cleared her head. "I just need some time alone, to think. Get my head around this, you know?"

"Yeah, I do."

James didn't sound convinced, and it scared her. At the same time, he didn't seem bitter or hostile.

"I mean it. I just need a little time alone. Just a little time. That's all. Okay?"

James nodded. He told her he understood perfectly. Even though Laurie wasn't sure he was okay, she hugged him and said, "Thank you."

After another half hour or so, Laurie stood up. "I've got to go to the office tomorrow. I've got some things to take care of. It might take a little while to get all my shit together, but I promise I'll come visit you in a few days. A week, tops."

James's mouth worked, and he forced a smile. "Sure."

"Anyone else would have called the looney bin," Laurie said.

"Oh, it's crossed my mind. Several times, actually. I still might call 'em."

James escorted Laurie back to her car.

She kissed him passionately, but he felt distant. She pulled back and met his eyes. He gave her the same patient smile.

"I'll see you soon. I promise," she said.

James nodded. "Okay."

"Please don't sound so morose."

James offered nothing but a warm smile.

"Okay?" Laurie reiterated.

James laughed. "Yeah, I'll see you in a few days."

Laurie looked at him for a few long moments. Finding him impossible to read, she touched his cheek and got into her car.

"I'll probably just pop in on you if that's okay. Does two thirty in the morning work for you?"

James shrugged. "Yeah, why not?"

Laurie smiled at him, started her car, and left.

Laurie snuck into the office at eight o'clock the following evening. She was dressed down to say the least, wearing a pair of faded jeans she normally reserved for gardening detail, a light-green shirt, and a dark windbreaker.

She was surprised to find several people still working, including two members of her own team. One was Jed Beckman, the research analyst. He was a tall, thin man with short hair, who wore Buddy Holly glasses. The other was Kim Trisham, a graphic designer.

"What are you two doing here?" she asked Jed and Kim, who both seemed worn to the bone.

Kim, a soft-spoken petite blonde with big blue eyes, hopped up out of her chair. "Laura! Oh. Did she call you in, too? Maybe something will get done now." She elbowed Jed and winked.

"Did *who* call me in?" Laurie's brow furrowed with suspicion, and her eyes narrowed. Her two subordinates looked nervously at one another and said nothing.

"Come on, out with it, guys—it's *me,*" Laurie coaxed.

"Um, Kate assigned us to work with Libby's team to help finish—"

"*Kate* assigned you?" Laurie felt the heat rushing to her cheeks.

"Yeah. She said you wouldn't have a problem with it, since we were so far ahead." Jed forced a smile and rubbed the back of his neck.

Laurie clenched her teeth and stowed her anger. She narrowly avoided unleashing a heated stream of obscenities about Kate. "How long have you two been here?"

"Since this morning, at about seven," Kim said.

Laurie stepped back into the hall and glanced in the office, where three of Libby's team members—a stocky man in a gray suit, a small man in a black suit, and a woman in a white blouse and navy skirt—all sat, lounging around. The stocky man was in the middle of telling a dirty joke, the small man was listening with a bored expression, and the woman was cursing under her breath as she consulted her watch. They weren't doing much of anything.

"Come with me, both of you." Laurie headed for her office.

As she marched past, the lounging trio began to busy themselves. The stocky one muttered, "Oh shit," under his breath.

"Too late," Laurie said dryly. "Next time, post someone by the door as a lookout."

Kim and Jed followed Laurie to her office. She flicked on the lights and booted up her computer.

"Sit down, you two," she said.

Jed and Kim seated themselves on the soft leather couch and relaxed.

Laurie rattled away at her keyboard. She guided the mouse along and clicked. The printer hummed, and several pages dropped into the tray.

Laurie gathered the dozen or so pages and scrawled her signature across the bottom of each one. She rose from her desk and approached her subordinates, who promptly rose to their feet.

"Jed, this one's for you, and Kim, this one's for you." Laurie handed each of them one of the signed papers. Jed and Kim read over what Laurie had handed them. They glanced at each other then up at Laurie.

"Letters of recommendation. I wrote them up last week. No, I'm not being fired. Listen, I want you to know it's been a real pleasure having you on my team. I feel the same way about every person I printed one of these for. You both know I've been with this company for quite a while. I've satisfied a hell of a lot of firms in that time. People know me by name. You hear what I'm saying?"

Jed and Kim nodded.

"A letter from me is worth something out there. You know Darren Fisk? Sara Mattucci?"

Jed and Kim nodded with wide eyes. The names belonged to two people who worked for a very high-paying firm on the West Coast.

"They used to work for me. Now they work for Tom Hendricks at Lyntec Media because I recommended them. Jed, since you're senior, I want you to distribute these letters tomorrow morning—by hand. And keep it quiet."

"Yes, ma'am."

"Between us, I'm fed up with this shit. You're the elite among the elite in this company—the hard-working. That doesn't mean a hell of a lot to some people around here, but it sure as hell does to me. And I'd bet my life that it means a lot to more than two dozen firms I've represented in the past. I want you to have the opportunity to excel. You've both earned that."

Kim sniffled and wiped her eyes.

"Don't worry, Kim. There's something a whole lot better waiting for you out there. I'm going to make some phone calls in a few days. Don't be surprised if there's an offer or two in your hands by the end of the week. The same goes for you, Jed. I hope you'll forgive me for not doing this for you sooner, but…" Laurie paused, smiling at them both. "I needed you."

Before leaving Laurie's office, Kim insisted on hugging Laurie. Jed shook her hand and gave his assurance that the letters would find their addressees in confidence.

"I wouldn't be surprised if this office looks like a ghost ship by the end of the month," Laurie said, eliciting a laugh from Jed and Kim, who walked beside her.

Laurie poked her head into the office where Libby's slackers still pretended to be working. "You shitheads have fun with whatever the hell it is you're supposed to be doing. My team's going home."

The trio stared back silently at Laurie with dreadful, weary expressions.

The undeniable sense of elation Laurie experienced faded the closer she got to Don's house.

Her thoughts scattered again like the pieces of so many crushed leaves in the wind. Large, enveloping hands of panic seized her, squeezing tighter as the little flakes few farther apart.

She pulled into the driveway that evening and noticed a metallic emerald-green Volkswagen Beetle parked across the street. She remembered how Sarah used to drive a car just like that.

Then she looked up and saw Sarah sitting on the front porch.

Laurie turned off the engine and exited her car. Sarah stood up and stuffed her hands into her front pockets. The beginnings of a smile formed as she came down the stairs.

"Sarah?" Laurie's jaw went slack.

True to her nature, Sarah wore loose-fitting pants made from canvas or something, a beige cotton shirt, and sandals.

"Hey, baby girl." Sarah smiled and gave her a little wave.

"What…what are you doing here?" Laurie's mouth felt numb as she spoke. Sarah was like a beautiful specter drifting across the lawn, her mouth bending into a wider smile as she came closer.

The way Sarah walked took Laurie back to the days when she would hold her small hand and lead her to the pond near the house, where they would swim in the nude, unconcerned about anyone watching. She was so unpredictable. As a child, Laurie had become especially familiar with the word *spontaneity*.

"I wanted to see you." Sarah shrugged, as if this would smooth over the shock of her showing up unannounced.

Laurie blinked at her and licked at her bottom lip. "So you just drove up here from Savannah? Are you crazy?"

"Silly question. Of *course* I'm crazy." Sarah touched Laurie on the cheek.

"It's not funny, Sarah. Jesus, to come home and find you on my porch—"

"*You* called *me*. Remember? A couple days ago?"

"It was like a week ago." Laurie started toward the house.

Sarah walked beside her in the grass, making the blades hiss with her feet. "Ah, so I *didn't* imagine it." Sarah stuck her left hand into Laurie's short hair and stroked her head for a moment before Laurie took her hand away.

"Well, just because I called doesn't mean I invited you here," Laurie said.

"That's true." Sarah's gaze wandered over Laurie's face, her eyes sparkling with wonder.

Laurie knew there was little point in asking why she'd come. Sarah didn't need a reason to do anything. She never had. She made her living as a marginally successful artist and craftswoman the last Laurie knew, constructing little Civil War dolls and other "Old South" paraphernalia. Most of the real work took place during the winter months, freeing up her schedule during the spring and summer to do damn near whatever she wanted.

"Might as well come in." Laurie held the door open for Sarah, who didn't hesitate to start in with whistling and comments.

"My god, will you look at this place?" Sarah craned her neck toward the vaulted ceiling.

"It's not mine, so be careful." Laurie gave Sarah a sideways glance. "Please don't touch anything. You always make a mess."

"What are you worried about, Laurie? You think I'm gonna squat down and piss on the floor?" Sarah let out a short, raspy chuckle.

"Nice image, Sarah. Real nice."

Sarah explored the house while Laurie ducked into the bedroom and closed the door. She grabbed onto the bedpost for support and closed her eyes, hoping that when she opened them again, her life wouldn't be caught in a reckless spin she couldn't control.

After several deep breaths, Laurie emerged from the bedroom warily. Sarah, however, behaved as if nothing had ever gone wrong between them, throwing Laurie completely off guard.

"Music!" Sarah looked around the great room. "Where's your stereo? I need music."

Laurie pointed the way, and Sarah hurried over to the cabinet.

"Damn radio died in the Bug," she said. "Had to drive all the way from Florence with no music."

Sarah found the Bose stereo and started fiddling with it.

"I still have a crappy CD player at the house. This is fancy. Look at all these songs!" She turned to look back at Laurie, her face wrinkled in distaste. "Who loaded Kenny Rogers onto this thing? Please tell me it wasn't you."

Laurie shook her head and crossed her arms.

Sarah turned back to the stereo and hit a few buttons. The great room came alive with the Queen of Soul, Etta James, singing "Only Time Will Tell."

Laurie studied Sarah as if she were a stranger. She swayed to the music, brushing at the air with her hands.

"Tell me about your job. Advertising, right? How's that going?" Sarah danced her way toward Laurie.

Laurie fidgeted and stuffed her hands in her pockets. The last thing she wanted to do was tell Sarah she was quitting her job. "It's marketing, and it's fine. There have been some personnel changes recently. Other than that…"

"Hmm. As long as you're happy." Sarah studied Laurie again, wearing her faint little smile. Her expression told Laurie she wasn't convinced, that she knew Laurie was going through a difficult time. Sarah was the non-threatening type—she would never try to force her way in, like some mothers. Instead, her brown eyes wandered over Laurie's face again, and her smile grew wider. She hummed along with Etta James as she danced into the kitchen.

"I should cook dinner." Sarah started rummaging through the fridge, taking things out as if she lived there. She banged her way through the cupboards then yanked a pan off the rack hanging from the ceiling. Laurie opened her mouth to say something, but held her tongue.

Sarah set a few vegetables on the counter. "Lynn's daughter just had a son. Fat little bugger, too. He weighed in at nine pounds, eight ounces. Lynn says he'll be a linebacker for Georgia State before he's finished the second grade."

Laurie sat on one of the stools and watched Sarah go to work chopping onions, carrots, and mushrooms. A skillet with oil and garlic hissed on the stove. Sarah tossed in the onions and carrots, and in no time the air thickened with the aroma.

"Oh, and Miss Larkson's old place finally burned down." Sarah glanced over her shoulder at Laurie. "Remember that old house? The one you always said was haunted? I knew it was only a matter of time. Something that old and dry, kids sneaking in at night to do God knows what. Apparently, someone was playin' with matches or candles and touched the curtains. That old place lit up the whole neighborhood damn near half the night. In the morning, it was nothin' but a pile of ashes."

Laurie considered the old mansion, left to rot after Miss Larkson had died. It had been there since before Laurie was born, standing alone at the end of the street, empty and forsaken. It was suddenly gone, poof. Laurie felt strange when a flicker of remorse touched her. She hated the place, had been terrified of it all the way through high school, and yet she couldn't imagine it not being there.

"No one was hurt," Sarah added. "Fire department just contained it. Let it collapse in on itself." Sarah fell silent and didn't move for several moments. Laurie knew she was thinking of the one true love she'd lost so many years ago—Laurie's father.

Laurie nodded, mute herself.

Sarah finally snapped out of it. She went on about the local politics, filling Laurie in on all events great and small, most of which Laurie had no interest in. But as she listened to Sarah talking, a familiar calmness washed over her, and a little smile shaped Laurie's mouth before she grew pensive.

As Laurie watched Sarah and listened to her voice, she pretended that her mom was just a woman she really didn't know that well, an acquaintance whose life had been littered with far more debris and pain than her own. Not a mother, a friend, or a sister. Just a woman. And when Laurie removed herself from the mother-daughter connection, a painful lump grew in her throat.

She hasn't had the easiest life, you know? Laurie's eyes welled with tears. *She always protected you. She always loved you no matter what. It was just a mistake. That's all. It was an accident.*

The stained-glass globe over the light near the sink sprinkled colored gems over Sarah's face, enhancing the depth of her beauty. Her dark eyes looked bold and alive with the strength and courage she'd always displayed. Like her beauty, it hadn't faded in the slightest. Nor had the kindness, the patience, and everything else that was good about her. It left Laurie feeling ashamed and angry with herself. She wanted Sarah to stroke her hair again the way she had when Laurie was a girl.

A full minute passed, with Sarah chattering away and Laurie watching her, seeing her not as a mother who'd made a terrible mistake, but as a woman who'd been challenged in ways most people hope never to be. And Sarah had faced those challenges with a bright smile on her face. She'd battled poverty. She'd fought illnesses. She'd endured the loss of her one true love. She'd taken on the rigors of motherhood. All of it, all by herself. So, perhaps for the first time in her life, Laurie realized that Sarah wasn't really to blame for the accident. No one was.

As Laurie stared at the woman sautéing vegetables on the stove, Sarah turned to face her. As her deep-brown eyes settled on Laurie, they filled with concern. All Laurie wanted to do was apologize for all those years of hatred and silence. But she couldn't move from where she stood. Her lips wouldn't move. Even when Sarah started toward her, Laurie remained frozen in place. The only movement came in the form of tears running down her face.

As always, Sarah was gentle in the way she took Laurie into her arms. Whether it was a scraped knee, the loss of an animal she loved, or the cruel words other children said about her secondhand clothes, Sarah always treated the injury with the same care. As for Laurie, she might have been a child again, the way she clung to Sarah and wept.

"I'm sorry, Mom," Laurie whispered. "I'm so sorry. It wasn't your fault. It was just an accident."

A familiar sensation tickled her, a lightness of her inner being that she had first felt in James's presence—another splinter removed.

Sarah sighed and laughed with relief. She didn't say anything, but she rarely did at such times. She didn't have to. That was part of her gift.

In the back of her mind, Laurie could still hear the screams echoing inside the car as it rolled again and again. Glass was breaking, and the night was a cluster of shadows and slivers of recklessly spinning light. And yet, Laurie felt safe. In Sarah's arms, there was no blame, hatred, or fear. Not anymore.

Sarah consoled her, kissing her the way she used to. Laurie felt even more debris from the bitter past leaving her soul. For over twenty-nine years, she'd carried the animosity, the poison, and the rage. Its absence awarded her with a sense of relief unlike anything she'd ever known. She looked her mother in the eyes and saw something in them she couldn't define. *Doubt? Apprehension? Wariness?*

"What is it?" Laurie asked.

Sarah shook her head and smiled. "Nothing. I've just missed you a lot."

Laurie looked into Sarah's eyes, but whatever she'd seen there a moment ago was gone.

Sarah sat in one of the kitchen chairs and pulled Laurie into her lap, where she hugged and kissed her as if she were six years old again.

After a dinner of pasta primavera, Sarah stood by the open kitchen window and lit up a cigarette. When Laurie leaned against the counter, sneered at her, and waved her hand in the air, Sarah exhaled out the window and said, "Don't give me any shit, kiddo. I'm down to three a day. One after each meal."

Considering that Sarah used to smoke two to three packs a day when Laurie was a teen, she supposed that was a notable improvement. She asked Sarah about coming so far just to see her, and Sarah shook her head and exhaled with a laugh.

"I didn't come all this way to see *you*. God! You have become the narcissistic one, haven't you? Bratty little shit. Can't even be bothered to pick up the phone."

Laurie smiled, and Sarah leaned over and kissed her on the forehead. She ruffled her hair and laughed.

"So where are you off to?" Laurie asked.

"Kentucky. Visiting Jane and Judy for a little bit. Remember them? You know, the twins I went to school with till I had to drop out? Anyway, I'm going to see 'em." Sarah dowsed her cigarette under the tap and tossed the butt in the trash.

"What if I hadn't wanted to see you? Where would you stay?" Laurie asked.

Sarah chuckled and sipped her tea. "Hotel, where else? I got money, honey. You'd be shocked stupid by all the things tourists snatch up nowadays. Me and Annie are doin' real well down there." After a pause, Sarah poked at one of her rear molars with her tongue. "I'm glad you invited me in. Can I stay the night?"

Laurie made up the guest room, and right before Sarah was about to go to bed, Laurie found her fluffing up her pillows and tugging at the sheets.

"Sarah?"

"Mm?"

Laurie stood in the doorway and watched the bizarre activity. Sarah never fluffed pillows.

"You okay?"

Sarah stopped and faced Laurie, squinting at her. "Of course. Why do you ask? God, I'm just tired, babe. Come here."

She hurried over to Laurie and embraced her. Sarah was trembling.

"Mom, what's wrong? You're shaking."

Sarah laughed and looked Laurie in the eyes. "I just missed my best friend, and…"

"Me, too. But you're here now, and all that other stuff is behind us. So you can stop shaking. Okay?" Laurie tried to put her at ease, acting more like the adult.

"Okay." Sarah turned away from Laurie's gaze.

"Okay. Goodnight, Mom." Laurie kissed Sarah on the cheek.

"Goodnight, baby girl."

Laurie heard the pounding of her heart, the thumping of a wheel going around and around. Then she was rolling over and over again. A scream rattled inside her head, but it could not escape.

Her body struck one door then the other. Her head smacked the seat, the hard metal of the door, the steering wheel, and the dashboard. Glass shattered and rained down on her. Steel twisted and crumpled.

The rolling came to a stop with a broken thud. A tree shook from the impact. Acorns rained down onto the underside of the car, drumming like little feet running away from something. She was bleeding, moaning, unsure of where she was or what had happened.

Where is…where is Jimmy? He'd been with her, just before… *Sarah?*

Laurie lay in a bruised and bloody heap across the metal strip of the T-top ceiling. An open gash on her arm was just beginning to sting. Her head swam from the combination of reckless motion, drugs, and alcohol. She vomited, coughed, and started wailing for someone to help her.

Laurie was crawling out of the window when she saw Jimmy twenty yards away. The car had left a path as it rolled down the hill.

Jimmy was sprawled out almost in the middle of it, his lifeless body twisted and unnatural—a secondhand marionette with broken strings.

Laurie's shrieking rang out in the night. She hated Sarah. She wanted Sarah to die because she was supposed to be okay to drive. She was supposed to protect her daughter.

Laurie opened her eyes and sat up in bed. She swore she could still feel the fresh bruises on her arms and legs. Her forehead throbbed, prompting her to touch her scar. She blinked and looked about the room in a daze, trying to decide if she was still asleep, still dreaming.

The pinkish gray light of early morning trickled in through the blinds. She heard movement downstairs in the kitchen, indicating that Sarah was already awake.

Laurie turned her head toward the window. The milky reflection in the glass of her pale face and troubled expression made her look like a shock victim. She supposed she looked the way she had on the night it happened. When she'd come to, broken and bleeding, lying on the ceiling of her overturned car…

And just like that night, she felt nauseous and unstable. She stared at her reflection in the window, lost in thought.

On the ceiling of her overturned car.

And then she knew why she'd been so terrified of opening her ragged box of sour memories. She sat there in bed, staring into that box, stunned silent and unable to look away. It was all there, right in front of her—everything she had blocked from her mind.

Laurie slipped out from under the covers and rose from the bed. Her legs felt numb and rubbery as she stepped out of her bedroom and padded down to the kitchen.

She found Sarah at the table, stirring cream into her coffee, staring intently into her cup. When Laurie stepped onto the tile floor, Sarah looked up and smiled. It was a forced smile, and her eyes were pink from crying or lack of sleep, perhaps both.

"Morning, baby girl." Sarah sniffled.

Laurie's stare fell to the floor. She trembled all over, feeling as if she were about to be sick.

"Laurie? Honey, what's the matter?" Sarah started to get up from her chair.

Laurie raised a hand to stop her. "Wait. Just wait."

Sarah sat back down, her eyes wide with confusion and concern.

"Something…" Laurie's mouth tried to form the words. "I had a dream, and…I remember something…about the accident."

"Laurie, forget it, honey. It was an accident, and it's over. You forgave me, and it's done. Okay? Just forget it." Sarah rose from her chair again, but Laurie held up her hand.

"I had bruises," Laurie said. "I was bruised all over my body."

Sarah closed her eyes and sat again, as if stunned. "Laurie—"

"My arms and my legs…"

"Laurie, *please*. Please…"

Laurie looked up at Sarah, tears standing in her eyes. "I was really banged up—"

"Laurie, don't do this! It's over, and you need to forget it."

"I was bruised because…"

"Oh, Jesus…" Sarah muttered.

"Because…I wasn't wearing a seatbelt…"

Sarah pressed her eyes closed. Tears spilled from her eyes.

Laurie stared off into the far corner as her own composure began to crumble. "And I wasn't wearing a seatbelt because—"

"Laurie, please don't!" Sarah sobbed.

"You weren't in the car. Were you?" Laurie asked.

Sarah clamped a hand over her mouth and said nothing.

"You…you weren't driving."

Laurie's legs folded beneath her as her strength suddenly left. Sarah rose to her feet and rushed toward her, embracing Laurie as she slumped to the floor. They folded into a heap together.

Laurie pulled in a breath, and her throat burned from the scream she forced out like fire.

She pinched her eyes closed and pressed her hands over her face. She let out another burning scream, and in the darkness behind her closed lids she saw it.

The night of the accident, sirens had filled the air. And through the obscurity of her tears, Laurie had seen someone walking down the hill, coming to help her.

Balled up on the kitchen floor, Laurie wailed as if she'd been stabbed in the stomach with a red-hot blade. She clung to Sarah as the pain flowed out of her like blood. And when she closed her eyes again, she saw the face of the person coming to help her. The woman who'd told Laurie she would drive her and Jimmy home. The woman Laurie hadn't listened to. The woman Laurie had been too stubborn to wait for. Sarah.

Laurie's convulsive breaths shook her to the core. The visions filled her head, flashing horribly like a damaged reel of film.

Sarah ran to the car and pulled Laurie free. There was no sound, but she was asking if Laurie was okay. Sarah was crying in an uncontrollable panic. She kissed Laurie, and all Laurie could do was look on in a daze. She was losing blood. She would be out in a few seconds, immersed in darkness and perfect silence. She was drifting away when Sarah rested her head on her jacket and stood up.

Laurie didn't know what to make of it when Sarah wiped her eyes, picked up a piece of glass from the rearview mirror, and cut her own arm with it. The sourness of wailing sirens clawed at the shattered night air. Voices blossomed atop the hill. People were talking up there. Confused little beams of light bobbed along the grass. The last thing Laurie saw as her lids closed on the horrible scene was Sarah crawling into the wreckage of the car.

Laurie's wailing subsided. Her breathing slowed, and she accepted the comfort of Sarah's arms and voice. "What was I supposed to do, baby girl? Let you go to jail?"

Laurie said nothing. There was nothing to say, even if she'd been able to form words.

"I should have made sure you didn't leave with Jimmy. I never should have let you out of my sight. But I did. I let you down because I wasn't watching."

Laurie felt as if she'd just killed Jimmy five minutes ago. That, combined with her remorse for blaming Sarah for so many years, left her floundering in a cold abyss. The only warmth she felt, the only chance she had at finding sunlight again, came from Sarah's gentle hands and her soothing voice. Laurie remained in a little ball and clung to her mother, who had shielded her from this pain for so many years. And now the weight of it pressed down on Laurie's soul, and she could no longer breathe.

I *killed Jimmy. Me. I killed him.* Laurie punished herself by repeating the words over and over.

I killed Jimmy. Me. I killed him.

The truth burned deeply, and recalling the good memories of Jimmy became impossible. She had no right to those memories anymore, knowing what she'd done. No right at all.

Sarah stayed with her, holding her. Laurie suffered a multitude of storms that day. Her mouth felt numb. Her entire body went from burning up to shivering. She felt like a hopeless addict trying to get clean, while Sarah tried in vain to shield her from the black clouds of shame and regret.

Laurie lay in bed, her knees pulled in close to her body, staring at the wall. The next moment, a wave of anguish stabbed her in the gut, and she was sobbing uncontrollably. She shrieked a time or two, like a small child who'd just skinned her knee on rough pavement.

Moments later, she felt Sarah lie down behind her on the bed. Sarah wrapped her arms around her, kissed the back of Laurie's head, and whispered, "Shhh. It's okay, baby girl. You're gonna be okay." Laurie heard Sarah's voice catch in her throat, the sound of her sniffling as she fought back tears of her own.

Sarah made lunch, but Laurie wouldn't eat. She stayed in bed all day, staring at the wall. The sobbing fits became less frequent then stopped altogether. Laurie supposed that was an improvement, but the numbness that replaced her pain chilled her. She didn't feel sadness anymore. She didn't feel hunger despite not eating. She didn't feel anything.

I killed Jimmy. Me. I killed him.

After a second torturous night of fitful, broken-glass nightmares, Laurie awakened to find Sarah sitting on the bed behind her, stroking her hair. "Morning, baby girl."

Laurie reached back and took Sarah's hand. "All those years we lost…"

"I'm so sorry about all of this. This is my fault, too. Sometimes I just don't know when to…"

"Let go?" Laurie rolled onto her back and looked at Sarah.

Sarah smiled. "No. Be a mother. I should've been a mother to you that night and many other nights, instead of your friend." Sarah's eyes filled with tears. "Then I tried to fix what was broken, and I never thought about—"

"Sarah, listen to me—"

"I was so fucking selfish. I martyred myself to protect you, and I never thought about what would happen if you ever remembered the truth." Sarah kissed Laurie's hand. "I never should've let you out of my sight."

Laurie squeezed Sarah's hand and shook it. "Jesus, Sarah. I was old enough to know what I was doing. You couldn't be there every second to keep me from fucking up."

"But where was I? Dancing with kids half my age? Having a drink at a teenage party?" Sarah pinched her eyes closed and shook her head.

"I pulled you into all that," Laurie said. "If I hadn't pushed you so hard to come out with me that first night, you probably would've been at home reading." She forced down a lump in her throat. "And Jimmy would still be gone."

Sarah faced her and shook her head. "I was old enough to know what I was doing, too. And I should never have gone, that night or any other. I should never have let *you* go. You were only sixteen!"

"Yeah, and when you were sixteen, you were raising a three-year-old. *Alone*." Laurie forced a laugh. "Christ, Mom. You went to *jail* for me, and I blamed you for almost thirty years. Now you're trying to take the blame again? Stop it. Okay?" Laurie's head throbbed. "*I killed Jimmy. Me. I killed him.*"

She expected to shatter completely as she had so often over the past day and a half, but instead, she felt relieved to hear her own words—her admission of guilt. "I didn't mean to do it. It was an accident, a horrible, stupid fucking accident. But it was *my* accident, not yours." Laurie smiled at Sarah and kissed her hand. "I loved Jimmy. I really did. And I hate myself for losing him the way I did. I know you were just trying to protect me. But, Sarah, in a lot of ways, losing you was so much worse."

She rested her head on Sarah's shoulder and thought about how the accident had changed her, how she had resented Sarah and turned down the wrong path, and how James had helped steer her back to the right one.

Laurie's phone rang. Sarah had been screening her calls, so she picked it up without thinking.

"Hello? No, Laurie has been ill. This is her mother, Sarah. Who's calling? James? Let me see if she's feeling up to it." Sarah looked at Laurie then held out the phone to her.

Laurie's heart pounded. She slowly raised a trembling hand to take the phone. But she froze. Her fingers curled inward, and she lowered her hand. Laurie met Sarah's eyes and shook her head.

"I'm sorry, James. Laurie isn't feeling well enough to talk right now. Can I take a message? Okay, bye." Sarah ended the call and put down Laurie's phone. "No message. Says he'll try again tomorrow."

Laurie nodded, smiling faintly. "He doesn't leave messages."

"You hungry? I'll make French toast," Sarah offered.

Laurie smiled a little wider. "That sounds great."

True to his word, James called again the next day to check on her. And again, when Sarah offered her the phone, Laurie slowly reached for it, froze, and shook her head.

"James? She's still not up to it. No, no. It's nothing like that. I just happened to be in town when she got sick. She's fine. It's just some kind of flu, I think." Sarah made a face and shrugged, unsure if her lie was convincing enough.

A wave of panic washed over Laurie. She reached for the phone, but—

"Okay, bye now." Sarah ended the call. "Did you want to call him back?"

Laurie took her phone, started to call, and stopped. "No. Never mind."

"Do you want to tell me about him?" Sarah asked.

The question lingered in Laurie's head. A faint, bittersweet smile came and went. "Right guy at the wrong time."

"So what about...*Don*, isn't it?"

Laurie shook her head. "Wrong guy. He failed your test."

"Yeah, that's a tough one."

Sarah gave Laurie a sympathetic smile and rubbed her back.

Kate called three times to ask about Libby's accounts and why Laurie had pulled Jed and Kim. Sarah did well to block her from bothering Laurie. "She's still exhausted. She's sleeping right now." She said winked at Laurie. "But I think she's doing better. She hopes to be well enough to come back in to work soon."

That was the plan anyway. As emotionally shattered as she still felt, Laurie knew she couldn't stay home and hide forever. Despite the suffocating weight of her guilt and anguish, she had set a plan in motion, and she refused to turn around.

"A couple more days? Are you sure you'll be up to it?" Sarah asked.

Laurie frowned. "Not really. But I don't have a choice. I have a lot of things to do. And I can't do them if I'm hiding out here."

"I can stay as long as you need me. Or until Don gets home and throws us both out. Speaking of Don, are you gonna be okay to handle that on your own?"

Laurie hugged her. "Don't worry, Mom. I'll be fine. Eventually."

"Part of me will always worry about you, at least a little bit. Comes with the job, kiddo."

That night Laurie didn't sleep much. She lay awake thinking about the accident and about losing Jimmy then finding James. The discovery that she was responsible for Jimmy's death was still as fresh and painful as the wounds she'd suffered on the night it happened.

I killed Jimmy. Me. I killed him.

Tears flowed. "I'm so sorry, Jimmy. It was an accident. Please forgive me. If you can hear me, help me let this go, because I can't do it on my own."

Laurie closed her eyes and pictured Jimmy's smiling face in a halo of sunshine. The weight on her chest, the cold lead in her heart, and the painful tumor in her throat—they all went away. She desperately wanted to believe that, wherever he was, Jimmy forgave her. She took a deep breath and exhaled long and deep. The tide of slumber enveloped her with warm currents and gentle motion, carrying her far away.

Laurie walked along a beach at sunset. In the distance, she saw Jimmy standing ankle deep in the water. She started toward him but forced herself to stop. He smiled brightly and waved to her. Laurie watched him turn and walk deeper into the ocean as the sun set. As he waded deeper in, he swept his hands along the surface of the water. He looked back, flashing his trademark smile one last time. And somehow, it was all she needed to see. Without a word, she knew he would be okay. She knew he was not sad, angry, or afraid. He was forever. And knowing that washed away most of her pain, enough so that she found the courage to feel again.

Jimmy looked at her for a few moments longer. Then he turned back toward the fading sun, and together, they became one with the sparkling, eternal sea.

Early the next morning, Sarah gathered the few items she'd dragged in from her little car and shuffled to the door. Laurie told Sarah her plans for starting her own horse ranch, possibly somewhere in Georgia so they could be closer. But before she started down that road, Laurie needed some time alone to sort everything out. She wasn't surprised when Sarah offered her full support.

"I think it's a wonderful idea, babe," Sarah said. "You're still a baby, but at least you know how to walk. Maybe you just haven't been so sure where to go until now."

Framed by the open door, Laurie squeezed Sarah tightly.

"Don't you be scared now, you hear?" Sarah caressed Laurie's short hair.

Laurie nodded against her.

Sarah pulled back and rested her hands on Laurie's cheeks. "I'll say it again, baby girl. I think it's a beautiful idea. It's not a *dream*. A dream is being married to Hugh Jackman, like I was last night."

Laurie laughed and shook her head.

"Listen to me, 'cause this is the last I'm gonna say about this. You listenin'?"

Laurie nodded and sniffled.

"You deserve to be happy. Okay? You've earned it. How and when you make that happen, that's up to you. But I know whatever it is you choose to do, you'll be terrific at it. I always said that, didn't I?"

Laurie smiled and nodded again.

Sarah wiped Laurie's cheeks and kissed her on the forehead. "You know, for some people, the possibility of happiness is more appealing than happiness itself because a possibility can never be lost. But I'm telling you, happiness—*real* happiness—is better. Even if it doesn't last as long as you want it to."

They hugged again, and Sarah headed for her car. She waved at Laurie, and when she smiled, Laurie could see her mother's eyes sparkling in the early-morning light. Sarah hopped into her little green Beetle and poked her head out the window.

"I'll call you later tonight!" Sarah tooted the horn, and the Beetle chirped its way up the street.

Laurie waved until Sarah's car was out of sight, then she went back inside and closed the door. She considered what she was about to do.

Am I being too spontaneous? Does leaving Don make any sense at all?

Good questions. A fog of doubt clouded her thinking, until she asked herself one more. *Do you love him?*

That question helped dissipate the fog. Laurie marched upstairs, took the folded boxes out of the closet, and started popping them open. Packing up everything she didn't want or need anymore was liberating. The local Goodwill store did pick-ups, so once everything was boxed or bagged, one phone call would make it all disappear.

Laurie didn't collect a lot of things. She had a lot of clothes for work, sure—most of which she wouldn't need anymore. She had a photo album, several pieces of art, and a few other odd and ends that she wouldn't part with, but most everything else was replaceable or expendable.

Whatever wouldn't fit into her car, she would sell or put into storage.

Whatever she couldn't sell or store, she would give away.

Whatever she couldn't give away, she would leave behind.

Packing up almost everything she planned to donate, except for the bulk of her dress clothes, took most of the day. She stuffed the items into boxes and garbage bags, labeled and staged them in the garage for easy access when the Goodwill truck came.

Laurie separated out everything she wanted to keep into half a dozen boxes. She packed a week's worth of dress clothes into her garment bag, and five changes of casualwear, along with a few pairs of shoes, into a little carry-on bag then stuffed the rest into a duffel bag. She could deal with everything else the next day.

She walked through the house several times to make sure she'd properly packed and staged everything she owned. Deciding what to keep and what to ditch had been surprisingly easy.

Don would make out pretty well in the bargain. Laurie hadn't packed any sheets, towels, flatware, silverware, glassware, or cookware. It wasn't that she wanted to buy all that stuff over again, just that she couldn't remember which of them had purchased what. In her present state of mind, a clean break was more valuable to her than a set of king sheets and a few wine glasses.

After a long day of packing and moving boxes up and down stairs, Laurie showered then realized she'd packed all her pajamas and sweatpants. So she dropped her towel on the floor and hopped into bed wearing nothing.

She was asleep in five minutes.

Laurie woke early the next morning and put on the same dirty clothes from the day before. She tucked her hair into a tattered ball cap and drove across town to a storage rental place. A stocky gentleman with bushy hair and a beard greeted her with a crooked smile.

"Mornin'. How can I help ya?"

Laurie returned the greeting and asked for a price list. She settled on a small five-by-eight container then glanced at her little roadster and frowned. Some of the boxes she'd be putting into storage would never fit, even with the top down.

"You could almost park your little car in there." The stocky manager chuckled at his comment.

Laurie flashed a troubled smile. "I don't suppose you rent little trailers, do you?"

"Uh, no." The stocky manager leaned to one side and pointed down the road. "But there's a moving truck place just over there. They rent by the hour."

Laurie looked down the road and saw the place. She was so relieved she could have hugged the manager. "I think you just saved my life. Thank you."

"Heh heh. You're most welcome. Saving someone's life always makes my day. And it ain't even nine o'clock yet!"

After renting her storage unit, Laurie drove up the road and parked at the moving truck rental place. A teen boy with a black

Mohawk was busy washing down the trucks lined up in a neat row. He stopped what he was doing and wiped his hands on a dirty rag.

"How ya doin'?" The teen's soft voice made him sound much younger than he was.

Laurie's gaze ran up and down the long row of trucks. Their sizes ranged from giant box trucks over twenty-five feet in length, to full-size pickup trucks.

"Doin' fine, thanks. I need a pickup for an hour or so."

The teen nodded and waved her toward the office. They went inside, and the teen filled out the paperwork. Laurie fought to suppress a bittersweet smile when she heard REO Speedwagon on the radio singing "Time for Me to Fly."

The teen handed over the keys with a grin, and Laurie was on her way back to Don's house.

She listened to the rest of the song from the truck. As she drove along she imagined herself as an organized criminal preparing for a complex heist that would stump even the most talented veteran detectives. She made a game of it by adding her sunglasses to her ball cap to complete an effective disguise.

Back at Don's house, she loaded up the half dozen boxes and closed the tailgate. After a quick stop to unload the boxes at her storage space, she returned the pickup with ten minutes to spare. And just like that, she had completed a big step toward pulling off her disappearing act.

Laurie spent the rest of the morning going through the house and writing down what she planned to sell—which was pretty much everything she owned in the house. She went into the basement, brought up the original boxes for several newer appliances—they were more like statues, considering she never used them—and boxed them all up. Once everything was set out and arranged just so, she wrote prices on a roll of blue painter's tape, tore off the marked strips, and stuck them on everything she wanted to sell. In less than an hour, she had tagged over a dozen pieces of furniture and close to two dozen smaller items, like framed artwork, decorative rugs, and appliances. After finishing all the dirty business, she showered and changed clothes.

The doorbell rang just after one o'clock. On her way to the door, Laurie paused and looked around at all the furnishings, hoping she was seeing most of them for the last time. She continued to the door and opened it to see Irene's smiling face. The younger woman was bursting with joy and excitement, and her smile was contagious.

"Hi, Miss Alman!" Irene beamed at her.

Laurie noticed her stealing a glance inside the house. "Please, call me Laurie...I mean *Laura*. Thanks for being so punctual." She chuckled when she saw a newer SUV with a long moving trailer attached to it sitting by the curb. A stocky man with bushy hair was busy fussing with the rear doors. "You came prepared, didn't you?"

"Yes, we did." Irene turned to check on the man by the trailer. "That's my husband. Rick! Don't worry about that right now!"

Rick abandoned the trailer and strode up to the house. "I might need a blowtorch to get the damn doors open."

"Just... Let's not take up too much of Miss Alman's time, honey. Okay?" Irene sounded nervous and a little bit like she was biting back frustration.

Laurie gently rested a hand on Irene's shoulder. "Relax, okay? I'm in no rush. And you're kind of doing me a favor here—both of you." Laurie made eye contact with Rick, who responded with a muted smile. "The less I have to post online, the better."

Irene exhaled as if a great burden had been lifted. "Thank you so much."

"Come on in." Laurie opened the door wide and extended her arm.

Irene and Rick entered slowly, their eyes wide.

"Anything with blue tape on it is up for sale. All prices are negotiable, so if you like something, make an offer. I'll stay close by, but I won't be breathing down your neck," Laurie said with a smile.

"Okay." Irene took a small notepad out of her purse and started shopping. Rick followed close behind. Their oohs and aahs started the moment they saw the Italian leather sofa, loveseat, and matching chairs a few feet away.

Laurie returned to the master bedroom to sort through the rest of her clothes. She planned to donate most of what she hadn't already packed up and hauled off to the storage unit. If only Irene weren't three inches shorter and two sizes smaller, with tiny feet.

Half an hour later, Laurie found Irene and Rick huddled together in the living room, looking over Irene's notepad.

"How did we do?" Laurie asked.

Irene looked up and smiled brightly. "I think we're going to almost clean you out."

"Good!" Laurie sized up the two of them. "You, uh, gonna need any help moving everything out?"

Rick held up a hand, as if to stop Laurie from doing something. "Oh, my brothers are on call. Didn't know how long this would take, so I told 'em I'd call when we were ready. Excuse me a minute." Rick took out his phone and headed for the door.

Laurie held out her hand to Irene. "Let's see what you've got."

Irene handed over the small pad. Indeed, she had jotted down almost everything Laurie was selling—only a few smaller appliances and the large antique mirror remained.

Laurie checked the list and noticed that Irene had added up the items at Laurie's asking price. The total came to $7,345. Laurie had paid more than that for the living room set alone, so Irene had done very well. In a sense, they both had.

"It was really nice of you to think of me, Miss Alman. Thank you so much." Irene handed Laurie a check. "It'll clear, I promise."

Laurie took the check. "Since you work in accounting, I'll take your word for it."

"It'll be so nice to have decent furniture in the house." Irene crossed the living room to caress the leather furniture she'd just bought. She stopped before the large antique mirror, one of the few items she hadn't taken.

Laurie noticed how Irene lovingly admired it and wondered why she hadn't bought it. The price might have been a deterrent. Laurie had spent four thousand on it and was asking twenty-five hundred.

Irene gently touched the mirror's hand-carved wood frame. "When I was a kid, we had all this great furniture. It was older, but it was all handcrafted and sturdy, you know?" Irene looked back at Laurie.

"Yup, I do. That's why I bought the good stuff. Lucky for you, I guess." Laurie chuckled.

Irene turned back toward the mirror. "The furniture in our house had all been passed down from my grandparents. My grandfather was a woodworker, and he'd made most of the furniture himself. It felt really solid, like it would never break, like it would always be there. And then a few years after my grandfather passed away, there was a big flood and…" Irene shrugged and sighed. "It was all gone."

"I'm sorry to hear that."

"Yeah, it was pretty tough losing everything. Anyway, after that, we never had nice furniture. It barely lasted long enough to get through the warranty—if we were lucky. So I always promised myself that I'd never buy junk. *Never.* I'd rather pay more for something that was made by someone who really took pride in what they were doing. Someone like my grampy."

Laurie glanced back and forth between Irene and the antique mirror. "You like this mirror, don't you?"

Irene nodded. "We had one something like it years ago. Grampy carved the frame by hand. It had all these little branches and vines in the wood."

Laurie reached out and slowly peeled the painter's tape from the mirror. "Why don't you take it? Call it a housewarming gift."

Irene faced Laurie with wide eyes. "What? I can't accept this.

It's—"

"It was a gift," Laurie lied. She'd bought it in Charleston five years ago, without knowing why. She'd never even liked it all that much. "If you like it, I want you to have it."

Irene turned back toward the mirror. She reached for the sides of the frame, as if touching something magical. She faced Laurie again. "I have to give you something for it."

Laurie thought about that a moment. "No you don't. It's okay." She gave the mirror one last glance. "I don't need it anymore."

Rick's two brothers showed up, both of them stocky and more than capable of moving furniture. An hour later, they had everything loaded into the trailer. Laurie stood in the doorway as Irene and Rick walked to their vehicle, chattering about what piece of furniture would go where. They got into the SUV, and Irene waved as she and Rick pulled away. Laurie waved back then watched the long trailer full of things being hauled out of her life forever.

She stepped back into the now-empty living room, called Goodwill, and scheduled a pick-up for that afternoon. A pair of workers, one wiry and the other like a bowling ball with arms and legs, showed up an hour later. Laurie opened the garage. They exchanged hellos, the boxes and bags were loaded, and off they went with a little toot of the horn.

Back inside, Laurie looked around at the bare living room. It was shocking to see it in such an empty state.

"Wow," she muttered. "Don's gonna be pissed."

After gliding about in the shadows of the house like a brooding specter, Laurie finally sat at the small kitchen table and looked around. So empty now, these rooms that had once been filled with expensive furnishings and the smells of what she'd always assumed to be normalcy: aromatic traces of a meal cooked minutes before, a whiff of cologne, the scent of a damp towel draped over a chair...

On the table sat the paper she'd set out hours ago, with the intention of writing out an explanation to Don. She wondered what she ought to write. A passing whirlwind of something invisible collected her scattered thoughts and spun them about. Anger. Guilt. Frustration. How to begin.

An expression of anger felt wrong, as did her feelings of guilt. Finally, she started writing, allowing the honesty of her emotions to guide her.

Dear Don,

I've never said anything about the problems in our relationship. It's probably reasonable to assume you never thought we had any. Maybe this is because you never listened to me, and maybe it's because I didn't try hard enough to be heard. I can't say for sure. But I'm leaving. Lately, there have been some changes in my life, questions I've been asking myself, and the first indications that I'm still alive.

For a long time, I had my doubts. I came close to giving up, and I know it sounds terrible, but part of that surrender was accepting your proposal. I'm sorry, but I'm not ready to give up. Not yet.

I'm walking a tightrope as I write this, trying hard not to fall on the side of guilt or anger. There's a certain negative balance to us, I think. Whenever I'd try to let something bad out, you were never there to listen. And whenever you were happy (which is often), I could never let that in. So where does that leave me? Standing outside of a life I don't want anymore.

I think part of me wants to leave this note because facing you frightens me. It frightens me because I don't blame you, and whatever pain this might cause would be hard for me, too. I'm so much like a child right now: confused, excited, scared, and ready to discover the world again. There aren't enough pages in front of me to explain what happened to me as a teenager, and it's not important that you know. I've tried to tell you, and you didn't listen. In that absence, I grew numb and cold. I felt sorry for myself, and I allowed bitter thoughts to poison me. And I don't want to feel that way anymore. So I'm saying goodbye before I'm too scared to leave. Before I forget myself again.

I wish you the best in whatever you do. I don't resent you, and I hope you won't hate me too much for this, either. I also wish you luck with your future wife, whomever she may be.

Take care of yourself,

Laurie

When she had finished writing, Laurie grunted angrily, crumpled up the sheet of paper and tossed it away. She missed the can and didn't bother to retrieve the wadded-up note from the floor.

"This really sucks." She capped the pen and tossed it onto the table. Her eyes felt dry and tired.

Yawning, she rose from the chair, and when the chair legs rubbed against the hardwood floor, a loud moan filled the hollow room. Laurie looked around at the naked walls that had once been adorned with the many pieces of artwork she had thought she liked. The floors, once blanketed with lovely intricately patterned rugs, felt cold against her stockinged feet, vacant and unfamiliar, the way her life was beginning to feel. She allowed herself a chuckle and shook her head.

"Fuck you, *Laura*," she whispered to the hollow chamber. "I'm not going back. I'm *never* going back."

Laurie surveyed the room again, seeing it as an open space with innumerable possibilities. She climbed the stairs to the mostly empty master bedroom and slept, dreaming quietly in a place that was colorful and warm.

A loud thud downstairs stirred her, but Laurie ignored the sound and drifted back to sleep. She was normally a light sleeper, but the bed was so warm, the darkness of her closed lids so infinite and pleasing.

Then there arose another sound—one that struck her the way a callused finger plucks a guitar string. She sat up against the headboard immediately, eyes wide, heart pounding.

The front door had slammed closed. She heard shoes scuffing the floor. Someone sighed through his nose. A piece of paper crinkled. The realization was no less terrifying than the idea of a burglar in the house.

Don was home early.

Laurie slipped out of bed and got dressed. She gathered her purse and started for the door. She crept to the stairs and peered over the bannister. Don stood at the edge of the living room, dressed in jeans and a cream-colored shirt. He looked around in bewilderment at the empty room. He then gazed about at the naked walls in the hallway. He stepped over to the window and drew back the lacy curtain with two fingers, looking out at the little green car he didn't recognize, presumably.

"What the hell?" he muttered.

When Laurie stepped off the stairs and into the hallway, Don jumped. He slapped a hand to his chest. "Jesus! What—what the hell's going on?"

He looked around again. "Where's all our furniture?" His eyes flitted to the top and sides of her head.

Laurie guessed he was wondering where the rest of her hair had gone, as well. She took in a deep breath and watched as he turned in circles, looking around at all the empty space. His eyes shifted to her several times. "Well?"

"I'm leaving," she said.

"*Leaving?* What do you mean you're *leaving?* To go where?"

Laurie shook her head. "It doesn't matter where."

Silence fell between them while Don appraised her, his expression bordering on devastation. His eyes were wide and still, like those of a person who has died unexpectedly. His mouth, slightly agape and twitching, uttered words and sounds that collapsed before they could form.

"What…? Laura, what happened? What's the matter?" he asked. Laurie closed her eyes. The letter would have alleviated this, what she was seeing and hearing in his voice. Now she had to endure his pain, anger, and whatever else came with it.

She opened her eyes, forcing herself to look at him. "I don't know what happened. Or *when.* Or *how.* I only know that I can't do this anymore."

"Do *what?*" A flicker of anger rose in his voice.

"*This!*" Laurie waved at the empty house. She spaced her thumb and forefinger an inch apart. "I came this close to just giving in to…whatever the fuck this is, and—"

"What? *Marriage?* To a man who loves you? Jesus, Laura, have you lost your mind? Our wedding is in less than three months—"

"*Was. Was* in less than three months," she corrected.

Don blinked at her and scowled. "Just like that? Without the slightest hint of a reason? Well, that's just terrific!" He fell into the only chair left in the living room—a recliner he'd bought before they met and was particularly attached to.

Laurie crossed her arms and exhaled. Being in the room with Don made her feel heavy.

Don jabbed a finger toward the window. "Whose car is that out there? Is it *his*? Is someone else helping you make this decision?"

"No," Laurie said. "It's my car."

"Yours?"

"Yes, mine."

Don shook his head and dragged a hand down his face. She'd never seen him so upset before. He got to his feet again, hands stuffed in his pockets as he paced about the room. "How can you just spring this on me? I come home early, and you have *this* waiting for me? What kind of person does something like that?"

"I'm sorry it had to come to this—"

"You're *sorry*? That's it? You ruin my life and you're *sorry*?"

"I didn't ruin your life."

"Oh no, you're just running off with someone right in front of my face! It would have been behind my back if I hadn't come home early."

"There *is* nobody else."

Don gave a little grunt and threw himself back into his chair, then he immediately stood up again. "I want an explanation. Something better than *this*."

In the brief silence that followed, Laurie looked at him. Shame for leaving him faded, and anger took its place. "No, you don't. That's why I'm leaving. Okay? You never want to know *why* unless it affects you."

"Just get out, then. Go on and leave." Don turned his back on her and stomped into the kitchen.

Laurie laughed and shook her head. She followed him. "How dare you! You selfish son of a bitch! You're doing it right now!"

"I said *go*!"

"I didn't want to blame you. I really didn't! But now I think I was right!"

"Get out of my house!"

"No! You're gonna listen to me! This time, you're gonna fucking listen!"

Her narrowed eyes swelled with anger, and the sharpness of her words stopped him in place. He crossed his arms and tried to stare back at her, only to look away.

"Even now you want me to leave because it's the only way to preserve your precious silence. Just usher me out of your fragile little world unless I enter with a smile on my face. Well, fuck you, Don! I'm not smiling now. And I haven't for a long time. It's so convenient for you to ignore it all so you can be happy, pretending that I'm happy, too, and not really caring one way or the other."

Laurie heaved in and out like an angry bull. "You're like a little boy. You know that? All you care about is toys and sunshine. You're so selfish, you don't even realize it. You never listened to me. Just *listened* to me. Do you have any idea how painful that is?" Laurie crossed the room. "You want a reason? That's the biggest one. And because of that, I don't *know* you. I don't know who you are. And now I don't want to. I listen to you and all your stupid goals for acquiring this toy or that one, and all the while, I'm suffering because something's not right inside me—and you don't want to hear it." She put a hand to her mouth and sniffled, fighting off tears. She didn't want him to see her cry. "I don't think that's what marriage is supposed to be like. You know? I can't just pretend that I'm okay to please you, to keep from bringing you down. I won't." Laurie picked up her purse; everything else was already in the car. She looked at Don. He stood by the table, looking down at the floor like a scolded child. Laurie felt a twinge of guilt. "I moved all my stuff out already. Good luck with everything."

In the silence following, she left Don standing there in his big empty house, staring at the bare floor. He never called out to her, never tried to halt her retreat.

And she was glad he didn't.

That same morning, Laurie went to the office to make some phone calls and to grab a few personal items she'd left in her desk.

She arrived in a stale, gray state of mind. She felt smothered, as if by a wool blanket, itching and anxious to execute these petty matters, the same way a child hurries through her chores—quickly, quickly, because the promise of freedom beckons.

Laurie pulled into the garage beside Kate's car, freshly waxed and sparkling.

"This ought to be fun," she muttered.

Dressed casually, far too casually by company standards, Laurie walked toward her office. The menacing little ghosts of a dozen whispering voices trailed her. Yes, the rumors were as thick as April pollen, drifting about in plain view. And she really didn't care.

The cleanup inside her office was a simple matter. She collected the few items she'd forgotten: a teal scarf, a cotton shirt, a pair of sunglasses, and an opened pack of gum.

Laurie sat by the phone. Knowing that her welcome would soon expire, she opened the little notebook stuffed with business cards and dialed.

A sunny receptionist answered. "Lyntec Media, this is Amber. How may I direct your call?"

"Good morning, may I speak with Tom Hendricks please?" she said. "Tell him it's Laurie…*Laura* Alman. Thank you."

After a few moments, Tom's booming voice came on the line. "Hello, Laura," he said.

"Hey, Tom. How've you been?"

"Never better. Busy as hell, but that's when I'm happiest." He chuckled.

"Glad to hear it. Listen, do you remember asking me if I knew any good people looking for work?"

After making half a dozen more calls, Laurie hung up the phone for the last time and grabbed her bag. She would have stopped off at Mason's office to make the resignation official, but he was still away on business. Besides, a clean escape seemed much more appealing.

No such luck.

Kate emerged from around the corner with an ashen expression and a mixture of rage and terror in her eyes.

"Laura? Jesus, what the hell is going on?" Kate kept her tone down as she looked around at all the curious subordinates.

Laurie wrinkled her brow with mock concern. "What on earth do you mean?"

Kate ushered Laurie into a corner, taking her by the right forearm and squeezing too hard. Laurie pulled her arm free and glared.

"McKinley Corporation is on the line. They're saying they don't have the marketing plan we promised them for their new line of scuba equipment. The launch is supposed to be tomorrow and their board meeting is in less than an hour. What happened? I assigned some of my people to finish it last week."

"And some of *my* people, too. Right?" Laurie asked.

"What? Yes, of course. I *had* to assign some extra help. It's a big project, and the deadline is up. Look, this company is a major account, and if this thing doesn't get fixed by tomorrow…" Kate paused to look around. "They'll be out for blood."

"Hm. That's a damn shame isn't it? Well, I gotta go, Kate. Talk to you later." Laurie started off.

Kate grabbed Laurie by the arm again. "Wait! Go? Go where? You need to find Jed and Kim and ask them why they didn't work through on this project like I asked them to."

Laurie pursed her lips and removed Kate's nail-polished talon from her arm.

"First of all, Jed and Kim are part of *my* crew. Secondly, the three shitheads from *your* side of the house weren't doing anything when I came in last week, so I—"

"You were here? Last week?"

"Don't interrupt. I told you before about commandeering members of my crew to pick up the slack from other departments. I don't like it—or *didn't* like it."

Laurie's last remark bunched Kate's eyebrows.

"Anyway," Laurie said, "I spoke to HR a moment ago. Jed and Kim are both leaving. Tomorrow's their last day."

"What? I need them *here*! Now!"

"Don't yell at me."

"You call them and get them in here right now! Do you *hear* me?" Kate shrieked.

Laurie pressed two fingers against Kate's sternum and pushed her up against the wall hard enough to knock a picture askew. Laurie's face molded into a mask of rage. "You raise your voice to me again, and I swear to God, I'll rip your fucking head off."

The office fell dead silent.

"Do *you* hear *me*?" Laurie's eyes burned into Kate.

Kate's wide eyes stared into Laurie's with an expression normally reserved for encounters with a grizzly bear.

Laurie leaned in close. "Jed and Kim are leaving. *Period.* You need something fixed? *You* fix it. Do your fucking job. My former crew—what's left of it after today—is done doing it for you. Do you understand that?"

Kate blinked, her stare wandering briefly over Laurie's shoulder to glare at the curious gathering of witnesses. Laurie lowered her hand and adjusted the bag on her shoulder.

"Tell Mason it's been a real pleasure. I'll be sending him my official resignation directly." Laurie started down the hallway.

"Laura?" Kate said meekly.

Laurie turned and faced her. Kate looked scared. Terrified. It occurred to Laurie that the aggression she'd exhibited was but a small part of it. Kate had looked uneasy even before their little chat. Her mouth worked, and Laurie realized that Kate didn't have the authority to use anyone from Laurie's crew. Kate had never asked Mason for permission to do what she'd done. That was a big deal all by itself, reassigning personnel. And it looked as if she would lose at least one account over it—a *large* account.

"I need you for this. Please," Kate begged, right there in front of God and everyone. Her hands trembled. Her face was pale. Deep down, in the most primal recesses of her soul, Laurie pitied the woman. A small part of her reached out, but Kate was just too far away.

"Oh, Kate…" Laurie shook her head with genuine empathy. "I could help you. A part of me really wants to. But I just can't. Not today."

Tears coated Kate's eyes, and Laurie wished, deep down, that she could have said something else.

A small woman with corn-silk hair in a tight braid inched toward Kate. When Kate saw her, the woman said in a very mousy voice, "Mr. Rockwell is on line one. He wants to speak with you. Right away."

A brief exchange of eye contact passed between Laurie and Kate—the escaped prisoner and the one sentenced to death. Kate surveyed her subordinates. Her expression hardened back into her usual countenance. She straightened her suit and turned away. Laurie watched her stroll confidently down the hall. She reached her office, entered, and closed the door quietly behind her, which seemed more frightful, more final to Laurie than a thunderous slam.

Laurie turned away from that quiet door, closed like the lid of a coffin, and walked past the many onlookers without saying a word. She saw them as wandering spirits she had once known, lost souls who could not follow where she was going. It didn't seem to matter at all that Laurie herself had no idea where that place might be. There might not be a place at all, only a road she wanted very much to travel on for a while, one that led her away from the routine stagnation that so many lacked the courage to reject.

As a teen, Laurie had been quite at ease with her poetic view of the world. She saw images and answers hidden in the clouds and in the trees, metaphors for life and the complex enigma of human understanding. For years, she'd felt as if her soul could no longer recognize such things. But as she drove along Stratford Avenue, she imagined a hot air balloon rising into the clear blue sky. From the ground, the people below could see the pilot cutting loose the sandbags that had kept it on the ground for so long. Laurie smiled widely, inhaling the clean air rushing in on her.

She instinctively headed toward James's place. Deciding that she ought to announce herself before arriving, she reached for her cell phone. She looked down at it, then hissed and shook her head. The battery was dead again. *Old habits…*

She put her phone down and proceeded anyway. "At least it's not two in the morning."

Laurie made the left turn and started down the road. And suddenly, she had a funny feeling—a cold feeling. An unnamable reluctance to proceed crept in, and she found herself crawling along at half the speed limit. It might have been her recollection of how James had behaved the last time she'd visited him, when he'd acknowledged then extracted the bitter nest of thorns in her side. The sense of dread, both odd and intrusive, hit her suddenly.

Driving around the bend, she looked away from the space between the trees, ignoring the absence of what she wanted to see. She'd seen the reflective skin of his blue-and-silver bus so many times glistening through the trees, providing a canvas on which the rays of the sun danced and glided. The sun beamed in the sky, but nothing glimmered behind the woods. James's bus was gone.

Panic seized her as she checked her surroundings, making certain she was at the correct driveway. She felt physically ill. In her mind, she pictured the hot air balloon, in which she'd been rapidly ascending, becoming heavy again, and falling back to the ground.

Laurie drove slowly up his drive, parked her car, turned off the engine, and got out. On shaky legs, she turned around like a frightened child playing a game of hide-and-seek gone terribly wrong. The bus really was gone. In its place was a large pale spot of ground. On the other side was the outdoor living room. Laurie approached the spot, certain it would vanish when she drew too close. Pausing, she looked back at her car. It seemed miles away, as did her adventure of self-rediscovery.

The flowers and shrubs remained, leaning when nudged by the wind. But it all seemed so dead. She had been surrounded by the aroma and the voices of that garden, immersed in a simplicity she adored. It had become a cemetery. Even the birds had abandoned the once-lively place. The air, devoid of their collective song, felt leaden with hopelessness. Laurie walked about the barren living room, taking only a few short steps in one direction before turning around again. Something caught her eye—an envelope hanging from a small branch by a piece of string. She approached it with the same sense of disbelief and dark wonder. The envelope had her name on it.

She took it down, opened the flap, and removed the contents. The first peculiar thing she noticed was that a large corner had been torn from the paper. The next was that the writing followed the length of the page, rather than the width.

Dear Laurie,

It was a difficult decision, leaving without saying goodbye. I wish you no misery, and I want you to know how much I enjoyed the time we spent together. I think I'm finally mature enough to appreciate the miracle of chance meetings and to cherish the peace they carry. That's what you are to me—a chance meeting I will never forget.

You're going through a difficult time right now. I know that. But difficulty doesn't always have to be unpleasant.

The words on the page blurred behind tears as she read the next few lines.

During many of our discussions, it was so hard for me to keep from just squeezing you tight without ever letting you go. And every time you'd leave, I'd suffer the chill of your absence (something I thought I'd grown accustomed to). I've been alone for a very long time, Laurie. I decided long ago that the numbness of being alone is much easier to endure than the pain of separation, or even the fear of it.

Laurie gasped as her eyes swept the next sentence.

There's no harm in telling you this now: I fell in love with you the first minute you walked into my life. My seasoned defenses couldn't—

Laurie turned the paper over.

—stop you, not for one second. You just walked right past them. And now I'm frustrated and scared, and I've chosen to cling to what I know.

I hope you forgive me for this selfish position and try to understand how terrifying it is to me that I might have only been able to love you for a short while. It's not the loving I'm scared of, but the emptiness I know will surely follow when it ends. This way, I will always think of you and smile. I may even allow myself to dream of how it might have been, and wonder at the idea of eternity with you.

With that I will end. I wish you all the happiness in the world and the freedom to see and enjoy it. I also hope you find Paradise one day. If you do, maybe I'll see you there.

With Love,

James

Tears flowed from Laurie's eyes, and she felt the promise of happiness bleeding out of her soul. The steady swelling of hope and joy had ended with a violent collapse. James's note was but a jagged crescendo to the past few hours. Her fight with Don and her departure from work were a swelling and collapsing that sickened her as completely as the violent sloshing of a troubled sea. It left her confused and lost, not unlike someone suddenly finding herself in a dark, unfamiliar wood, where not even the sun could be counted on for guidance or warmth.

Laurie retreated to her car and started the engine. She read through the note again, riding the icy wave of anxiety carried by certain lines—*I fell in love with you the first minute you walked into my life*—and shuddering with hopelessness at others—*And now I'm frustrated and scared, and I've chosen to cling to what I know.*

She stuffed the note into the center console box and shifted into reverse.

"How could you do this?" She smiled in spite of herself. "We never even got started."

Laurie's own words returned to haunt her. She'd informed James that she needed some time alone. She'd flat-out told him she wasn't ready for a relationship. She'd refused to take several of his calls. *What kind of message did I expect those words and actions to send?*

Only in that moment did she realize how stupid she'd been, saying such things only days after he'd told her the story of his ex-wife. To him, her words must have sounded all too familiar. Jeanie had left him, and Laurie had essentially done the same.

She felt like an idiot, although she was only trying to be realistic about the whole thing. As screwed up as her life would be for however long it took, hooking up with James didn't seem practicable. Not anymore.

"But making love to him, that was okay with you," she scolded herself.

Each time she paused to consider that James had confessed to being in love with her, Laurie gritted her teeth and groaned in pain.

When Laurie was six or seven, Sarah threw her a birthday party. The memory of it returned to her, as strange as it seemed. At the party, Laurie had been showered with gifts and attention, and almost a dozen other kids had shown up, in addition to her closest friends. One was a boy named Nicholas, whom she had a secret crush on. For a present, he'd brought Laurie a kite with a white tiger on it. Laurie remembered glancing over at Nicholas a dozen times and smiling. He smiled back once or twice. But before Laurie finished opening her gifts, Nicholas had left. There she was, surrounded by gifts, and bothered by the absence of a boy she didn't even know that well. Only the affection of her family and friends had softened the blow. There was so much to enjoy, after all, so many other things to be thankful for. But that day, Laurie allowed herself only a diluted happiness, all because Nicholas had gone home without saying goodbye.

The memory was fitting for her present situation. Again, she was allowing herself only a diluted version of happiness, born of possibility rather than substance. She resigned herself to the fact that, yes, she needed some time alone, and yes, she'd gotten her wish. Moping about in North Carolina hardly seemed like a sensible way to begin her journey. After all, she had picked the lock to her cage, and a big beautiful world awaited her.

Laurie sniffled and wiped her eyes as she drove in a blur of confusion. She'd packed everything she thought she might need in the trunk: a very meager cache of clothing, a bag containing a few items to maintain proper hygiene, and a few other personal items.

She thought about heading south to Georgia right away. And she supposed she would, someday soon. But for now, with the three horse magazines piled on the passenger seat, Laurie headed west. She'd never really been out west, and right then, she wanted to see wild horses running on the plains. And by heading west, she would have plenty of road to drive on and think.

It was a balmy day with patchwork clouds filling the sky, perfect top-down weather. Laurie started out on the highway, but wasted no time veering off onto less frequently traveled roads. The radio was tuned to a rock station, and the sleek rhythm of Dire Straits gave way to Bad Company. The song "Silver, Blue and Gold" was so befitting of Laurie's situation that she wore a bright smile all the way to Ashville.

Then came the Great Smoky Mountains, green and bold, with a smooth road snaking its way through them in wide, lazy curves. Laurie acknowledged and savored the peace that seeped into her. The farther she got from her old life, the clearer her future became. She didn't know what she would do, or if her dream of owning a horse farm in Georgia would ever become a reality. The trivial matters that had once imprisoned her blew away like dandelion seeds, and she embraced the boundless hope and the new sense of adventure and mystery. Where she went and what she did when she arrived there were of little consequence. All that mattered was that she was *going.*

Tennessee offered farmland and rolling hills. Shades of emerald, gold, and bronze danced before her eyes with a liveliness she couldn't recall ever having seen before. She appreciated the beauty and pulled to the side of the road from time to time to be someplace calm for a while. Sometimes, the radiance sprawling out before her brought tears to her eyes.

Not since she was a teen, back in those simple, timeless years had she stopped long enough to behold something so simple and quiet. And when she finally departed, it was never in haste. She pulled away slowly, allowing her gaze to separate gently from the scenery. Sometimes, she only drove another mile before stopping again.

On and on, she drove, seeing and feeling the serenity that did more to cleanse her than any therapist ever could. A mental housekeeping was underway. She discarded troublesome memories and worries, allowing ample room for new possibilities. Immediately, she thought about James's note and shook her head.

Why couldn't you have waited a little while?

Laurie's thoughts rang with confusion and yearning for an answer. But she could find nothing to supplement what he'd written. Unable to solve the mystery, she focused on the road and all the beauty rolling by.

Dusk had settled in by the time she arrived in Missouri, having zipped along a little faster than she should have at times. It also could have been that nothing inhibited her while on the road. The weather was perfect, the balmy haze lifting as the sun faded and the air grew cooler.

Laurie found a hotel in a small town. She'd never stayed at the chain before, and she'd stayed in many. Still, the idea of a hotel depressed her. The indifference of a cheap room, the hard bed, and the little soaps wrapped in paper made her shudder. A hotel room seemed too much like part of a life she'd turned her back on. It left her searching for options, and a glance across the road produced an unlikely one. Amid a small cluster of stores, one toward the middle had a canoe affixed to the roof.

Laurie parked in one of the spots out front and entered the store. Once she was inside, it all made sense. She went about gathering what she needed: a small tent, a light sleeping bag, a lantern, a flashlight, some matches, water bottles, and even a portable shower that was little more than a bag with a hose on it.

Luckily, she found a campground nearby and set up her tent. That evening, as she lay on her back with her head propped up on her hands, the stars were brighter than she'd ever seen them. The occasional cry of a bird or cricket made little ripples in the silence.

Later that night, the moon crept into the sky, and an owl began hooting. As she admired the countless balls of fire in the sky, Laurie's old life seemed just as far away—distant but still visible. And when she wanted to shut it out, all she had to do was close her eyes.

As midnight approached, Laurie crawled into her tent and slept. It was a peaceful sleep, awash with slippery dreams and optimistic wishes. James appeared, smiling and making jokes. He hadn't left her, after all. The note had been an illusion. And then she held him, and he held her back, gracing her with soft kisses and the loving caress of his hands.

When the sun came around the next day, Laurie awoke naturally to the sound of singing birds. She felt a sting of longing when she realized James wasn't there beside her. Then she reminded herself that one goal of exploring on her own was to clear away the cobwebs, as it were. She could already feel that it was working, but she also knew she still had a long way to go.

After eating breakfast at a small diner in town, Laurie stopped at a local bookstore to acquire a road atlas. She'd been lucky to make it as far as Missouri without getting hopelessly lost. She started poring through the atlas's large pages, tracing roads and trying to decide which way she might like to travel. Being in no particular hurry afforded her the option of taking mostly scenic routes.

By nine that morning, Laurie was on the road, heading north, toward Iowa. She'd always been told it was a boring state, flat and covered with nothing but cornfields. To some degree, she found that to be true, but to Laurie's eyes, wonder and beauty existed all around her. The simplicity of a lone farmhouse nestled in its own bounty inspired her with its subtlety and pride. The undeniable stitches of tradition and hard work could be seen in the tilled fields and across the endless plains where seeds had been sown and young plants sprouted into the world. The sprawling farmland displayed a way of life she'd never considered before—a lifestyle that she looked upon with humility and respect.

That evening, she set up camp in Iowa, in a small place far from everything. Another family camped nearby, and she welcomed the voices, the high-pitched laughter of the two children, and the warm light of their fire. When night blanketed the land, she marveled once again at the sky, alive with so many burning jewels. Her eyes burned from staring at them for so long without blinking. A shooting star raced by and faded. Laurie closed her eyes and made a harmless wish, the way she used to as a girl.

Lying in the cool grass, she felt some of that simplicity returning, the hope and peace of knowing that everything would be okay in the morning. Memories of her pre-high school days drifted by, complete with summers at the lake, fireflies, and drive-in movies with a dozen laughing kids her age all riding the carousel before it started. And then James found a way in again. She tried to make light of how wonderful she had felt with him, but she couldn't help longing for his company.

The next day, Laurie discovered a charming small town in western Iowa and stopped for lunch before crossing the border into Nebraska. She purchased some food for the road, including cans of soup and ravioli, crackers, and fruit.

Laurie found Nebraska more appealing than she'd expected. Of course, her attitude had changed, and everything seemed more agreeable in her present state of mind. Without all the bitter cynicism, she could appreciate what she found pleasing and disregard the rest.

The hills, most of which were beginning to assume a subtle shade of green, rolled up and down like lazy ocean waves. She pressed on, anxious to reach Colorado, where she planned to camp that evening. She set up near the border instead, in a quiet little campground beside a hiking trail.

It was still light when she stopped, and before setting up her tent, she took a walk, bringing the little pack and some fruit with her. The narrow trail was crowded by budding trees and grabby little bushes. She walked beside a small brook, which dribbled around large stones and under fallen chunks of rotten wood. The farther she walked, the wider the small stream became. The obstructions grew thinner, and the water flowed much faster and without as much sound. Finally, it bent and curved into a river in a steady transition that made Laurie smile.

By the shore of that river, she seated herself and ate one of the apples she'd bought in Iowa. She became thoughtful and started to explore the tiny splinter that had been bothering her since Tennessee.

It was James, but the problem involved the note. Only two, maybe three sentences stood out in her mind, the last of which had escaped her at first. One memorable line made her feel warm whenever she thought about it: *I fell in love with you the first minute you walked into my life.* She would never forget those words, even though she sort of hated him for leaving.

The note captured him so well that she could hear his voice whenever she read it. The one sentence that bothered her stood out because it *didn't* sound like him. It read something like, *If you find paradise, maybe I'll see you there.* It didn't fit with the rest of the note at all. She wondered why he'd chosen the word "paradise." To her, the word conjured images of loud Hawaiian shirts with too many colors, hissing palm trees, and exotic drinks served in coconut shells with little pink umbrellas.

Maybe she'd somehow given him the impression that she wanted to live in paradise. Perhaps he felt threatened or turned off by that. Considering the way he'd described his ex-wife, it didn't seem out of the question. Sitting there on the bank as the river rolled along, Laurie narrowed her eyes. Her stare shifted from left to right, the way it always did when she was working to solve a complex dilemma.

"What the hell was going on in his head when he wrote that? Maybe he was making fun of me." She hissed a laugh through her nose. After a few moments, she gave up the mystery for lost and allowed herself to enjoy the scenery.

That evening, she heated ravioli and ate it with crackers. No one camped around her, so she set up a makeshift screen with a poncho and washed with the little portable shower before it got too chilly.

When night closed in, she tossed and turned inside the tent as the same oddball sentence paraded through her head over and over again: *I hope you find paradise one day.*

"Jesus," she muttered. "It's not bad enough you leave me. You have to write some corny sentence that keeps me awake, too?"

The next morning, Laurie drove into Colorado, where she spent the whole day exploring the mountains. She drove south first and visited Colorado Springs, passing the campus teeming with students. Then she went north into the metropolis of Denver. From there, she proceeded into Boulder, where she walked about in the shopping centers beneath a canopy of young trees. She was off again after a quick lunch, heading west into cooler climes, where she hoped to set up camp for the night.

For her stay at the base of the Rockies, Laurie bundled up in a fleece sweater and built a fire to keep warm. This campsite was livelier than the previous ones. A group of students had set up nearby and were chatting noisily. A small family with two children had set up across from her, their golden retriever panting and racing about. The friendly pooch ran up to Laurie with a soggy white teddy bear in his mouth. He seemed to want to play, but when Laurie reached for the bear, the dog turned his head so she couldn't reach it, all the while staring at her with his human-like eyes.

"Dixon! Get over here. I'm sorry." The man of the family approached her campsite.

"It's okay, really." Laurie laughed as Dixon trotted over to the students' campsite to pester them.

Just before eleven, Laurie retreated to her sleeping bag with the flashlight and the atlas. She leafed through the maps so she could plot her course for the following day. Wyoming looked interesting, and she'd never been there before. She wanted to visit Yellowstone for sure. Flipping back to the map of the whole country, she thought she might go through Idaho and perhaps end up in Oregon before heading to California.

That night, Laurie dreamed of bison and bears, both of which she hoped to see at Yellowstone National Park—just not up close. Then came images and sounds of beautiful horses thundering across a broad, golden plain that belonged to her. She saw a huge barn, two large stables, and young men and women she'd hired to help her run the place. Laurie ran her hand through the silky coat of a smoky spotted mare. She leaned in close to the beautiful animal. "I'm naming you Valkyrie."

Then she dreamed of shapes, strangely enough—squares, oblong blocks, and narrow little forms she didn't understand at first. She finally realized, the way one can only in dreams, that they were the shapes of the many different states she'd passed through.

Wyoming was both old and timeless, with its jagged, rusty cliffs and rocky plains, horses dotting the landscape, and blue sky forever. And the farther west she drove, the bolder it became, until she was inside Yellowstone.

Having never seen a bison in the flesh, Laurie was amazed by how big their heads were. She'd once been told that all bison have an invisible ring around them. If anything stepped inside that ring, the bison would charge, so she kept her distance.

She saw whole families of antelope walking along the roadside. She saw a small bear sitting against a tree, eating something that looked like raw meat, and a silver fox prancing about in a field.

That evening, Laurie made camp inside the park, within screaming distance of the other campers, just in case one of the wild animals tried to get too cozy with her.

Over the next two weeks, Laurie meandered about, exploring the Midwest with no sense of urgency and no particular destination. She spent many nights sleeping under the stars and treated herself to a king-size bed and a hot shower now and then. As she drove along winding mountain roads and across flat plains that went on forever, she allowed her thoughts to wander, as well. The constant motion helped her think and helped her heal.

Not a single day passed that she didn't think about James. She tried to imagine where he'd gone and wondered if she would ever see him again. Along her journey, she kept in contact with Sarah, calling or texting at least once a day. Laurie promised Sarah that she would return to Georgia as soon as her head was clear or she got bored with the Midwest—whichever came first.

It turned out that there was far more to see than she could ever hope to in one lifetime. She ate at local diners and cafés, hiked on more trails than she could count, and witnessed more beauty than most people would see in a lifetime. Along the way, she bought a packable hammock, and during one short hike in South Dakota, she strung it up between two trees and settled in for a nap. As she lay there drifting in and out of sleep amid the warm breezes, a pang of loneliness emerged out of nowhere to disrupt the peaceful relaxation she'd been enjoying. She saw James's face whenever she closed her eyes, and more than anything, she wished that he were there with her.

The logical side of her argued that she wasn't ready yet, that she still had much inner healing to do. Her pessimistic side reminded her that she had no idea where James had gone, which made her fantasies about the two of them napping in a hammock together completely pointless. It was hopeless to argue against either of these facts, so Laurie closed her eyes and pushed them aside for the time being.

Despite the annoying reality of her situation, Laurie didn't feel ready to head back to Georgia quite yet. She was enjoying her expedition, and the countless miles she'd traveled had been good for her. Even though she longed for human company again, another part of her wanted to remain on the road a while longer. Her intuition had always been hit or miss. She'd been led astray by hunches and gut feelings more times than she would ever admit. For all she knew, it was happening again. But after everything she'd been through over the past few weeks, she decided to listen to her inner voice—however vague it might be—and give herself another day or two before returning to Georgia to begin the next chapter of her life.

That evening, she made camp at a small site near a rippling stream. Sleep finally came shortly before midnight, bringing with it dreams of James, the note he'd left her, and a cascading waterfall of square and oblong shapes flowing through it all.

The moment Laurie awoke the next morning, James's misfit sentence returned to pester her again. Uncertain of what he'd written exactly, she pawed through her belongings in search of the note. She found it and studied it more carefully. The sentence was, *I also hope you find Paradise one day. If you do, maybe I'll see you there.*

The first thing she noticed was the capitalization of the word "Paradise." She started to wonder about the page's missing corner, torn from the bottom, and tapering upward toward the top. It gave the note an odd shape that brought to mind all the shapes she had seen in her dreams. The page's shape left her wondering why James would have bothered to use a defective piece of paper to write such a note, and why he'd oriented his note in landscape on the page instead of the more traditional portrait. Laurie supposed that it was the only sheet of paper he had had at the time. Yet the shape looked familiar somehow.

She brought out the atlas and set it on the picnic table close to her tent. Page by page, she started flipping through it. As if stricken by some crucial recollection, she started flipping faster and faster. *Iowa, Kentucky, Louisiana...* Her heart pounded suddenly. Her hand shook as she tried desperately to locate something important. *Michigan, Missouri, Nebraska...*

On she went, stopping suddenly and flipping backward. When she found the page she wanted, she laid the note down beside the atlas.

"Oh my god. Montana."

The sheet of paper James had used to write his note and the shape of the state were nearly identical. She studied the map. Her stomach twisted and turned as her finger traced the northwestern side.

Her eyes widened, and she laughed as her hand came to rest. She'd stopped her finger on a place called Paradise.

Paradise, Montana.

And the town rested exactly where James had written the word on his note.

Laurie hurried back to her car, remembering what Sarah had said to her before she left. *"For some people, the possibility of happiness is more appealing than happiness itself, because a possibility can never be lost."*

Laurie wondered if James had secured the possibility of happiness by leaving a door open, without necessarily pointing the way. He had, in effect, created an illusion, but also a chance that one day, happiness might find him. To simply tell Laurie where he was going wouldn't be the same. That would only provide a short-term possibility of happiness—one that would end after a month or two, when Laurie didn't appear. But with the puzzle he'd offered her, chance was on his side. Maybe it would take a year for Laurie to figure it out, maybe ten. It was timeless, and as long as he believed that Laurie had kept the note, there existed a possibility that she would solve the puzzle and find him.

To Laurie, it felt as if James *had* secured his own possibility of happiness. And strangely, it made sense to her, as distorted as it might seem to others. She knew where he had gone, and she *would* find Paradise.

Laurie didn't intend to drive the whole distance in one day, but traffic was light, and she made excellent time. It took her about eight hours to reach Missoula, and she found the town of Paradise a little over thirty miles north of it. It was a place much too small for James to hide. Sadly, Laurie found no sign of him there. She drove about town and asked several locals if any of them had seen a large blue-and-silver bus, possibly towing a Jeep CJ-7. No luck.

Heading back toward Missoula, Laurie parked by the roadside and stepped out of her car to stretch her legs and gather her thoughts. She found little comfort in the beautiful surroundings, perhaps because her thoughts had drifted off to focus on other matters.

Why would he do this to me? Is this all just a bizarre coincidence?

She crossed her arms, heaved a sigh, and walked back to her car.

Before she could open the door, she saw something. It looked like a star gliding along the ground toward her. The shape of it was unclear, surrounded by a silvery-white light. She remained where she stood, watching the approaching star fallen to Earth.

The sun reflected off of the vehicle as it came, splashing the blue-and-silver sides and the long windshield with its rays. Laurie's mouth bent into a smile, and she laughed as the massive bus slowed down. It pulled off the road twenty-five feet away and stopped.

James stepped out. His mouth hung open slightly, his eyes narrowed in doubt. Laurie and James walked toward each other, she with a casual stride, James more slowly.

When they were two feet apart, Laurie said, "You didn't think you were gonna get rid of me that easily, did you?"

Silently, James reached up to touch her face, as if he doubted the reality of her presence. "I was hoping I couldn't."

Laurie held up the note and smiled. "Could'a fooled me. What if I'd never figured out your little treasure map?"

James shrugged. "I don't know what to say. I apologize, but—"

"Shut up. I forgive you." Laurie walked into his arms. She leaned away from him and gave him a light slap in the face. "But don't ever do that again."

James pulled her back in and kissed her on top of the head. She felt his heart pounding—the heartbeat of a frightened man.

"I didn't know how to say goodbye to you," he said. "I didn't want to."

Laurie inhaled and laughed. She admitted that it was as much her fault, citing her own words, how she'd felt a need to be alone for a while.

"You don't feel like that anymore?" he asked.

Laurie pulled back to look into his eyes. "I'm still gonna need some space, now and again. For a while, I don't know how long. I'm working through something right now. Someday I'll tell you about it. I won't always be good company. But it'll be easier to get through it if I know you're there."

James caressed her cheek. "Whatever you need." He leaned in and kissed her gently. "I don't know if I dare ask what you're doing way out here."

Laurie gave him a sideways glance.

"I mean, *besides* tracking me down."

Laurie shrugged. "I'm finally inside the circle of when. So now I'm trying to figure some things out, so I can be happy." She blinked at him. "Also, I robbed a bank before fleeing North Carolina. I'm now wanted in over fifteen states. So there's that."

"I see." James flashed her a smile. "Well, then, I guess I've got a few things to figure out myself."

Laurie pressed her hand to the back of James's neck and pulled him in for a long kiss.

"If I have to choose between the possibility of happiness, and happiness itself—even it doesn't last forever…" she kissed James on the neck and let out a long sigh of relief. "I choose *this*."

Laurie and James remained by the roadside, locked in their embrace, immersed in a single moment that went on and on.

Author's Note

If you're reading this before reading the book for some reason, you might want to stop now to avoid having the whole book spoiled for you. Okay, you've been warned. Here we go…

Funny thing about this book: I was living a pretty secluded life in North Carolina when I wrote it, working swing shifts at a cryogenic production facility at the time. As it turned out, life imitated art when I left that comfortable job to strike out for parts unknown. Well, that's not entirely true—the destination was Beaverton, Oregon by way of a one-year pit stop in Kansas City, Missouri. Upon tendering my resignation at the cryogenics plant, I went into survival mode the same way Laurie did and sold everything I owned to stay afloat. Every possession I had that wouldn't fit into the long bed of my '88 Chevy truck had to go. The experience was equal parts exhilarating, frustrating, and terrifying. But it all worked out in the end, more or less.

There's much to be said for simplifying one's life, for casting off the anchors—both mental and physical. In my case, I was fortunate to not have to fight through a tortured past the way Laurie did, but I owned a house and more possessions than I could take with me. Shortly after resigning from my position (for reasons I won't go into), I lay in bed wide awake, staring at the wall thinking, *What the hell have I done?* The house was a project I'd been working on for years—a project I had yet to complete. And so, I found myself with a mortgage on a house with several renovations I hadn't finished, and no income with which to pay for them.

What am I going to do now? I thought. And a sense of calm washed over me as I received an answer—from where it came, I can only guess. That answer was this: *Sell everything you own.* And that was exactly what I did. I used the money I raised to pay my mortgage, and for some of the renovations I had left. Unfortunately, it wasn't enough. However, luck was on my side, and I found work as an electrician's helper. The work was brutal and often exhausting, but I was glad to have it. And through a bizarre twist of fate, it was a fellow I worked with who ended up buying my house, essentially cutting away the last anchor and setting me free.

That was how I began my journey from isolated stagnation to something better. The journey continues to this day.

Please take a few minutes to **Rate and Review** this book online! It helps other readers and it greatly helps the author.

Acknowledgements

With regards to this book I can only thank the circumstances and mysterious forces that yanked me away from a life of safe comfort and stagnation before it was too late. I imagine my muse had something to do with it, so I thank her as well. Shedding one's skin—so to speak—can be a frightening ordeal, but it can also be rejuvenating and empowering. Doing so enabled me to live out certain aspects of this story in my own life, and for that I am forever grateful.

About the Author

D.E. Ladd has written short stories, novels, and screenplays in multiple genres, including fantasy, action, horror, thriller, science fiction, and drama. Derek is a PAGE Awards winner, and his work has been featured in *Four Hundred Words* magazine, and the *Stories of Oregon* audiobook. He spent thirteen years working with clients as a professional content editor and story consultant, and currently resides in Portland, Oregon, where he spends a great deal of time preparing for an alien-zombie-ninja warrior invasion.

For more about Derek and his work, please visit **www.deladd.com**.
Join D.E. Ladd's mailing list at **www.deladd.com/connect**.

Books by D.E. LADD

A Dreamer's Dance

A Dreamer's Dance flings the reader from a hopelessly romantic "serial idiot" in clumsy pursuit of a woman's affection, to a dark comedy involving an old barn, an abusive ex-boyfriend, and a chainsaw. A mother of two struggles with self-doubt over her parenting and shopping skills on Christmas Eve, and a dumbfounded teen joins an alien invader on a mission to deliver an ominous warning to the people of Earth. Unique characters and worlds align to tell stories that are dramatic, sometimes dark, and often comical—but never dull.

Circle of When

Laura Alman's drizzly morning commute is disrupted by a ghost from her past—a scruffy free spirit in a Jeep singing without a care as he's pelted by the rain. Laura starts to question how she went from being a blue-jean girl working on a horse ranch to a refined and polished marketing executive. A journey of transformation and discovery forces her to redefine happiness, reconnect with her estranged mother, and revisit a past she's spent the past thirty years trying to forget.

Moonlight Roses

A husband and wife science team creates an organism designed to consume all human waste on the planet. Serve time with a woman held in a cramped dungeon, tormented by shattered memories and the sound of her ex-boyfriend's insane laughter from an adjoining cell. Ride along with a young man as he gears up for the race of his life against a deadly opponent known as the Road Ripper. As you scurry from one tale to the next, you will come to realize that evil takes root at night…and terror blossoms best in the moonlight.

Without Wings

At 26, William Nedeau has a couple of weeks left on his parole sentence. Between the strained relationship with his father and the torturous reminders of his failed life, he clings to childhood memories of Christina Averly, someone he could never forget. After learning that Christina is in a bad situation, Will violates his parole to cross the country. His actions ignite a chain of events he is powerless to stop or control, turning his virtuous journey of personal redemption into one of jeopardy, chaos, and sacrifice.

For more information please visit **www.deladd.com**